ABSENCE OF CERTAINTY

Allan McGregor

ABSENCE OF CERTAINTY
Allan McGregor

ISBN 9781914615900
A CIP catalogue record for this book is available from the British Library.

Published 2023

Tricorn Books
Treadgolds
1a Bishop Street
Portsmouth
PO1 3HN

ABSENCE OF CERTAINTY

Contents

PROLOGUE
The Northern Irish
Border 1977

The bullets screamed past his head, missing him by inches. He had no plan, but he knew he had to get away fast. He began to run, swerving and keeping as low as he could. The car was about thirty yards in front of him, no one was near it. Crouching down, he felt for the car key in his pocket.

The others were dead, he knew that. He needed time to think – time to clear his head. *Head back to the house*, he thought.

More shots rang out and voices shouted. They were looking for him. If they found him, he knew it would be over. No mercy, just death. Shoot to kill.

He realised he was breathing heavily. Stumbling over some rocks, he cursed silently to himself. The mud patch softened the impact as he fell to his knees. He used his left hand to push himself upright and, in a second, was up and moving again. The gun in his right hand was heavy but still clean. He needed it.

The voices behind him had gone silent; weapons quiet. They couldn't see him, that much was clear. The small undulating hillocks and surrounding bushes had blocked their sight, at least temporarily.

He sprinted the last few yards and crouched down beside the car. His left hand reached into his pocket for the key. He opened the door and slid silently into the driver's seat, guiding the key into the ignition while pressing the clutch and putting the car into first gear. The engine burst into life, and the car screeched away up the dirt track.

He gripped the gun and the steering wheel together. He knew these minor roads well and now had the advantage – at least for a short time. The house would give him some respite and the chance to think. There was that fucking Brit to deal with. His mind continued to race as the car sped onwards.

As he entered the outskirts of the town, he deliberately slowed down to avoid undue attention. He pushed the pistol in between his legs; out of sight, but close enough if it was needed. He threaded the car through the empty streets, making a decision to drive around the back of the house to the lane used for the dustbin lorries. It would alert fewer people of his presence and it was more likely the back door wouldn't be locked.

As he got out of the car, he reached for the gun and swiftly tucked it into the back of his jeans, hidden under his jacket. Only he would know it was there.

He approached the house. He was right. The door wasn't locked. He opened it and stepped into the kitchen.

Before he could do anything else, he heard the front door open. Footsteps came towards the kitchen. Was it one person? The steps were light. He was pretty sure it was the woman on her own. Good. He moved quickly and silently to the other side of the room.

The woman entered the kitchen, carrying a shopping bag in each hand. She became aware of him standing there and smiled.

'You're back early. Where are the others? By the way, we're not stopping. Just popped back to drop these off.' She lifted both bags a little.

'Where is he?' he snapped.

'Jack? Why? He's waiting in the car. I said I'd just pop things in the fridge first.' She looked at him. 'You seem agitated, Rory. Are you OK?'

'I need you to sit down,' he barked. 'Now!' He pointed at one of the kitchen chairs.

She stared at him. 'Who are you to tell me what to do in my own house?'

He moved towards her. 'Sit the fuck down, Maggie! We're gonna wait for that English traitor to come in here. And then I'll show him what I think of him.'

'You're not making sense. What's going on?'

He reached into his waistband, feeling for the weapon's grip. 'I told you to sit down!' He pulled out the Browning and with shaking hands pointed it towards her.

She dropped the bags to the floor and stumbled backwards onto a chair.

Rory stood over her, sweat dripping from his face. 'Now,' he said through gritted teeth, 'we're going to wait here so I can give that fucking English cunt some of his own medicine.'

She nodded, trembling. Eyes focused on the gun barrel pointed straight at her.

PART I
Chapter I
November 1975

The bar area of the Liverpool to Belfast overnight ferry was heaving with drunken Northern Irish football supporters. The noise was deafening. Terrace songs shouted out tunelessly and aggressively. Spilt beer covered the floor, waded across by hundreds of Dr. Martens boots. The bar staff were doing their best to serve the rabble as quickly as possible but were struggling.

The tiny number of passengers sitting around the edge of the area who were not football supporters looked on with anxious faces. Instinctively, they knew violence could erupt at any second. Testosterone, alcohol, youth and tribal loyalties were not a good mix in this setting. The two friends knew to keep a low profile.

Jack's eyes were drawn to a petite young woman standing a couple of yards from the bar. She had long blonde hair and was wearing tight faded jeans and a dark blue top. Jack found her incredibly attractive. He watched as she tried unsuccessfully to make her way to the bar. The crowd would not let her through.

He rose to his feet.

'Leave it, mate,' Steve said as he nodded, almost imperceptibly, towards the loudest of the group downing pints. 'Those guys are pure trouble and now is not the time to be a hero. That one's already got his eye on her.'

'I just want to help her get served.'

'Then let me do it. They're pissed loyalist thugs. If you go near them with your English accent, they'll have you.'

'Maybe, maybe not. But don't worry, I'll be careful.' Jack smiled mischievously and put his hand on Steve's shoulder to stop him from getting up. His friend shook his head.

'I'm telling you; this is not the time or place to be a hero.'

Jack ignored him and approached the bar, stopping about a yard behind the girl. She was now the attention of a small group of men who had almost encircled her. He felt a sudden rush of adrenaline and shouted out, 'For Christ's sake, Liz, what's the hold-up?' The girl turned immediately, giving Jack a quizzical frown. He willed her to understand.

'Who the fuck are you?' The Northern Irish accent was harsh and the tone threatening. The owner of the voice stepped in front of Jack, blocking his view of the girl. Thickset, with shoulder-length greasy brown hair, an ugly face and a nose that looked as if it had been broken more than once. Jack flinched. He hoped no one noticed. The face leant in closer, only inches away. Taking a step backwards, Jack tried his best to look unthreatening.

'She's my girlfriend, mate.' He tried a smile. 'I was thinking she'd never get to the bar. Then I saw her standing next to you and realised at least someone was going to help her. Thanks, mate!'

Jack locked eyes with the girl and nodded. She stared back. After what seemed like an eternity, she finally spoke:

'Sorry – just couldn't get served.'

The ringleader looked at the girl, then back to Jack. He turned to his mates and grinned.

'I'm a white knight, me. So I am there!' He raised his pint and bowed as his audience laughed and cheered. In a second, the aggression towards Jack dissolved.

'OK Englishman, no problem. Yeah, I saw your wee girl trying to be served and thought I'd help her.' His mates clearly thought this hilarious, but nevertheless created a space for them to get to the bar.

'Thanks again, mate.' Jack tried to calm his beating heart as he followed her through the gap.

At the bar, she turned to him and started to say something, but Jack put his finger to his lips. She got the message and went silent. Having bought the drinks, he led the girl back to the table where Steve was waiting.

'Who's your friend?' he asked Jack, nodding at the young woman.

'No idea,' Jack said, with a smile.

The girl sat down.

'I'm Roisin,' she replied before turning to Jack. 'And you must be Sir Galahad?' She raised her glass and took a sip, eyes sparkling at Jack over the rim. 'I can look after myself, you know!' The indignation was apparent.

Steve laughed aloud. 'There you go, Jack. Told you Northern Ireland was difficult to comprehend.'

Jack smiled. He liked this woman. It wasn't just her physical attractiveness; it was the way she spoke, the way she moved. She was different – and Jack liked that.

Chapter 2

'Excuse me, sir.' The smartly dressed man, in his early forties, stood directly in front of Jack and produced an identity card. He held it right in front of his face.

'RUC. Security check. It won't take long. Follow me, please.'

'You're OK,' Steve interjected. 'It's standard procedure. I'll wait for you.'

The man led Jack away from the stream of disembarking passengers, and towards a nearby door marked 'Security'. He levered the door handle, stepping back as it swung open and nodded for Jack to enter. Jack walked past him, noticing a strong waft of cologne as he did so.

The officer followed him in and closed the door firmly behind them.

The windowless room was brightly lit with fluorescent strip lights protruding below water-stained ceiling tiles. The only furniture was a wooden table in the centre of the room with two plastic chairs either side of it. It was functional, austere and depressing.

'Take a seat, sir.'

The Northern Irish accent was strong and harsh; Jack had to concentrate to get every word. He'd become accustomed to Steve's way of talking over the last couple of months, but this accent was something else. He sat down and pulled his small, faded holdall up onto his knees.

The officer stared at him for a few more seconds. 'Now, sir, with your full cooperation, this should only take a few minutes.'

'Sure,' Jack nodded. 'No problem.' He wasn't sure he really meant that. After all, this was Belfast – in the Troubles – and he was English.

'Let's start with your full name, occupation and usual place of residence, please, sir?'

'Jack McLaughlan. Student. Manchester University. Ridgemont Hall of Residence.' Jack felt brevity was appropriate.

'Thank you, sir,' replied his questioner having made a note. He looked Jack squarely in the eyes again, unblinking.

'And what's your reason for this visit to Northern Ireland, sir?'

'I'm here for a few days with a friend from university. He's from Larne, and we're staying with his parents.'

'Mr McLaughlan, as pleased as we are to welcome you to Northern Ireland, there must be more than that to bring you here?'

'I'm not sure what you mean.' *What's he getting at?*

'I'm wondering if there are any other reasons for your visit to Belfast?'

'No,' Jack replied. This time, the man leant forward intently.

'Has anyone asked you to bring anything into the province for them?'

'Like what?'

'I don't know, sir. Anything at all?' The repeated use of *sir* was beginning to irritate Jack.

'Not to my knowledge.' He tried not to show his annoyance.

'Has your bag been with you at all times during your journey? Could anyone have had access to it? Perhaps without your knowledge?'

'No. I'd have noticed if anyone had touched it.'

'Even when you went to the toilet, or the bar or the shop on board?' Jack had done all those things. Had he been watched throughout the ferry journey? It was unsettling.

'Yes, I'm sure. Whenever I did any of those things, my friend kept an eye on my bag.'

'Do you mind if I look inside your bag?' came the reply.

'Not at all,' replied Jack.

The man stood up, indicating the table between them. Jack placed his holdall on the scuffed table.

'Open it please, sir.' The tone was civil yet abrupt. Jack did as he was asked and unzipped his bag.

The officer proceeded to take out the contents, placing them in precise little piles on the table. Jack grimaced inwardly as they appeared. Faded boxers and old socks, and then his toilet bag, or to be exact, his dad's somewhat dated washbag. That too was opened, and the contents put on display: a cheap disposable Bic razor, a well-used toothbrush, half a tube of Colgate toothpaste, two condoms and a plastic soap container. The officer took out the small bar of soap and held it to his nose before returning it to the box.

'Are you aware of any concealed parts to your case?'

Nonplussed, Jack didn't reply immediately. 'Nope,' he said eventually. 'Not to my knowledge.'

'So, just to be clear, sir. No one has asked you to bring anything into the country. And neither you, nor your friend, let your bags out of sight at any time during the journey?'

'Yes. That's correct.'

'Did you sleep at all on the boat?'

Jack's mind slipped back to the ferry bar, and the hours spent with Roisin. He smiled as he recalled her lilting accent.

'No,' he answered. 'Well, I only dozed. And I'm sure one of us would have noticed if our bags had been tampered with.' The officer made no comment. A few moments passed silently as he made more notes on the notepad.

'One last question, sir, if I may?' Jack thought silence was enough to convey his assent. 'What are you studying in Manchester?'

What's the relevance of that? thought Jack.

'Politics and economics. I'm in my first year.'

Again, notes were made.

'Right you are, sir. Thank you for your cooperation. You're free to go now.'

The man stood up abruptly and walked out of the room. He said quietly, 'Don't forget to take your possessions, sir.' The last *sir* seemed to have a pointed ring to it.

Jack hurriedly, shoved everything back into his bag and re-zipped it. *Thanks for your help*, he thought.

When he emerged from the room, the officer was already talking with a group of policemen. He appeared to nod in his direction and Jack felt an inexplicable sense of guilt as the officers' heads turned towards him. His eyes were drawn to their black leather belts, with sidearms attached. They stood out on their dark green uniforms. *Time to get out of here* he thought.

Looking around, he saw Roisin getting into a taxi. She waved at him as it drove off.

'See you around, Jack! Enjoy your visit!' she called out of the open window. He smiled and waved back, his hand going instinctively to his back pocket to check the scrap of paper with her number was still there.

'Over here, Jack!' a voice called behind him. He spun around. Steve was waiting for him as promised. 'What did they ask you?'

Relieved to see his friend, Jack told him.

'I can't believe how many questions he asked,' he said finally. 'I thought he'd never end. Is that normal?'

'It sounds like you had the usual routine,' said Steve. 'It's the English accent. They know you're not from round here. They're suspicious of everyone, but particularly strangers. To the RUC, you could be an IRA sympathiser smuggling in weapons or information; or on the other hand, you might be an innocent person who's been used.' He looked at Jack's incredulous face. 'The IRA sometimes plant weapons in passengers' bags,' he explained. 'It's zero risk for them, and if no one searches the bag, they can create a distraction later and recover the item.'

Jack thought back to the night before. 'What about the fuss in the bar? Could someone have tried something then?'

'Great minds think alike,' said Steve. 'The RUC always have plain-clothed officers on the ferries looking for anything suspicious like that. I suspect the guy you just spoke to was one of those. He'd have observed what happened last night – and he'd have known Roisin was Catholic, and therefore could have been IRA.'

'Jesus!' Jack whispered under his breath. 'That's pretty serious shit. I had no idea. How on earth would he have known Roisin is Catholic?'

'People's names are a giveaway, Jack. *Roisin* is SO Catholic. It's the same with school names and certain words and expressions. You'll soon pick it up. Come on. Forget all that for the moment. Let's find some breakfast. I'm starving.'

It was drizzling as they left the dock and the sky above Belfast Harbour was a slate grey. Jack felt apprehensive. He put it down to the security check and a poor night's sleep. Some food would help, he told himself.

Chapter 3

Steve was a good, if concise, tour guide as they walked into the city from the docks. He would nod in the direction of something, pause, make a comment, and then move on.

The black letters H&W appeared prominently on most of the towering yellow container cranes that dominated the scene. Even walking away from the harbour, they formed a distinctive feature of the landscape.

'Harland & Wolff. Biggest ship and engineering employer in Belfast – Protestant that is,' explained Steve.

As they walked, Jack was aware of the biting wind that swept down from the steep, dark hills above Belfast. Gradually the port area gave way to the city, with wide roads, department stores, cafés, restaurants and offices.

'Look out!' Steve shouted.

Coming from the road behind them, a large grey armoured Land Rover with a wire mesh grid welded over the windscreen appeared from nowhere. It sped past them, a soldier wearing a beret at the steering wheel. Both back doors were wide open, and two soldiers perched on the benches inside. Facing the street, they quickly scanned from left to right, cradling their rifles in their arms.

'Fuck!' exclaimed Jack as it sped by.

He'd seen newspaper photos of such things but seeing it for real was very different. He caught the eye of one of the soldiers and instinctively smiled in relief. English soldiers. A natural bond he thought.

That thought was dispelled in an instant when the soldier returned the smile with a prolonged stare. No mistake, it was distinctly hostile, and there was certainly no hint of a smile. Jack suddenly realised the soldier would have no idea that he was English.

Steve nodded as the vehicle sped away.

'They prefer to keep moving. It lessens the chance of someone taking a pot shot at them. IRA snipers killed a few soldiers in the early days, so they got wiser and changed their tactics.'

It made sense to Jack.

They approached a large imposing building. Another nod from Steve. 'City Hall.' Jack followed his gaze but was distracted by a gaunt steel barrier blocking the road next to the building. It was a forbidding piece of engineering about eight feet high and stretched across the entire width of the street. Uniformed police and army soldiers milled about the various entrances, eyes constantly surveying the scene around them.

Steve read his mind.

'Yep, that's what the city centre has become these days. Barriers and no-go areas. No one gets through unless they're authorised. All vehicles are security checked with dogs and mirrors. Pedestrians are searched.' Jack marvelled at the ugliness of it all. 'We go through here,' said Steve, indicating a metal shed-like structure with two entrances marked *male* and *female*. 'Get your bag ready.'

The search was carried out by silent security men who, when satisfied, nodded them through the turnstiles. *Deliberately intimidating*, thought Jack, as he emerged on the other side.

'The place I have in mind is just off the main street up there,' Steve announced, nodding in the general direction before setting off again. Jack followed, trying not to look like a tourist.

The Teapot Café, when they got there, seemed small from the outside and the front window was misty with condensation. Jack followed his friend inside and realised the place was much bigger than it had appeared. Immediately the warmth hit him.

Two dumpy women were struggling to get to their feet, vacating a small table near the window. Steve and Jack stood politely, waiting for the women to gather up their various bags and move towards the door. Once they'd gone, Steve sat down and handed Jack a slightly stained and dog-eared menu.

'Choose what you like. This first breakfast is on me. You're my guest. You'll need to decide if you want soda bread, wheaten bread or just pan with your fry.'

'What's the difference?'

'Quite a lot,' Steve smiled. 'Soda bread is made with buttermilk. Not available in England,' he explained. 'Wheaten bread is denser and darker.'

'And pan?' Jack asked.

'You Brits call it sliced white bread. Pan over here.'

Jack decided to try the soda bread. As he bit into the hot buttered bread, he was aware that he'd never tasted anything like it before. He looked up at Steve.

'Bloody hell, that's delicious,' was all he could say.

The rest of his breakfast proved to be just as good, and he began to feel human again.

'We'd better be on our way,' said Steve as he finished his third cup of tea. 'Don't want to miss the train.'

Back on the streets, Jack's impression of Belfast that grey Sunday morning continued to be coloured by the constant presence of army Land Rovers, soldiers and policemen and endless security barriers. Steve kept up the 'nod and talk' routine.

They passed rows of shops, often with gaping holes in them.

'See this one here? That was an IRA bomb. That one over there? That was the UVF.' He looked at Jack and realised more explanation was needed. 'The nationalist Irish Republican Army and the loyalist Ulster Volunteer Force both operate in the province. You can see the consequences. Pretty, isn't it?'

Jack grimaced; he had not experienced his friend's irony before.

'It's depressing,' he said quietly to his friend.

'You got it. And more than a bit intimidating. Now you know why I came to England to study.'

They arrived at the station and bought their tickets. As the train pulled out, Jack found he was relieved to be leaving the city.

'Don't worry, mate,' Steve said reassuringly. He looked around the train carriage and lowered his voice even though their carriage was largely empty. 'Belfast and Londonderry are the worst. Maybe some of the towns near the border too, but the rest can be OK.'

Jack nodded.

'Be happy I didn't expose you to some of the nastier areas. In West Belfast, nationalist areas face loyalist ones just yards away from each other. Rioting, shooting and petrol bombs are the norm. Have you heard of the Shankill Road?'

Jack had.

'Well, the Shankill is strongly loyalist, but it's right next to the Falls, New Lodge and Andersonstown – all nationalist areas. It's a recipe for disaster, and a no-go area for most people. It would have been too risky to take you there.'

Steve continued to educate Jack about the Troubles, and their impact on Northern Ireland, throughout the journey. As the train lumbered north, Jack looked out at the increasingly beautiful scenery. The rolling hills and coastline were in direct contrast to the depressing tales his friend related.

Chapter 4

Steve's parents turned out to be both welcoming and friendly. His dad offered them the use of his car, so they planned to explore the province while using the house as a base.

Jack retired early that evening, leaving Steve to catch up with his mum and dad in front of the fire.

Inside his bedroom, he stripped down to his boxers and climbed into bed. As he lay there, he pictured Roisin's petite figure waiting by the bar on the ferry. With all he had learnt today, he realised what a dangerous situation it could have been. He smiled wryly, thinking he'd do it all again if it meant another evening with her. Rolling over, he drifted gently off to sleep, images of her laughing face playing through his mind.

The next day proved to be a complete contrast to the Belfast experience. They took the coastal road north from Larne through a couple of small seaside towns. No one seemed to be in a hurry, which was a pleasant change to England.

'The Eagles OK for the journey?' Steve had enquired and soon they had both been singing along to 'Take it to the Limit'.

Now and again, Steve went back into tour guide mode, pointing out features of the Antrim mountains to their left and the shoreline to their right. They stopped at a few of the beaches he had mentioned, and they were indeed stunning.

'I can't get over the size of them,' said Jack. 'And they're almost deserted. It's so different to the crowded seaside resorts back home. I'm used to arcades, donkey rides and candyfloss.'

Steve laughed. 'Thought you'd like it. How about we stop for lunch in Ballycastle? It's the most northerly town of the province and Scotland is only a few miles across the water.'

'Sounds great,' Jack replied.

They entered the town just after midday, and as they drove through an estate on the outskirts, Jack found his eye drawn to the side of the road. He was mesmerised. The kerbstones were painted orange, white and green in rotation.

'Presumably a nationalist street?' he queried.

'I should have mentioned that Ballycastle is mainly Catholic,' replied Steve smiling, 'but you worked it out for yourself. You're learning!'

'Why do some communities need to go to such lengths to stress their religion and their territory?'

'Don't think it's just the Catholics,' Steve replied. 'In some Protestant areas, the kerb colours are red, white and blue. It serves as a warning to the other side. Tells you know when you're taking a risk. If you don't do anything to draw attention to yourself, all is fine – usually.'

Jack was genuinely surprised. He'd never seen anything like it before.

'Mind you, it's a different logic after dark,' Steve continued. 'At night, you either avoid these areas altogether or just don't stop – even at traffic lights. In the worst areas, people can be stopped at random and interrogated as to why they're there. If their answers are wrong, they might be beaten up or even shot. Stupid, but there it is.'

As they got closer to the town centre, normality returned. The kerbstones retained their drab grey and neutral colour.

'Pub lunch, then?' Jack inquired, holding up his wallet. 'My shout this time.'

Over a pint and sandwich, and again checking that no one was listening to them, Steve added a few more insights.

'At some point, you should see the murals that are painted on gable ends in Belfast and Londonderry – or Derry as the Catholics call it. They'd be works of art if they weren't so bloody evil. The Protestant ones celebrate the Battle of the Boyne, the Red Hand of Ulster and the UVF and UDA nutters; the Catholic ones celebrate the IRA triumphs, the hatred of the Brits and the IRA/ INLA nutters.'

'What do you think will happen going forward?' Jack asked.

'That's the sixty-four-million-dollar question. No one knows. Both sides are polarised, there's no middle ground. I think it's going to get far worse before it has a hope of getting better.'

They lapsed into silence and Jack found himself wondering how Roisin felt about all this. He hoped she didn't hold extremist views but couldn't help remembering Steve's comment about the IRA working tourists on ferries. He couldn't let the thought rest. *Surely, she couldn't be involved in something like that.*

His thoughts were interrupted by his friend.

'Let's get back home. Supper with my mum and dad and then I'll show you the delights of Larne at night. We'll go to my old watering hole and meet a few of my mates. You'll like that.'

Jack wasn't sure whether Steve was being ironic again but said nothing.

On the way back to Larne, a repeat performance from The Eagles helped lighten the atmosphere. Jack found he was able to push his doubts about Roisin to the back of his mind and enjoy the journey.

That evening, in downtown Larne, everyone they met seemed to know Steve and invariably asked him about life in England.

The stock answer was 'Good, thanks mate,' and that was where the dialogue about England stopped. They had recognised their friend wasn't around as much as he used to be, but their lives were locked in Northern Ireland and conversation revolved around local events.

Jack was often asked to repeat himself as many of Steve's mates simply couldn't understand him. His English accent, together with his slight Nottingham burr, caused quite a few laughs, as did his inability to follow their conversations.

The only time the atmosphere chilled was when one of Steve's old friends was first introduced to Jack.

'Jack, this is Billy. An old football mate of mine. Billy, meet Jack, a mate of mine from England.'

'So, what foot do you kick with then, Mr Englishman?' Billy's manner was decidedly hostile. Jack had no idea why.

'Mainly right foot but occasionally I can …' Steve suddenly interrupted.

'I said he was my mate, Billy. Did you hear me? My mate. And that's all you need to know.' Steve snarled the words, and Jack realised he'd never seen his friend talk to anyone like that before.

'Oh, for fuck's sake,' replied Billy leaning away and putting on a forced grin. 'I was just joking with you. Any friend of yours, Stevie boy, is a friend of mine. Want another pint, Jack my lad?'

Jack was confused. A short conversation about football had gone badly wrong, and he had no idea why.

'I'll explain later,' said Steve putting his hand on Jack's shoulder and leading him to a table where a group were laughing over their pints.

It was on the way home that Steve finally said, 'Remember I mentioned about you learning more of our quaint Northern Ireland expressions?'

'I do.'

'It's simple. If you kick with your right foot, you're Protestant, and with your left, Catholic. It's a quick way to find out if you're on the same side from a religious and political perspective. Billy shouldn't have asked you that. I'd introduced you as my mate. That should have been enough. He's always been a bit of a dickhead and obviously hasn't changed! Sorry.'

They walked on for a few minutes in silence. Then Jack noticed a large graffiti sign on a brick wall nearby.

'What does that mean?' he asked, pointing at it.

'Try not to point over here, Jack. Just draws attention to yourself.' He turned to look.

'*Ulster Says No*. You mean that one?'

'That's the one. What does Ulster say *No* to?'

Steve smiled back and took in a long breath.

'Everything,' he exclaimed. 'And that's a big part of the problem over here.'

Chapter 5
Manchester University – December 1975

He was jolted into reality as his politics professor suddenly announced, 'Make a note of your next essay question, please.' Jack and the other four students grabbed their pens. The professor read slowly and studiously.

'Power politics is a tautology, as all politics is an exercise in power. Discuss.' He looked up at them and added, 'Thank you, everyone. Leave your completed questions in my pigeonhole before the deadline please.'

Jack wrote it down, but it made no sense to him at all. He didn't know what a 'tautology' was to start with, and he certainly had no interest in discussing it. *Bloody hell. Where do I start with this?* he thought. He left the tutorial room confused and demoralised. The next few months were going to be heavy going.

He passed the phone booths in the lobby and decided he needed a distraction. Consigning all thoughts of tautologies to the back of his mind, he reached into his back pocket for some coins and the scrap of paper he carried with him at all times.

He dialled the number and waited. After the fifth ring, and just as he was about to hang up, the phone was answered.

'Student Nurse O'Malley speaking. How may I help you?'

'Roisin, it's me, Jack.' The joy he felt when hearing her voice lifted his depression immediately.

'Hi Jack! Great to hear from you again.' She sounded genuinely pleased. 'Do you have the dates for your visits to RAF Woodvale?' *No messing around. A good sign!*

On their last phone call Jack had explained he was in the University Air Squadron and his pilot training was at RAF Woodvale, a few miles from where she worked in Ormskirk. He had tentatively suggested that they might meet up when he was next there.

Jack smiled. *She's as keen as I am.*

He outlined his plans for the next few weeks – which weekends he'd be at Woodvale and when he might be free to meet her. Once again, the conversation flowed freely, and he was sorry when she finally said:

'Jack, I'm due to start my shift. I can't believe how time passes when I'm talking to you! I'll see you in The King's Arms in Ormskirk at 7 pm on Friday. I'm looking forward to it.'

'Me too,' said Jack. And he was. Very much so. 'See you then.'

He put the phone down and realised he was grinning. Friday couldn't come soon enough.

Chapter 6

Jack was in luck. An air squadron colleague owned an old Mini and offered him a lift to Woodvale that weekend.

Andy could be a bit dry, but Jack decided he could put up with him for the hour-long journey, especially since he had also offered him the use of his car to go to Ormskirk that evening.

The routine on arrival at the RAF station was always the same.

'Please sign in, gentlemen. Good to have your company this weekend. I hope the weather treats you favourably.' It was the standard opening line for the duty sergeant at the gatehouse.

At the officers' mess, shortly after, the administrative corporal announced, 'Your briefing tomorrow starts at 08:30 as usual, gentlemen. Squadron Leader Mellish will expect you there a few minutes before.'

Jack noted the start time and was pleased. He'd be able to get back to Woodvale after last orders and still have a good night's sleep in preparation for the next day. Squadron Leader Ian Mellish, the air squadron senior officer, was known for his strict attention-to-detail attitude to flying and Jack knew that being late for the day's briefing was not an option. Mellish had been Jack's instructor three times before and the experiences had generally not been good ones.

Jack had flown in Chipmunk training aircraft in the Air Training Corps and they had a front-and-back configuration. Here, Bulldog aircraft were used. More spacious, with a side-by-side arrangement. Having his instructor sitting beside him had made Jack a little uneasy. He'd messed up the pre-flight cockpit checks and then forgotten routine instrument checks whilst airborne. Worst of all was his airsickness the last time they'd flown together. He'd had to give control back to Mellish only seconds after taking official control of the aircraft, and immediately vomited into his sick bag.

Jack blamed the smell of the rubber mask he was obliged to wear over his nose and mouth, but Mellish had been unsympathetic, to say the least.

Let's just hope tomorrow turns out better, he rationalised to himself and focused his thoughts more positively on his evening out with Roisin.

There was a chill in the air as he made his way to the car. It was one of those winter evenings when the temperature plummeted in direct proportion to the waning sun. He drove to the gatehouse and as he went inside, the duty sergeant looked up from his desk.

'You're leaving the station already, sir?'

His accent was unmistakably Scottish. Jack guessed Glasgow.

He was still not used to being called *sir*, however as a trainee pilot he carried the rank of acting Pilot Officer and as such, RAF personnel were obliged to reflect his rank in all communications.

'Yes, that's right, Sergeant. Just for the evening. I'll be back later.

It appears I have a full day's flying ahead of me tomorrow.'

'Would you mind signing out then, sir? We have to keep a close tab on people coming and going from Woodvale. Levels of security remain high. A result of the bombings down south,' he added.

'Of course,' replied Jack. He'd remembered seeing the recent news. A popular Irish pub in London had been bombed. No one had been killed but five people had been wounded.

Jack reasoned that an RAF station, even a small one like Woodvale, would be deemed an appropriate target. Especially by the IRA, who seemed to associate anything British as a legitimate target.

He took the pen the sergeant offered him, duly signed his name and entered the time. As he turned to go, the sergeant added, 'Could I remind you, sir, that the latest time for returning to the base is midnight? I'm sure you understand.'

'That's fine. I'll be back before then. I'm only meeting a friend in a pub in Ormskirk.'

Chapter 7

He was pleased to find the pub wasn't too full. He looked around and identified a couple of small tables and alcoves that offered a little privacy. There was a small jukebox mounted on the wall adjacent to the bar, and he noticed that the track playing at that moment was 'Glass of Champagne' by Sailor. Another good omen.

As he got to the bar, a pretty red-headed barmaid came from the other end of the bar towards him. She smiled at him.

'Hello there, I haven't seen you before. What can I get you?'

Jack pointed to one of the pump handles.

'I'll try a pint of Cutlass, please.' She reached above her, took a glass from the shelf and began to pour the amber-coloured liquid into the glass.

'Good choice, Cutlass,' she said. 'Very popular in Ormskirk.'

The silence that followed was interrupted by another voice.

'So, you've started without me? Have you British men no manners?'

Jack spun round to find Roisin's smiling face looking straight at him. He was taken aback by those sparkling blue eyes he remembered so well and found himself lost for words.

'Is that all?' the barmaid said loudly. 'Or can I get you something else?'

Jack managed to find his voice. 'Do you still drink cider?' he finally asked Roisin.

'A pint of cider would be very welcome after the day I've had,' she replied. 'Three bed baths for horny old men, two coughing fits and a messy case of projectile vomiting.' Jack laughed out loud, possible too loud. It was such an incredible feeling just being near her and hearing that soft Irish accent again.

The music had changed, and he became aware of the Four Seasons belting out 'Oh What a Night'. *Perfect*, he thought to himself. He reached for his wallet, but she raised her hand.

'You're on my patch now. The first round is on me.'

Jack was pleasantly surprised and had a feeling she'd have been offended if he had forced the issue. She smiled and paid for the drinks. They found an empty alcove away from the bar and sat down.

'Thanks for coming this evening, Jack. I hoped we'd meet up again. How was your journey?'

He brought her up to speed on developments with the car.

'Sounds like Andy is a wee star, then,' Roisin offered.

She's gorgeous, he thought. *Now to keep her talking.*

'So, tell me a bit about your work,' he said. 'Is every day like today? It sounds exhausting.'

'It can be hard, but I love it. And where I am, the staff are great. I had wondered if it would feel strange coming to England to study – all my family are based in Northern Ireland, and I think, despite the Troubles, my parents would have preferred me to be closer to them. Not that they've ever said that of course!' She laughed and took a sip of her cider. 'As it is, I've settled in really well and made some great friends.' She looked at him over the rim of her glass. 'You never know, maybe you'll meet them sometime,' she added cheekily.

Jack's heart skipped a beat. 'I'd like that,' he replied, trying to keep his voice calm. 'So, were you visiting family when we met on the ferry?'

'Yes. I try to get home as often as I can. It's expensive and takes big chunks out of my time, but family is important. My Ma is a real matriarch and loves it when we're all around. My Da's pretty special too – he owns and runs a small bar attached to our house.'

'That sounds convenient,' chuckled Jack.

'Ah yes, but you need to be aware the police station is right next to it,' she laughed. 'The bar is tiny but very popular and my Da is a good man because he lets the RUC officers drink there at the end of their shifts. Not everyone would allow that.'

Jack nodded, encouraging her to keep talking. As she told him about life back home, he listened intently for clues as to whether she had a boyfriend. There were none. In the end, he took his courage in both hands.

'So, is there anyone special waiting for you back home?' he asked quietly when there was a lull in the conversation. She looked at him, with mock surprise.

'A boyfriend, you mean?' she said, smiling. 'No, I don't have a boyfriend.'

Jack could barely contain his delight as she continued.

'Well, I was seeing someone for a while, but it wasn't serious. He'd have liked it to have been, but it would never have worked. You see, I want to specialise in post-operative care when I qualify. That means, in reality, Belfast or somewhere in England. He was a local boy and wanted me to stay in Newcastle. We fell out about that a while ago and haven't seen each other since.' She looked at

Jack. 'I'm sort of pleased about that. Does that sound bad?'

'Not at all,' said Jack honestly. 'I'm not seeing anyone either.' It was her turn to smile. She leant in close to him as she talked. Her scent was heavenly. Everything felt effortless and natural; conversation flowed and time sped by. Her words and expressions were refreshingly different and while he didn't always know the precise meaning, he got the gist. He could have listened to her forever. The gentle rolling accent was unlike anything he'd heard before.

The bell for last orders eventually interrupted their conversation. As they finished their drinks, Jack offered to drop her home. She happily accepted the offer.

'Thanks for a super evening,' Jack said as he pulled to a stop outside her house. 'It was lovely to spend some time with you.'

She turned to face him and smiled.

'Can we see each other again soon? I'd really like to see you again.' Jack's heart leapt again.

'What about next weekend?' he said, trying not to sound too eager. 'Does that work with your shift pattern?'

'I'll make it work,' she smiled. 'I have some friends who owe me a few favours. But if I'm to keep them onside, I'd better go in now. They'll be wondering where I am.'

He felt a strange sense of impending loss but managed to return her smile.

She opened the car door to get out, and then leant across to give him a very gentle kiss on his cheek.

'Thanks, Jack. Lovely evening. Talk next week.'

He watched her get her front door key from her jeans pocket and unlock the door. Before she went inside, she turned back to him and waved. The door closed, and with a smile on his face, he drove slowly away.

Chapter 8

Jack arrived back at the RAF station before the midnight curfew. The duty sergeant looked up and smiled as Jack walked through the door of the gatehouse.

'Evening, sir. I hope you had a good evening.'

Jack's mellow demeanour must have been apparent. 'Yes thanks, Sergeant. My first date with a girl I met a few weeks ago.'

'I'm envious, sir. Is she from these parts?'

'No, she's from Northern Ireland. She's over here studying to be a nurse.'

'Is she attached to the hospital in Ormskirk?'

'Indeed, she is.'

'Well, sir, I'm very pleased for you,' the Sergeant smiled again.

Jack thanked him and made his way out of the building. It appeared no one else was awake and all was silent as he made his way back to his room.

His alarm clock woke him the next morning at 7 am. He took five minutes to wake up properly, slipping back into thoughts and feelings about the evening before. He couldn't get Roisin out of his mind. Once dressed in his blue RAF trousers and shirt and standard polished black shoes, he knocked on Andy's door and when the door opened, he held up the Mini's keys.

'Thanks again.'

'I thought you might have spent the night in Ormskirk,' smirked Andy.

Jack laughed but said nothing.

They headed to the officers' mess for breakfast, and both helped themselves to scrambled eggs and sausages with some toast and butter. This was standard breakfast fare on flying days and tasted pretty good. Jack hoped he wouldn't see it again in a sick bag a few hours later.

After breakfast, they headed over to the ops building near the air traffic control tower to get ready for the morning's training. Jack's flying suit, helmet and other items such as navigation maps and pens, were kept in his locker in the changing area. It didn't take long to get ready and by 08:25 all the student pilots were kitted out and sitting in the briefing room.

At 08:30 precisely, Mellish started the briefing.

'Good morning gentlemen. Essentially a clear morning predicted with good visibility, but rain and mist scheduled to roll in early afternoon. Standard flight circuits, climbing to around 12,000 feet to practise stalling and recovery, and a few aerobatics over the Irish Sea if time permits before returning to base. That OK, everyone?' The trainee pilots all nodded.

Jack heard the word 'aerobatics' and hoped his stomach would not let him down.

He was scheduled to be second up so had about forty minutes to wait while Andy completed his flight. Eventually he saw the aircraft start its downwind leg and knew he had to don his helmet and start walking. He left his face mask dangling at one side to minimise the time it would be clipped firmly over his nose and mouth.

He was waiting at a safe distance as Andy taxied into position. Within seconds of the aircraft coming to a halt, the canopy opened and Andy began hauling himself out. Another few seconds and he was on the ground in front of Jack.

'Watch out, Jack, he's in a foul mood.'

'What's new?' Jack shouted back with a forced grin. He stepped up onto the wing and climbed into his seat. Looking across to Mellish, he nodded as he connected his microphone lead into the aircraft. Mellish nodded back and then Jack heard him speak through his earphones.

'OK Jack, let's hope for a better session today, shall we?' For a second Jack thought his instructor might have mellowed slightly but realised he had misjudged the comment when Mellish growled, 'We haven't got all day. Get your mask clipped on.'

Jack did as he was instructed. The unmistakable smell of rubber returned. Not a good omen.

After being airborne for about twenty-five minutes, with the temperature inside the cockpit arguably frostier than the air temperature outside, Mellish abruptly announced:

'OK, let's try a few stalls and recovery. I'll demo first, and then I want you to have a go.'

As he pulled the joystick back, the horizon disappeared, and Jack noticed the engine start to labour. The aircraft's nose continued to go up, and the speed dropped noticeably. Seconds later his stomach began to protest in tandem with the engine. *Concentrate,* he thought to himself. *Mind over matter. The feeling will pass. All will be good in a few seconds.*

At the moment the aircraft stalled, Jack knew his self-talk was to no avail. The aircraft slewed to the right, the nose dropped rapidly, and they were plummeting downwards again.

His stomach took over, sending a message to his brain: *STOP AND STOP SOON*. To his right, Mellish was pushing the throttle forward to power them out of the stall.

The engine noise increased in sync with Jack's nausea.

His forehead was sweating, his brain was foggy, and he was dimly aware of Mellish looking at him.

'Are you ready to take control, McLaughlan?' It was a rhetorical question.

'No sir, I'm not. I'm sorry, but I'm pretty sure I'm going to be sick.' Jack was already reaching up to unclip his mask.

The need to throw up was accelerating. Pure instinct took over. He unclipped one side of his mask, and it fell to one side. There was a degree of relief as fresh air replaced the horrible rubber smell. Then he reached into his flying suit trouser pocket and withdrew the folded sick bag and had it open in a flash.

He vomited into the bag and felt slightly better despite the chills that now overtook him. He felt as if he'd been punched in the stomach.

'So,' said Mellish sarcastically, 'I assume you're not going to attempt the stall and recovery. We'll head for home.'

He set the aircraft's new direction, and they flew on in silence. Jack remained one step away from being sick again. He did not attempt to re-attach the mask and Mellish thankfully didn't ask him to do so.

As they started their descent to Woodvale, Mellish finally said, 'You're going to have to get over this sickness if you want to qualify for your pilot's licence. Believe it or not, I think you have the makings of a fine officer. Maybe aircrew, maybe not, but you're good with people and seem to have a sensible head on your shoulders.' Jack felt a glimmer of hope.

'Thank you, sir,' he said trying not to sound too relieved that he wasn't being cut from the squadron. 'I'll definitely try to get over it.'

'Good lad,' said Mellish. 'That decision takes guts.'

Stuff that, Jack thought. *Roisin is definitely worth the occasional bout of airsickness.*

Chapter 9

It was Roisin who took the initiative in moving their relationship to the next level. One evening, a few weeks later, as Jack drew up outside her house to drop her off, she asked him in to meet her housemates. After the introductions had been made, Roisin invited him into her room.

'Mr McLaughlan, it's good that we're getting to know each other better but I need to run something past you.'

Jack wondered what was coming.

'You are aware I'm Catholic.' He nodded. 'And no doubt, you're also aware there are certain rules we are supposed to abide by.' Jack thought he knew where this was going and prepared himself. 'I know I'm supposed to wait until you walk me down the aisle before suggesting this, but there's something about you.' She smiled at him as she pulled him closer. 'And I have to admit, I'm not that devout either,' she added, with a wink. 'How would you feel if I asked you to stay here tonight?'

Jack felt a shock of electricity surge through his body. He could feel her body against his. Her smell, her warmth, was irresistible. 'Will your housemates mind?'

'Of course not. The girls want me to be happy, and they can see I am.'

'So, I passed the inspection then?' he laughed.

'Of course,' she laughed back. 'Well, part of it at least.' She pulled him gently over to the bed. 'Part two is coming up.'

What followed fulfilled all of Jack's dreams. They had undressed each other, gently taking in each other's bodies, and had made love through the night. In between, they shared more about their lives and what their dreams were for the future.

He had never met anyone like Roisin and had to admit he was well and truly hooked. As the morning light began to fill the room, he turned onto his side to face her, and put one hand gently on her stomach. Her skin was silky soft and warm. Her long blonde hair tousled and framing her beautiful face on the pillow. He felt so close to her, the thought of losing her was almost unbearable.

'Do you think you'll return to Northern Ireland when you finish your training?' he asked in a whisper.

She paused, a thoughtful look on her face.

'I love going home for short visits,' she answered. 'But it's very depressing over there. People try to go about their lives without making waves – or they get out. I remember your friend on the boat saying he feels the same?'

'Yep, but he says he'll almost certainly go back to work there after he gets his degree.'

'I understand that. As bad as it's become, it's important to focus on the longer term when there'll be an end to the violence.' She leant up on one elbow and looked at him. 'That's why I want to do post-operative care. The Royal Victoria in Belfast has done some brilliant work in the last few years, treating the victims of bombings and shootings. I could learn a lot working somewhere like that, and at the same time make a real difference to people's lives.'

'But wouldn't you be nervous, being at the centre of all the violence?'

It was her turn to reflect for a few seconds.

'Maybe, maybe not. Anyway, I haven't decided yet.' She lay down again and snuggled up to Jack. 'I've got to finish my training first. And even then, it will all depend on where the job opportunities come up.'

There was another pause before she said, 'Can I ask you a question?'

Without waiting for an answer, her hand moved to his. She gently but firmly picked it up and moved it further down her body.

'Can we make love again?'

He felt the magnetism of her body, pulling him towards her.

'I'll take that as a yes, then,' she murmured.

Jack laughed to himself. She was full of such lovely little idiosyncrasies.

The bus pulled up at the gates to the RAF station. Jack had spent the entire journey re-living the previous night, but as the door opened, he was forced to put those thoughts from his mind. Picking up his bag, he made his way into the security office.

The sergeant looked up at Jack.

'Morning, sir. You didn't stay here last night?'

Jack returned his gaze. 'I spent the night at Roisin's house.'

'Things are getting serious, then?' asked the military man. 'You're lucky she's based so near here.' He handed a pen to Jack to sign in. 'Lovely Irish name, Roisin. You did say she was from Northern Ireland, didn't you?'

He walked back to the accommodation block, planning to freshen up before reporting for duty. The day was crisp and chilly with a clear blue sky above. It looked like it would be a minimum of two training flights for each pilot. Added pressure. Mellish had been marginally more sympathetic recently, but Jack's persistent airsickness meant he was falling behind his peers. He knew that wouldn't be tolerated for very much longer.

The 'freshen up' worked well. Shower, shave and fresh clothes. It was time to focus on flying.

Two flights, each of over an hour, were interspersed with feelings of nausea. He'd overcome it on the first flight, but the sick bag was needed in the afternoon. With Mellish's encouragement, he'd managed to continue, but persistent air turbulence at whatever altitude they tried, meant he continued to feel mildly queasy for the rest of the flight.

As the aircraft taxied to a stop and Jack started to unbuckle his harness straps, he had earned a 'Better, Jack. Better,' from Mellish. 'We might just get there. Well done for battling through it.'

Jack was pleased. His efforts had been recognised. His flying days weren't over yet.

Chapter 10

So it was, that a pattern became established. Jack spent the weeks in Manchester, attempting to focus on his studies and would travel up to Woodvale or Ormskirk at the weekends.

As Easter approached, Roisin mentioned that she would be going home for a few days. 'Would you like to come with me?' she said. 'My parents have said you'll be welcome, and it'll be a chance for you to meet my brothers. They'll be home too for the Easter weekend. You'll like them, I'm sure. They're all very different, but I love each one of them. I'm sure they'll all like you,' she said with a smile. 'Who wouldn't?'

'Well, I suppose this will be the time to find out,' Jack laughed.

'Good,' she said. 'You'll need to keep your handsome head down though. My dad said the UVF have been targeting Catholic bars and clubs near them. Your accent will raise suspicions.'

'I'll be careful, Roisin. Trust me.'

'I do trust you, Jack,' she replied.

They travelled together on the overnight ferry.

The RUC detained Jack once again. A different policeman but the same procedure.

Roisin's dad met them at the docks, and warmly shook Jack's hand. 'Seamus,' he beamed. 'I hope you're ready for a true County Down welcome,' he added, leading the way.

Roisin's mother was standing next to the car as they approached. Facially she looked very much like Roisin and was about the same height with the same bright blue eyes. Without waiting to be introduced, she grabbed Jack in a big hug and kissed him on the cheek. 'So glad that Roisin has met you, Jack. Call me Siobhan. I'd like that.' She released him as Seamus opened the car door for him.

'That's what we call a proper Irish welcome,' Roisin laughed as he climbed in beside her.

On the journey to Newcastle, Jack picked up about sixty per cent of the conversation. He knew Roisin would bring him up to speed later, so contented himself with gazing out the window. Now and then she would squeeze his hand and look expectantly at him. He worked out this was a prompt for him to answer a question or make a comment. Invariably he had to ask for the last bit of the conversation to be repeated – leading to more smiles and laughter.

As they left the city, heading south, the graffiti and slogans gave way to beautiful green countryside with gently rising and falling hills. After about twenty minutes, Roisin pointed out the approaching Mourn Mountains. High and impressive, almost daunting as they swept towards the sea.

Newcastle lay at the foot of the mountains, next to a lovely beach. A combination of well-maintained hotels and shops seemed a million miles away from the stark and oppressive streets of Belfast. As they drove down a broad road towards the O'Malley's home however, Jack saw massive concrete roadblocks and barbed-wire fences. An ugly grey observation tower stood above the town's police station situated next to the concrete blocks. The building had no windows, just narrow slats.

They parked the car in the nearest designated parking space, about fifty yards away, and headed to a small door at the side of a bar next to the police station. Jack grabbed Roisin's hand.

'Bloody hell. When you said where your parents lived, I had no idea that it would look like this.'

Roisin looked around her. 'Well, this is what it's like now. It used to be a very pretty street. That was until the bombings and shootings started. The police station was attacked a few times in the early years of the Troubles. The tower, barriers and wire have all gone up since.' She pushed him gently in the direction of the house door. 'Go you on,' she said.

As he entered, there was a long, wide hallway leading to the rest of the house at the back. He estimated the bar itself, adjacent to the house, was probably the same length as the hallway.

They walked into an enormous kitchen. 'This is where we eat our meals,' announced Seamus. 'And where we share the day's events as a family.' Jack noted the large wooden kitchen table with lots of chairs scattered around it, and the Aga along one wall. He could imagine everyone enjoying time together in this space.

The rest of the house was just as large and airy, and while Siobhan began to prepare the evening meal and Seamus disappeared to the bar, Roisin showed Jack upstairs, into the spotlessly clean guest room.

'Remember,' she whispered, pulling him closer, 'stay in your room tonight. If I can, I'll come to see you for a short time.' Jack put his arms around her and gently kissed her, wondering if he could wait that long.

They were interrupted by voices calling from downstairs. Two of Roisin's brothers had arrived. Neil, a teacher from Derry, and her youngest brother, Rory, who'd driven over from Belfast.

'Now then, you must be Jack,' said Neil, taking Jack's hand and shaking it firmly as they entered the kitchen. 'The Jack that is romancing my wee, innocent sister. I'm Neil.'

He leaned in towards Jack. 'I hope you two are not doing anything that my Ma and Da wouldn't approve of Jack?' he added mischievously.

Jack was caught off guard. He mumbled what he hoped was an appropriate response.

'That's OK, then,' Neil grinned. 'Now, has anyone offered you a drink yet? You'd think my Da, running a bar and all that, would have sorted you out before now, wouldn't you? Beer or something else, Jack?' Again, the Northern Irish brogue was strong, but this time understandable. Jack opted for a beer and turned to the other brother.

'You must be Rory. Nice to meet you. Roisin tells me you live and work in Belfast.'

'Aye, I do that,' Rory replied somewhat cautiously with no attempt to smile. 'I understand that you've been to Belfast and Larne before? What do you think?' His tone was slightly hostile.

'Much like other big cities,' Jack responded. 'But the security was all new to me.'

'That's true,' Rory said. 'Some areas are not safe for Brits.' He was clearly about to say more, but Roisin interrupted him.

'Now then Rory, Jack's only here five minutes, and you're trying to scare him. Plenty of time for you to bore him with your views of this happy province.'

Her tone was friendly, but it also contained an unmistakable warning to her brother.

'Sorry Rosh,' Rory said, still not smiling. 'Jack's our guest. And he's your boyfriend. I'll give him the inside track on Belfast another time.'

'I'd like that,' said Jack. 'It would be great to see things through local eyes.'

'I'll hold you to that.' The comment was accompanied by a silent stare which rattled Jack.

The arrival of Conor, Roisin's eldest brother, broke the tension. And shortly after that, Seamus emerged from the bar.

Supper with the family was loud and fun. Siobhan's cooking was marvellous, and the beer and wine flowed all evening. Jack could sense that Roisin was relaxing as the evening wore on, pleased that her Protestant English boyfriend seemed to be making a good impression on her family.

Once the meal was over, Roisin and Jack excused themselves and went for an evening walk along the beach.

'I suppose I should have warned you about my brothers. They're always up for pulling someone's leg – especially someone who's not from around here. Don't take it personally – there's nothing in it.'

'I'm glad. It didn't bother me with Neil and Conor – I knew they were joking. But Rory? Well, he didn't seem that pleased to meet me.'

She went quiet for a moment. 'I do worry a bit about Rory. Because he lives and works in Belfast, he's the one with most sympathy for the nationalist cause. He's basically a great guy but after Bloody Sunday things changed for him.'

Jack knew that bit of Northern Irish history. Thirteen civilians shot dead in Derry by British paratroopers. People were still very angry about it. Understandably. It made him wonder how Roisin's brothers really felt about an Englishman dating their only sister. She somehow sensed this and tried to reassure him.

'Come on,' she said, taking his arm again to lead him back along the beach. 'I know my brothers are going to be just fine with you.' She looked up at him with a grin. 'Believe me, we'd have known already if they didn't think you were right for me!'

When they got back to the house, Siobhan and Seamus had retired to bed. Roisin's brothers were chatting and sipping Bushmills. He was offered a glass and sat down in an armchair to join them. Roisin declined and bid them all a good night.

'You boys never change. Your whiskey nightcaps keep the distilleries in business. I'm up early to help Ma with the church, so I'll leave you to it.'

Jack found he was tuning in more quickly to the conversation. All three brothers had slightly different accents reflecting where they were based, but they all used the same sayings and idioms he had become used to with Roisin.

'So, I've heard that you were our sister's saviour on the boat over a few months ago,' Conor smiled.

'The way I heard it, you were a bit presumptive about her need to be saved from the Proddies.' Rory's tone was accusatory.

'That's unfair,' countered his older brother. 'You know how dangerous those situations can become. If they'd found out she was a Catholic, who knows what would have happened.'

Jack tried to explain himself. 'I just felt for her. The way to the bar was blocked, and the guys were pretty drunk.' He addressed his comments to Rory and stared over his glass.

There was a long pause.

It was Neil that spoke next, turning to Rory. 'Now, is that any way to talk to our wee sister's boyfriend? Listen to the man. He was there, and you weren't. I suggest you butt out of things that you don't know anything about.'

Rory raised an eyebrow towards his brother.

'Suppose so,' he mumbled before changing the subject. 'Shall we have another wee one then?' He held up his empty glass. Jack took that as his moment to retire to bed. 'Thanks, but another time maybe. It's been a long day and I'm ready for bed.'

Conor and Neil seemed to accept his decision graciously, bade him goodnight and returned to their conversation. Only Rory's continued gaze made him feel a little uneasy.

He climbed the wooden staircase and went to his bedroom as quietly as he could. As he opened the door, he was pleasantly surprised to find Roisin lying in his bed. 'I can't stay long,' she whispered, 'but I needed to be with you tonight, just for a while. You've been amazing all day. The fact that you stayed up and had a drink with them will have meant a lot. I think you've won them over.'

Jack chose not to mention the dialogue with Rory.

'Well, we'd better not give them a reason to change their minds then, had we?' he chuckled. With that, he reached for her hand and snuggled up quietly against her warm body. They made love quietly and easily, and just as Jack was beginning to fall asleep, he became drowsily aware that she had slipped out of her side of the bed and put on her dressing gown. She came round to his side of the bed and bent over Jack's face, kissing him gently.

'See you in the morning, Mr McLaughlan,' she whispered. 'Breakfast is at 08:30ish. Sleep well.'

Chapter 11

The next day started well enough with a full breakfast and people appearing in the kitchen at different times. No one minded. Whiskey sipped and appreciated the night before, usually came with some form of consequential hangover.

It appeared to Jack that Roisin's brothers had continued drinking and chatting until the 'wee small hours' and were suffering the full effects. He was glad that he had gone to bed when he did.

Throughout the day, family seemed to pop in and out, simply doing their own thing, chatting to whoever was around at the time. Siobhan was content to cook and talk to whoever was in her line of sight, always smiling and upbeat. Jack loved the happy atmosphere that existed in the house.

It was only that evening, when the news broke, that the mood changed. A bomb had exploded in the town of Dungannon.

Early reports said it had been a car bomb detonated outside the Hillcrest Bar and opposite a school where a teenage disco was in full swing.

Roisin's family sat in silence as the news came in, trying to make sense of what they were hearing: three people, some children, were thought to have been killed and scores seriously injured. The bar had been full of Catholic revellers celebrating St Patrick's Day. The news team blamed the Protestant paramilitary force – the Ulster Volunteer Force.

As it began to sink in, tears appeared in Roisin's eyes. Seamus put his hand over his mouth, muttering incoherently.

'You bastards,' Rory snarled at the TV. 'You cowardly bastards!'

Jack tried to comfort Roisin, but to no avail.

'Oh God,' she said. 'This is why I chose to go to England. Won't this ever stop?'

Rory continued, his voice raw with anger.

'Innocent Catholics are being butchered on the streets while the RUC and UDR do fuck all to stop it.' He was out of his seat and pacing around the room. 'They tolerate this, you know. The fuckin' British establishment tolerate this! They know who these bastards are, and they do nothing to stop it!' He glared at Jack. 'The Brits are behind everything!' he shouted.

Jack didn't know what to do or say. There was nothing to say. He turned back to Roisin whose eyes remained focused on the horror unfolding on TV.

He was beginning to understand the family's sense of powerlessness at a society that was tearing itself apart. At that moment he understood why Roisin had left Northern Ireland and why Rory was increasingly falling behind attempts to *respond in kind* to the savagery and unfairness they considered they were faced with. It was dawning on him that this was no longer just a localised conflict, in a relatively unknown part of the UK. This was a bloody civil war – savage and unforgiving.

The rest of the evening was very subdued. Nobody spoke much. Siobhan phoned a few of her family and friends who lived near Dungannon to check they were OK. They were. Seamus absorbed himself silently in the bar. Roisin's brothers went out to see their respective friends, all assuring their mother that they'd take extra care wherever they were.

Roisin, uncharacteristically quiet, agreed to Jack's suggestion of a walk along the beach. They walked silently hand in hand. No words were necessary. When they reached the end of the beach, she turned to him and hugged him hard.

'Jack, I hate what this war is doing to our country. Over the water, all this brutality seems so far away but being here now it brings it all back to me. I feel so guilty running away from it.'

Jack knew what she meant. The need to be careful seeped into people's psyches and their daily activities. Caution had to be used before entering bars, clubs, hotels and even individual shops. If there was any doubt, then they were avoided. People went out infrequently and were careful about what they said and to whom.

His heart went out to her.

He wondered how he would feel if she ever did return over here when her nursing training was over. If she did, fear and terror would be a part of her life. Some would see her not as a nurse dedicated to saving lives, but as an enemy who supported Catholic paramilitaries. The thought sent waves of emotion through him.

He didn't want that to happen to her.

Chapter 12

Back at university, the week dragged for Jack. Deadlines for meaningless assignments were looming. He felt disengaged and flat. The only thing that kept him going was the fact that he'd see Roisin again at the weekend.

The mid-week phone call helped a lot and broke up the academic grind. She sounded more like her usual cheerful self, and Jack was much relieved.

When he finally knocked at her door on the Friday evening, she welcomed him with an enormous hug.

'Come on in,' she said excitedly. 'I've had some news.'

'What is it?'

She said nothing but led him straight to her room and closed the door behind them. Her face told him this was serious.

'I've been offered a job after my training finishes. A really good job. It's on a post-operative ward. Just what I wanted.'

Outwardly, Jack smiled. Inwardly, his stomach lurched.

'Where?'

She sat down on the bed. 'Well, there's the thing. It's at the Royal.' She looked up at him. 'The Belfast Royal Victoria Hospital.'

Jack felt like he had been punched. He sat down beside her, trying to tame the emotions running through him.

What about us? What about you!

After a long pause, he looked at her. 'Well, part of me – a big part of me – is delighted,' he eventually said. Another pause. 'The other part of me – the selfish part – wants you closer. And definitely not in Belfast!'

'I know, Jack, and it's that that's making me think I should let this pass and wait for something else over here in England.'

He cupped her face in his hands and said, 'Listen, we both know it's a great opportunity. You might not get another chance like it. You've got to take it.'

She moved forward and hugged him tightly. 'Let's talk about it later.'

She'd cooked them both a fish pie, and they ate it at the kitchen table with a bottle of white wine. He'd had to use the kitchen sieve to remove the bits of cork that had dropped inside. They both laughed, and he was relieved to see the sparkle in her eyes had returned.

Afterwards, they went to the pub and continued to talk. 'I just feel it's the right thing,' she said quietly. 'At the Royal, I could make a difference. If I can't stop the violence, I can at least help save them.'

She looked at him with a pained expression.

'I don't want to be away from you, Jack, but I think this is something I have to do.' He saw the conflict in her eyes.

'Let's try to find a way to make it work,' he finally offered. She nodded and was about to reply when Jack continued. 'You and I want the best for each other, don't we?' He paused, and she nodded again. He made an effort to keep his voice positive and upbeat. 'Why don't you take the job, and we'll work together to see each other regularly. I still have long summer breaks, lots of long weekends, and there will be opportunities to get over to see you. We could make it work.'

Her eyes filled up with tears.

'Hey, the more I think of it, the more I know it's right,' he added with a smile.

'I do so love you, Jack.' She took his hand and squeezed it tightly.

He stayed over at the house that night. Their lovemaking had an added intensity and, as they lay together afterwards, Jack found himself holding her just a little more closely than usual.

He didn't sleep well. His dreams were weird. In one he was in prison for a crime he hadn't committed; in another, he was the passenger in a car accident but couldn't remember who was in the car with him.

Each time he awoke, he was reassured to find Roisin breathing gently beside him.

Chapter 13

The journey back to Manchester took about two and a half hours. He stared out of the window for most of it, thinking through the possible options. No matter what he came up with, it still meant time away from Roisin, and the thought filled him with despair.

He busied himself with planning his lectures and tutorials for the next week and actually managed to finish an essay he'd been struggling with for a few weeks. He knew full well it wasn't his finest piece of work, but really didn't care.

By the time Friday came, he was more than ready to get away from his studies.

'Good afternoon, sir,' the duty sergeant announced. 'You are requested to report immediately to Squadron Leader Mellish in the officers' mess.' The sergeant's tone of voice was more formal than usual.

Bloody hell, thought Jack. *That's all I need now.* 'Any idea what this is about?' he enquired.

'No, sir. Just that I was to let him know as soon as you arrived.' With that, he picked up the handset next to him and dialled a three-digit extension – presumably the officers' mess.

'Good afternoon, sir. You wanted me to inform you when Student Pilot Officer McLaughlan arrived.' He paused for a few seconds listening. 'Yes sir, he's in front of me now. I've informed him that you want to see him immediately. He's on his way.' He put the receiver down.

'He's waiting for you.'

'Thanks, Sergeant,' replied Jack. 'Wish me luck.'

'I do indeed, sir.' The sergeant looked up and smiled. He meant it.

Jack made his way to the officers' mess, glad that he had shaved that morning and was looking smart. He was pleased Mellish wouldn't be able to criticise that at least.

On arrival, a steward was waiting for him at the main entrance.

'Follow me please, sir,' was all he said and led Jack along a long corridor to a wood-panelled door. The steward knocked on it, and Jack heard Mellish's muffled voice: 'Come in.'

Jack found himself entering a small lounge. Three high-backed leather armchairs faced away from him, arranged around an ornate metal fireplace. Mellish got up from one of the armchairs and came towards him, arm outstretched. *That's unusual,* thought Jack as he shook his hand. 'Good afternoon, sir.'

'Afternoon, Jack,' said Mellish. His tone was friendly and welcoming. *Even more unusual.*

'I appreciate you coming over. I'd like to introduce you to Lieutenant Colonel John Turner.'

Jack was momentarily taken aback as a tall man with short fair hair stood up from one of the armchairs. He had not been aware anyone else was in the room.

'The colonel is based in Northern Ireland. A senior member of military security there.'

'Good afternoon, Jack.'

The man spoke in a crisp English accent. He offered his hand, and Jack shook it. The grip was firm and prolonged. He looked directly at Jack as he continued.

'Please sit down and let me explain the purpose of this meeting.' Jack realised in an instant, and with a certain amount of relief, that the subject matter was not his flying record. His curiosity increased.

'Squadron Leader Mellish has briefed me about your time with the Air Squadron. You're training to be a pilot but have yet to decide upon a military after you graduate. Correct?'

'Yes, sir,' replied Jack. 'My original intention was to try for RAF aircrew, but that could all change.' He looked at Mellish.

'You are aware Jack has an ongoing issue with airsickness,' Mellish explained before turning to Jack. 'This meeting however is about something completely different.'

Turner spoke again. 'As you are no doubt aware, the situation in Northern Ireland continues to worsen. Innocent civilians, soldiers and police officers are all targets. Paramilitary organisations, on both sides, are becoming increasingly violent both in Ireland and the UK.'

The man paused, looking for a sign that Jack understood.

'Yes, sir,' Jack answered. 'I've been over myself a couple of times in recent months, and I'm aware of all you've said. But what has all that got to do with me?'

'I'll explain, but before I begin, I must remind you that you signed the Official Secrets Act upon joining the University Air Squadron. The contents of this meeting are bound by that. Do you understand?'

Jack nodded.

'At present, you currently hold the rank of Student Pilot Officer. That is an official rank in the British Armed Forces.'

Jack nodded again.

'Within the past year, you have been to Northern Ireland twice. You will have seen the level of security for yourself and must also be aware that violence and brutality are commonplace.'

Jack continued to nod as images came flooding back into his mind.

'It is unusual to find somebody that has experience of Northern Ireland, is already a member of the armed forces and yet is not actively involved in events over there,' the colonel continued. 'You have also been exposed to, and presumably accepted by, both Catholic and Protestant communities since your girlfriend is a Catholic from County Down and your university friend is Protestant and from Antrim.'

Jack was stunned.

'I'm sure you are wondering how we know this.' Turner had read Jack's mind. 'Let me simply say that anyone travelling to or from Northern Ireland triggers interest from the security services. It's our way of checking who are the "good guys"' and who are the "bad guys". All information is fed into our security database.'

Jack instantly thought back to people on the ferries, the RUC searches, the gatehouse duty sergeant, people he'd met during his visits. My god, the list of possible options was enormous.

'We've carried out further research,' continued Turner. 'We know you're not enjoying your current university studies and also, thanks to Squadron Leader Mellish here, are aware that while struggling with airsickness, you have applied yourself consistently and professionally and that you are well regarded by your peers. You have excellent social skills, think quickly on your feet and generally have a very responsible attitude to life.'

He glanced at Mellish, who affirmed the comments with a nod.

Jack was still in shock. It was clear he had been *watched* and *reported on* for some time now. He was strangely uneasy about that.

Turner continued.

'What I'm about to say must remain strictly between the three of us in this room. None of it can be shared with your girlfriend, Miss

O'Malley. Have I made myself clear?' He looked directly at Jack. 'You must understand that. For her sake and that of her family.'

Again, Jack nodded, unable to find words to respond.

The colonel leant forward in his chair. 'This is what we propose. We need additional *eyes and ears* on the ground, primarily in Belfast. Despite having undercover military personnel, we have some blind spots. Queen's University is one of these – a significant gap in our intelligence. We need a full-time student, mixing with fellow students, who can provide details of bars, institutions and events that might become targets for the paramilitaries. We would like you to be our eyes and ears at, and around, Queen's. A student, unsuspected by his peers and privy to lots of data that will certainly be useful. We know young militants from both sides attend Queen's.'

Jack's jaw dropped.

Not waiting for a reply, the colonel added, 'As a British intelligence asset you would be helping to save lives by providing even small pieces of intelligence.'

Jack had not heard the term *asset* before, but he presumed it to mean some form of clandestine agent.

'We have provisionally cleared the way, through official channels, for you to transfer from Manchester University to Queen's University, Belfast to complete your second and third years of study. There is a psychology degree you would transfer on to. Assuming you agree, of course.' He smiled for the first time. 'We think psychology would suit you far more than your current course.'

Jack could not believe what he was hearing. How could they know all this?

Turner hadn't finished.

'We are also aware of your girlfriend's job offer at the Royal Victoria Hospital, Belfast. I'm sure you can see that by helping us, you will be able to keep seeing each other as well. All rather convenient, I would say.'

This last piece of information sent a chill through Jack. 'How do you know so much about my girlfriend?'

'It's our business to know. When Miss O'Malley first came to study in England, we had to check her out, and her family. Standard practice in these challenging times. Currently we have no concerns about her, albeit she has a brother who's on our radar. He's based, as I'm sure you're aware, in Belfast.'

Rory, Jack thought. He wasn't surprised.

Jack hardly had time to process this information before Turner continued. 'I'm sure all this has come as a bit of a shock to you, but as I say, it's a matter of the utmost secrecy and must stay within this room. You are regarded as a young man of potential, who possesses high intelligence and integrity. A rare combination. I'm appealing to your sense of duty. Your patriotic duty. Please think about it, and we can talk again before you go back to Manchester. I'm here for another couple of days.'

He paused for a moment and looked expectantly at Jack.

'It's a lot to process,' Jack replied honestly.

'Although the details of our conversation must remain confidential, it may help you to tell Miss O'Malley you have been exploring university options and there is a possibility of a transfer to Queen's.'

That was something at least. For now, he simply wanted to be out of this room and be able to think clearly. 'OK. I'll let you know on Sunday.'

'Good,' said Turner with a smile. He and Mellish both rose to their feet and shook Jack's hand.

'There will be no flying tomorrow,' added Mellish. 'The weather forecast is dubious, and in any event, you'll need time to think. Report back here on Sunday morning, please. 11:00 sharp.' Jack nodded and left the room, ushered out by Mellish.

'Think carefully and make the right decision, Jack,' he added in a low whisper before re-entering the room and closing the door behind him. The full enormity of what had just been suggested really struck home. Jack remembered Turner's words. 'Eyes and ears' on the ground around the University, an 'intelligence asset'.

He had just been offered the opportunity to become an informer. Basic level yes, just listening and passing on what he heard, but still an informer.

Possibly exciting, possibly dangerous. Mellish had been correct in saying he had to make the right decision.

Chapter 14

Jack spent the next few hours re-living the conversation with Turner and thinking through his options. He knew that Turner's offer ticked some important boxes for him. Being close to Roisin and changing to psychology were the obvious ones. He wasn't so sure about patriotic duty. *Serving your country* had always sounded a bit pompous to Jack and seemed more appropriate to a James Bond film.

In this new context, however, he couldn't deny the appeal. If he managed to do anything to help reduce the carnage over in Northern Ireland and move the province back towards a peaceful existence, surely that was good. And, he had to admit, there was a frisson of excitement about it all too.

Of course, he would not continue to fly over there but was surprised to find this no longer bothered him. The constant battle with nausea had worn him down. Now he would concentrate on a new part of his life. He would study psychology. He would enjoy that, and he and Roisin could share a life together, albeit in Belfast.

He tried to rationalise what Turner had proposed. The role in Belfast was essentially just to pass on information he would share with mates anyway. It was nothing really. If that contributed in any way to the peace effort in Northern Ireland, then that worked for him.

As he travelled the familiar roads to Ormskirk, he realised the sadness of the past week was now a thing of the past, replaced with growing excitement of what might be. His only concern was that he couldn't tell Roisin the full story. He knew that. And yet it didn't feel right to have such a huge secret between them. *It's worth it, in the long run*, he told himself, trying to put it out of his mind. But try as he might, his conscience nagged him all the way to Roisin's door.

'Well, my wee man, you're looking good.' She must have been waiting for him because she answered the door straight away, smiling as usual. That smile lit up his world.

'So are you, wee girl,' Jack mimicked the Northern Irish brogue.

She laughed. 'I'd put you somewhere between Belfast and Ballymena. Maybe nearer Ballymena.'

'Funny you should say that. I have some news for you. And I think you'll be pleased.'

She looked quizzical. 'Come on in then and tell me all about it.' She took his hand and pulled him in, closing the door firmly behind her with her foot. 'First things first,' she said, pressing her body against his and giving him a long kiss. 'Now then, what's your news?' she asked once she had released him.

He took a deep breath and began. 'Well, since your news last week, I've been asking a few questions back in Manchester about the possibility of changing courses. You know how much I hate the one I'm on.'

She nodded. Her silence suggested that he continue.

'Well, there's no chance of changing in Manchester.' He paused deliberately. 'But there is a good chance of being able to change to a psychology degree somewhere else.'

He paused again, watching her face, which as yet he couldn't read. 'Year 2, at another university.'

One last pause for maximum effect.

'At Queen's,' he announced with a flourish. 'In Belfast!'

She stared at him intently, her facial expression not changing. He began to wonder if he'd made himself clear. Or, worse, if she wasn't as happy as he hoped she'd be.

Her face still didn't change. He felt the need to fill the silence.

'I didn't say anything mid-week as I didn't want to get your hopes up and then find it wasn't possible. I only found out for sure yesterday.'

Slowly, her face began to break into a grin. 'So, you'd transfer to Queen's to do psychology?' she reiterated. 'Starting in September? Like me?'

'You've got it,' he beamed. 'So, what do you think?' He was teasing her.

'Oh Jack, that's so wonderful. More than I'd ever dreamed of but …' She paused.

'But what?' he asked, a little confused. 'I thought you'd be pleased.'

'I am of course, but it's so dangerous over there. You know that, and you're English. That makes it doubly dangerous for you. I couldn't live with myself if something happened to you there.'

Bravado, fuelled by a desire to be with her, flooded through his voice. 'I'll be fine. I've already had a glimpse remember, and I'll always be careful. Most of the time I'll be in and around the University area, and you've already told me that it's pretty safe there.'

She nodded but not convincingly.

Then she smiled again 'Is it certain – about the transfer? What's the probability it'll happen?' She was looking for catches, thought Jack. He'd been asking himself similar questions since the meeting with Turner and Mellish a few hours before.

'No catches as far as I can see at this stage. I'll have a lot of summer reading to catch up on, I'll have to get up to speed with what I've missed in Year 1, but that's about it apparently.' He looked at her to see if he had convinced her, desperately hoping that she couldn't read his conscience.

'That would seem sensible,' she said. 'Will your grant still be paid?'

'Apparently so. They're funding me to get a degree. I don't think they care what sort of degree it is.'

'What about your flying?' She looked worried.

'I've thought about that,' he replied truthfully. 'That's the one thing that's not transferable in the deal. And before you ask, I can honestly say that I'm not going to miss it. It's been more and more of a strain in the last few months, and I've not been enjoying it. I won't be sorry to stop. Honestly.' He emphasised the last word.

'Well, perhaps you could always pick it up again in a few years if you were still interested.'

'That's what I thought too,' he replied and then pulled her close to him. 'So, with all this news, we need to celebrate, don't you think?' He didn't wait for her to reply. 'There's no flying this weekend because of the weather, so we should use the time to make some plans, and I certainly need to break the news to my parents at some point.'

'How will they react do you think?' she asked.

'I know exactly. Mum will worry about the danger of violence, and Dad will just want to know why I've changed to psychology. I'll reassure my mum – you can help there – and I'll explain the logic to my dad. They will want me to be happy – and I will be if you're around.' He squeezed her hand as he said it.

∞

'I'll need to tell Mellish I've decided to resign,' Jack said as they lay together in bed the next morning. 'If I go back tomorrow morning, I can see him face-to-face. It's the least he deserves after all the time he's given me.'

It wasn't quite a lie and meant he could meet Mellish and Turner at the required time.

They spent the day making plans, walking hand in hand along the beach at Woodvale. The weather was blustery and the drizzle was constant, but Jack didn't care, he was with the woman he loved, and that was going to continue.

Chapter 15

Jack arrived at the RAF station just before 10:15 the following day. The duty sergeant was alert and professional.

'Morning, sir. I hope you had a good evening. Lieutenant Commander Turner will see you at eleven o'clock. Here are the keys to your bedroom. You will probably need a few minutes to collect your thoughts before the meeting.'

Very efficient, thought Jack. He was sure the man in front of him didn't know the full details of the meeting on Friday or the one today, but he clearly recognised Jack was involved in something serious.

He decided to go back to his room and make some notes for himself. By 10:45 he had a full page of questions. He felt prepared.

He had a quick shave and smartened himself up as best he could before making his way to the officers' mess. The same steward was waiting for him, and the same procedure followed, but it was Turner's voice he heard from inside as the steward knocked.

He walked into the room. Mellish was nowhere to be seen. As the door closed, Turner smiled and beckoned for him to sit down. 'Good to see you again, Jack. I trust you had a good visit to Ormskirk?'

Pleasantries over, Turner's tone became more serious.

'Right Jack, you've had some time to think about our conversation on Friday. What's your decision?'

Jack looked straight at him. 'I'm in, sir. I'd like to accept your offer. I do have a few questions though.'

'Of course. Let's hear them. I'll answer them as best as possible. After that, I'll talk you through the next steps.'

Jack opened his pad and looked at his list.

An hour later, the steward arrived with sandwiches and coffee for them both.

'I thought we'd have a working lunch,' Turner said after the steward had put down the tray and left the room. 'I suggest that it would be useful for us both to summarise what we've agreed up to this point. I'll go first while you eat your lunch.'

Jack helped himself to a range of sandwiches while the senior officer scanned his notes. When he sat back, Turner began.

'OK, Jack. We've agreed that in September you'll start Year 2 of a psychology degree at Queen's University Belfast. In all respects, you will behave as a normal student and will immerse yourself in student life.' He looked up. 'That won't be too hard, will it? An additional stipend of £200 will be added to your grant cheque at the start of each term. To avoid suspicion, this will appear to come from your county council.' He looked up at Jack and smiled again. 'That should allow you to socialise appropriately. You will be provided with additional funds should you need them.'

Jack smiled. *Beer money.*

'Nottinghamshire County Council will continue to pay your accommodation and tuition fees, and someone from Queen's will contact you in the next few weeks to talk about transition and arrange a visit to the University.'

Jack nodded. This was what he had understood.

'As far as your covert activities are concerned, you will be allocated a handler; an undercover RUC officer. This officer will be your only point of contact while you are in Belfast. You will meet with them on a regular basis in or around the University area. All information you deem useful will be confirmed orally to them, never in writing.' He looked at Jack again. 'I reiterate the need for extreme caution. Things are dangerous over there at the moment, and you cannot be too careful. Paramilitary organisations work hard to identify military and police informers.'

Jack nodded once again.

'You will be expected to pass on information about marches or demonstrations, visiting speakers – whether official or unofficial – and any special events that may require additional security measures. You need not worry if this information seems of little significance or appears to be common knowledge. That is not for you to decide.' He paused for a moment and scanned his notes.

'Your living arrangements with Miss O'Malley,' he said, looking up at Jack. 'While you are free to make whatever decision you like in the fullness of time, you will live in the University's student accommodation for the first year. It's simply not credible that you would move to Belfast and not make use of the halls of residence in your first year.' Jack knew this would disappoint Roisin but also knew it made sense.

'How you raise this with Miss O'Malley is of course up to you, but I think we can help your case by ensuring she receives a letter from the Royal requiring her, for reasons of security, to live in the hospital's nurses' accommodation. The same logic applies to her as to you. New faces in Belfast, having to play themselves in and all that.'

Jack rationalised that it would be a small concession in the bigger scheme of things. They'd still be able to see each other most days, and with a little creativity, all would still work for them. It could also allow them time to look for a house together.

Turner continued with his summary. Everything was entirely consistent with their discussions up to lunch. 'Finally,' he added, 'you will write a letter of resignation to Squadron Leader Mellish informing him of your decision to leave the Air Squadron. Effective immediately. At that point, to all intents and purposes, your association with the armed forces will end. You will be a civilian student. Only a handful of very senior personnel will know of your continued involvement with the military.' Jack nodded as Turner added, 'I suggest you cultivate a *student look* over the next few months. Let your hair grow longer, so you blend in with those around you. Tie up loose ends at Manchester and be prepared for your transition visit to Queen's. Perhaps take a holiday with Miss O'Malley.' He paused, and scanned his notes again, flicking backwards and forwards through the pages. Jack didn't interrupt him. 'Have I missed anything?'

'Just one remaining question, sir,' Jack replied. 'My handler in Belfast. How and when do I meet them for the first time?'

Turner smiled.

'Once at Queen's, they will make themselves known to you. They will initiate a conversation with you, and you will exchange code words. That first opening will seem a little strange, but it is necessary in order to maintain safety – both for you and for them.

'So, what is their code word?' Jack asked incredulously.

'Whippet,' Turner smiled.

'And my reply?'

'Bulldog.'

Jack burst out laughing.

Chapter 16

The summer months had seen everything fall neatly into place. Roisin started her new job, delighted that she had been lucky enough to get a place in the Royal's nursing quarters adjacent to the main hospital building and Jack was awarded a place at Alanbrooke Hall of Residence on the campus of Queen's University. They were both pleased that they were within walking distance of each other.

Politically, things in Northern Ireland were escalating. A few weeks before, a car bomb outside Dublin had killed the British Ambassador and his secretary. IRA snipers were active on the streets of Belfast, mainly targeting English soldiers and RUC officers.

Jack had started to listen more carefully to news of the Troubles and agreed with reporters when they said recent events heralded the start of a more severe security regime. He sensed he was to be a part of that.

And so it was that he boarded the Liverpool to Belfast ferry in early September. His black hair was longer now, and he knew he would blend in well amongst the student population in Belfast. He'd taken to only shaving twice a week, and his dark stubble gave him the 'hooligan edge' he was looking for. He had modelled the look on Roisin's brother Rory.

This time he was prepared for the security room interview routine as he disembarked from the boat.

As the officer closed the door of the interview room, he smiled. *Unusual,* thought Jack.

'Mr McLaughlan?' Jack nodded. 'I have a message for you.'

Jack tried not to show his surprise.

'We've been expecting you. As a precaution, my superiors decided you should receive the usual security interview. We wouldn't want anyone thinking you've been given special clearance.'

The smartly dressed young man extended his hand towards Jack, and Jack automatically shook it.

'Welcome to Northern Ireland. I don't know the details of your role, but I have been told to support you if required. Your handler will contact you over the next forty-eight hours.' *So that's how it's going to work.*

'OK, thanks. Anything else?'

'No. I must warn you, though, that paramilitaries are operating from the streets around Queen's when it suits them.'

'Noted.' Jack was appreciative of the advice.

'Good luck.'

The officer opened the door and walked over to his uniformed colleagues once again, leaving Jack to pick up his bag and make his way out of the room.

He took his time walking to the University area. He'd studied maps of the city and had memorised the key districts. It was good to reconcile the real terrain with those images. He knew to stay east of the Falls Road, the unofficial boundary of Catholic West Belfast.

He noticed the predominance of Union flags in Protestant areas, the murals painted on gable ends and the never-ending graffiti scrawled onto walls and windows. He spoke to no one for fear of showing himself as English. Tight security was everywhere, more so than on his previous visit. Armoured personnel carriers and other vehicles seemed to be on every street. Soldiers and police officers nervously scanned the crowds looking for signs of trouble.

What have I let myself in for? He asked himself and was relieved to see less of a security presence as he moved into the University area.

He went first to his hall of residence. His room was on the first floor. Standard student spec. A sink in the corner of the room next to a narrow chest of drawers. A single bed was along one wall, and there was a window at the far end. On the facing wall, there was a small wardrobe, and a wooden desk with a plastic chair tucked under it. He sat down on the bed, and a wave of relief swept over him. Despite what he had just seen, things were looking up. He had his own place, was studying something new and, best of all, Roisin was only a short walk away.

All he had to add was a little bit of data gathering for the security forces. He took a deep breath. His next appointment was the Psychology Department to pick up his lecture timetable and some books that had been put aside for him.

On his return, he saw a solitary female cleaner polishing the windows near the door. She seemed wholly absorbed in her job.

'Nice job,' said Jack as he approached. 'They're looking good now.' The woman looked startled and turned to face him. She was young and her dark hair was tied back in a ponytail. She smiled.

'Yes, they were boggin,' she replied in that now familiar Belfast accent. She paused and turned back to the windows but not before saying something that Jack didn't catch.

'I'm sorry I missed that,' he said. She turned back to face him, scanning the area around them. 'I said, just like my dog this morning when I took him for a walk by the Lagan River. It was muddy, and he was boggin by the time we got home.'

Jack nodded. He didn't know what to say in reply to her comment, so just smiled.

'He's a whippet,' she continued, looking intently at him. 'Do you have a dog?'

Jack stared at her. *Is this for real?*

'Not these days,' he replied. 'But I used to have a bulldog.'

Her face became more serious.

'So, hello, Jack. My name is Jane,' she said, still scanning the area. 'I think you know my role. I'm also a part-time cleaner here at the University. When I need to speak to you, I'll leave a note under your room door. If you want to talk with me, about anything, leave a message for me on this number.'

She quickly handed him a small business card with the name 'Elite Cleaning Services' in bold white letters under which was a telephone number. 'When I get the message, I'll find you.'

'OK,' he replied. He had always assumed his handler would be a man. *Mistake,* he said to himself. *Don't make assumptions.*

'You can bugger off now,' she said with a smile. 'But I'll meet you here again at 11 o'clock on Saturday morning.'

She turned back to her windows, dipping her cloth into the plastic bucket she had on the floor beside her and wringing it out before she lifted it to the next dirty windowpane.

He went through the main door, slightly bemused. He now had his official contact.

Almost operational. Eyes and ears. Asset.

He felt a surge of purpose, of mission and of direction. He was here to do a job. He was determined do it to the best of his ability and become a reliable source of information for the security forces.

His thoughts were still focused on his undercover role when he reached his floor. He heard voices coming from the communal kitchen at the end of the corridor. *No time like the present*, he thought, dropping his books and papers on the desk in his room. After all, he'd need to develop a network.

The kitchen had three other young men in it. Strewn around were the tell-tale signs of student life: cereal packets, tea and coffee, rice, pasta and the odd packet of biscuits. A faint smell of cooked bacon and crumbs of bread on the countertop made it clear the room was constantly in use.

As Jack entered, all three men turned to look at him.

Here goes.

'Hi guys. I'm Jack. Just moved in.' For a second or so none of them spoke and he realised that his accent had given him away. Then a tall, slim blond-haired man who'd been standing at the sink broke the silence.

'Chris. Chris Lorrimer,' the Northern Irish accent very evident. He brushed his hands together and wiped them on his grey jeans before offering one to Jack.

Jack shook his hand. 'Nice to meet you, Chris.' He turned to the other two who were sitting down and offered his hand to each in turn smiling as he did so. They seemed very friendly – John and Conor.

'I see you're getting the hang of the place already,' John smiled. 'Not too challenging, is it? What are you studying? I'm a chemical engineer.'

'Psychology,' replied Jack. 'I've just transferred over here from Manchester.'

'Interesting.' Conor grinned at Jack and raised an eyebrow. 'So, we have another foreign student here at Queen's. That makes two of us. Well, good for you. Do you fancy a coffee?' His accent was clearly Southern Irish. 'Chris just got the messages and was going to make us some toast before going down the Union bar for a few drinks. That right isn't it, Chris.' His friend smiled and grabbed a loaf of bread.

Jack knew *messages* meant shopping. Roisin had used it many times before.

'You want something Jack?'

'Yeah, a coffee would be great, thanks.'

They chatted easily for about half an hour. Chris, it turned out, was from the north coast of Northern Ireland, a little town called Portrush. A holiday town. Or at least it used to be before the Troubles started, he had pointed out. Jack found himself wondering if Portrush was Catholic or Protestant. John Campbell was from Armagh and Conor Butler from County Wexford on the southeast corner of Ireland. His first choice of university had been Trinity College in Dublin, but his grades had turned out to be not good enough.

'Queen's took pity on me,' he had said laughing.

'That's right,' Chris added. 'And now we have to put up with him. By the way, you two could be brothers. Stand up both of you a minute.'

Both duly obliged and moved next to each other.

'Fuck, you're right Chris,' added John. 'They do look alike. Peas from a pod. Sure, you don't have the same mother?' Everyone, including Jack and Conor, laughed.

'Thank god we don't talk the same way then,' said Jack. 'That way you can tell us apart.'

'And I have an Irish passport. That'll help,' Conor added amidst more laughter.

He noted that they all appeared to be good friends. Clearly Queen's students were both Catholic and Protestant, Northern and Southern Irish, and even English. Here at least, it seemed, they could co-exist amicably irrespective of religion and political persuasion.

As they continued to talk, others came into the kitchen, and Chris introduced Jack to each of them. They were all from Northern Ireland. Unlike Steve and Roisin, who had both deliberately chosen to study outside Northern Ireland, they had all chosen to attend university in the province.

'We normally celebrate the start of a new term with a beer or two,' Chris laughed. 'Good to line our stomachs first with some soda bread, before a session. We'll introduce you as we go Jack. It'll make for good craic that you're English and talk weirdly.'

That brought on another round of laughter.

As they left Alanbrooke, with Jack trying to remember names, a loud bang filled the air and interrupted their talk.

'What the fuck was that?'

They looked at him with a mixture of amusement and surprise.

'That's a bomb going off in the centre, Jack,' said Chris. 'You've obviously not heard one before. Sounds like it came from the Europa direction.' A few nodded, and the group moved on without further comment. Chris must have noticed the shock on Jack's face.

'Don't worry mate,' he said as he gave him a friendly slap on the back, 'you'll soon get used to it. A few beers always help.'

He was right. In the hours that followed Jack downed at least six pints. In amongst the noise of the bar, his ear adjusted to the plethora of Irish accents. He found it almost impossible to follow the conversation around the table, but whenever anyone looked his way, he would smile and respond with a loud '*Sláinte*'.

It was always met with good-natured laughter at the Englishman among them.

Chapter 17

He was perfectly on time for his meeting with Jane a few days later.

She gave him the merest of smiles and nodded to the door. They exited the building in quick succession. She spoke without looking at him. 'Let's walk and talk.'

With that, she set off in the direction of the students' union. It took him a few strides to catch up with her.

'So, anything I should be aware of?' she asked, continuing to look straight ahead as she walked.

'No, nothing of note yet,' he replied. 'I've met quite a few people – hall and union – and I'm assuming I will get to know more in my faculty once term gets fully underway.'

'That's good news. Try to focus on finding out where people meet and what they're concerned about. It might mean nothing to you at this stage, but we'll certainly find it useful. The students' union is a political hotbed. Lots of debates and arguments. Try not to write anything down. Give me the information verbally when we meet. That protects both of us.'

'Understood.' Jack found himself nodding, even though he realised that she wasn't looking at him.

'OK, we'll talk again soon. Be careful.'

She abruptly peeled off along another path, leaving him alone. If she hadn't appeared so serious, Jack would have laughed at the cloak and dagger style. He wondered how necessary it really was. Nevertheless, he kept up his pace and continued to walk towards the Union building as if this had been his intention all the time. He could always do with some pens and a pad of paper in preparation for tutorials.

Over the next few weeks, he began to settle into a routine. Psychology was challenging but strangely fascinating. He did the required reading and actually enjoyed it, managing to get his essays in on time without a struggle – a first for him. Hall life was sociable, and he was invariably asked to go out for a few drinks most evenings.

Roisin had started at the Royal, and he had seen her a couple of weekends in a row. As he'd hoped, she'd been able to sneak into Alanbrooke easily.

As well as the University Union bar, they also frequented pubs and bars in the city centre that were known to be 'safe' and student centric. It was common sense to avoid bars known to have either a Catholic or a Protestant orientation as strangers were viewed suspiciously. The Bot, near the botanic gardens and the Eg, the Eglantine, were favourites. Lots of girls from Stranmillis, the teacher training college, drank there too and so it was popular with male university students.

Roisin gladly embraced his growing circle of friends. The fact she was Northern Irish with a great sense of humour made her an instant hit with most of them. This group, with almost no sectarian angst, contrasted sharply with people Jack encountered on the few times that he left the University area. The two worlds co-existed side by side but he was always aware that the violence and fear were never far away.

In their times alone, Roisin would recount stories of the patients that she had to look after at the Royal. She operated at the front line, dealing with horrendous wounds caused by bombs, bullets and shrapnel. There was, she explained, a constant stream of casualties coming into her hospital. Operating theatres and post-operative wards were sometimes at breaking point. Triage had become critical. Most of them were innocent victims of indiscriminate sectarian violence.

She told him of a Catholic girl who had been brought in with a fractured skull and collarbone, a broken leg and other severe gashes and cuts. 'She was only eight years old, Jack. A lovely, sweet girl. Guilty of nothing apart from having a Catholic name. She was on an errand to the nearby butchers to get some pork chops for the family supper. On the way, a group of Protestant youths stopped her and asked her name. When she said it was Bridget, they called her a "*stinking taig*" and began pushing her around the group.'

Roisin looked up at Jack. He could see the anger in her face. 'No one came to help her. She was so scared. All she could do was run. Straight out into the road. She was hit head-on by a lorry returning to the Ormeau bakery nearby.'

Roisin shook her head as she continued. 'When an ambulance finally arrived, those same youths threw rocks at it as it drove off. What is this place coming to?'

Jack couldn't find the words to answer that.

'And you know what makes it even worse, Jack? When that poor girl finally regained consciousness in hospital, she was more upset that she had lost the five-pound note her mother had given her to buy the family's supper. She seemed to think her injuries were her own fault.'

On another occasion, Roisin told him of a British soldier who had been ambushed by an IRA unit while on patrol in Andersonstown.

'All he did was stop to talk to a young woman near a parked car,' she said. 'He was worried she had broken down. But as he stopped, two IRA gunmen jumped up from behind the car and in the blink of an eye had fired five bullets into him. They ran off down an alleyway between terraced houses a few yards away.'

'Was he by himself?' Jack had asked.

'No, some of his colleagues gave chase but their patrol leader called them back. Apparently, the passageways around those buildings are used to set further traps for those that follow.'

She explained that she had been part of the team assigned to him on arrival at the hospital. 'One of his patrol had used a beret to stem the loss of blood from the wound. He saved his mate by doing that. He'd never have arrived alive without it. One of the bullets was lodged millimetres from his femoral artery. He needed five pints of blood.'

The soldier was in intensive care for three weeks after the attack. Roisin was invariably there at his bedside nursing him and talking with him; keeping alive that critical spark of life he needed.

She shared these stories only with Jack. None of his friends would have known the reality of her day-to-day life and he admired her so for that. Even so, he couldn't stop himself worrying how all this would affect her in the long term.

Chapter 18

When he and Roisin were not together, Jack concentrated on his studies and tried to perfect a technique to remember key facts and observations about student gatherings and locations. He still didn't know what Jane would deem useful but tried his best to pass on as much information as he could.

Invariably they used the 'walk and talk' technique. It didn't matter what the weather was like. Jane would listen attentively, sometimes asking supplementary questions, and Jack would recount what he'd heard about various political meetings: the number and types of people attending, comments about the speakers and organisers, and his own view of their importance.

'I've heard there's a visit planned by a leading Irish Republican politician,' he told her on one of their walks. 'I'm not sure who they've got, but he's supposed to deliver a speech to the university union about the progress – or lack of it as he would say – of civil rights in the province. Most people don't seem too interested in it, but there's a group who are angry the visit is even under consideration.'

There were some of Jack's new circle of mates who were vehemently opposed to a '*fucking Republican bastard*' being given airtime on campus. They'd gone on to say what they planned to do to him '*if he ever sets foot on this campus*'. Jack relayed the story.

Jane paused noticeably before she responded.

'So, do you think any of them actually intend to cause trouble?'

Jack was a little taken aback. He was OK reporting on potential meetings but to be asked his opinion about one of his university friends was another matter.

'I don't think so. My view is that they simply don't like Irish Republicans and will try to drown out their arguments.'

Jane looked at him.

'This isn't England, you know Jack. *Drowning out* as you call it might be what happens over the water, but over here, it usually takes the form of physical violence towards the person whose views differ from yours. Listening is not a factor in Northern Ireland politics these days.'

'I get that, but some of my mates' families and friends have been murdered by the IRA. They're bound to feel strongly about things.'

'That doesn't mean they're allowed to incite a riot or cause trouble.' Jane's tone was quite emphatic. 'Allowing strongly opinionated politicians to address groups where it's known they will encounter equally opinionated people is a recipe for conflict. In this case, I think it is a mistake for the University authorities to allow this event to go ahead. I can envisage it will turn nasty if the police or military decide to get involved.'

'So, what will you do?' Jack enquired.

'Leave it with me,' she said. 'Just keep doing what you're doing.

It's good work, Jack.'

She looked at her wristwatch. 'Have to go now. I'll be in touch again soon.'

With that, she turned away from him and headed along a different track.

A few days later, he discovered that the Irish Republican's meeting had been cancelled. No reason was given, but Jack couldn't help wondering if his disclosure had been a significant factor in the decision.

Chapter 19

December was an unusually cold month in Belfast. Frost every morning and the cold, biting winds that characterised Northern Ireland, ever-present. Daylight was in short supply, and no sooner had the sun rose, it seemed to set again.

The political situation was dark and icy too. The IRA had planted a series of firebombs in Derry which caused millions of pounds worth of damage. There was widespread talk in the province that some loyalist politicians had been involved historically with arrangements to buy weapons and explosives as well as choosing potential bomb targets. The feud between the protestant UDA and the UVF was escalating; a member of the UDA was beaten to death by members of the UVF.

Jack sensed that the situation was deteriorating. The incidents of seemingly random acts of violence and brutality were increasing. Attacks on army patrols were increasing, some less than a mile from Queen's. Some car bombs exploded, and others had been defused. Innocent people were shot, sometimes because of mistaken identity. Bombs were detonated all over the province and Jack became less and less surprised when he heard them. He just stayed focused on his primary job of reporting back snippets of what he hoped was useful information for the RUC and military.

His one shaft of light was Roisin. Jack simply adored her. Their lovemaking had taken on a fierce intensity over recent weeks as if it was the only way to shut out the horror movie that Belfast was showing constantly.

Her shifts were long, and she would often stay for hours after she was due to finish because of emergencies, so when they were together, their time was precious. They both sensed that. Their hope, like many others, was that sometime soon there would be an end to it all. People would get sick of the fighting and start talking to each other. In the meantime, the survival strategy was to minimise personal risks and get on with life as best you could.

If Roisin had to work on beyond the end of her shift, she would call, or leave a message for Jack, if possible. She told him not to worry if she didn't show up on time. She had several routes that she could choose when walking from the hospital to the University area and sensibly chose to vary her way.

Jack had learnt not to worry. They'd fallen into a pattern of her coming to his hall of residence and if he wasn't there, he'd leave a note in his room explaining where he'd be. He'd had duplicate keys made for her so she could let herself in and out as required. She kept a pair of jeans and a few tee shirts, cardigans and items of underwear in Jack's room. She often changed out of her nurse's uniform there before joining him later.

Jack's university colleagues all knew her and would sometimes accompany her to wherever Jack was. The system worked well. Neither of them worried, as they always met up at some point in the evening.

Jack and his mates were in the Bot on a typically cold Wednesday evening in mid-December. There were about six of them altogether, laughing and drinking and enjoying the craic.

By 9 pm when Roisin still hadn't turned up, Jack presumed there had been some sort of major incident requiring her to stay on at short notice.

'That gorgeous wee woman of yours will be here soon, you mark my words.' The comment came from Chris Lorrimer, who noticed that Jack had checked his watch a few times.

'You're right, I'm sure,' Jack replied, smiling, 'I don't want to be too pissed when she gets here.' This time Chris was smiling.

'No, we wouldn't want that, would we? She's come to expect top-level performance from her English stallion, I'm sure.' Everyone laughed.

Just at that moment, another one of Jack's friends came through the door and announced, 'There's just been a soldier shot near Windsor Park. Sniper ambush seemingly. No news other than he was seriously injured and has been taken to hospital.' They all looked at one another and raised their eyebrows. Sad as it was, it was nothing unusual. 'He was UDR,' Roger added. The Ulster Defence Regiment was often the target of IRA gunmen.

Windsor Park, as Jack now knew, was the home of Linfield FC and was also the ground used by the Northern Ireland national team. He and Roisin had walked by it several times, and he could picture the area.

Roisin had not appeared before closing time in the Bot. He and Chris walked back to their hall, said their goodnights on the corridor and Jack went into his room. Roisin had not been there, he could tell.

The realisation that he would be sleeping alone that night kicked in. He climbed into bed, wishing she was there to cuddle up to. He always felt happy with the world when she lay next to him.

It took him a long time to drift off into a fitful sleep, and even when he did, he kept waking up with a sense of unease.

Chapter 20

He glanced at his watch, and it was 6:30 am.

He still felt uneasy. He knew that whatever shift she'd been made to work would have finished by now, and she would have gone back to her nurses' accommodation and crashed out.

He decided to walk over to the hospital to find out where she was likely to be. If she was still asleep, he'd leave a note for her; if she was working, he'd find out where she was and try to have a quick word with her.

The hospital was not far. Like Roisin, Jack knew several different routes, and none took longer than twenty-five minutes. He made sure he had his University ID card with him. Given the incident last night, he thought it likely he would be required to show it at some point.

As it happened, there was an unusually high number of uniformed forces about, and he was stopped twice before he reached the hospital. Each time, he waited patiently for his identity to be verified and then carried on with his journey.

He got to the hospital shortly before 7:30 am and went through the security channels to gain entrance, then onto the reception area to ask if anyone knew where Roisin was.

The woman on the reception desk had her head down as he approached her, and as she looked up, her face drained of colour.

Jack knew at that moment that something was wrong.

'You're Nurse O'Malley's boyfriend, aren't you?' She asked the question in a curious tone. The eye contact was intense.

'Yep, that's right. Jack McLaughlan.'

The woman tried a smile, but it wasn't convincing. 'I've been told, if you come in, to ask you to wait in the office over there. The duty doctor will come and talk with you immediately.' She pointed to a door about ten feet away to the side of her desk.

'You haven't heard, have you?' she added earnestly.

'Heard what?' Jack was getting more concerned by the second. 'I heard last night that a soldier had been ambushed near here. That's all.'

'The hospital didn't have a contact number for you, and we didn't know where you were living.' The woman seemed very upset. 'We thought you'd be around this morning.'

'Roisin knows my address. I'm in a hall of residence at the University. She's been there many times.' There was a knot of tension in Jack's stomach. 'Can you tell me what's happened?' he insisted. He was aware he was talking loudly.

'Please just go and wait in that room. Dr Prescott will be with you very soon.' She picked up the grey phone on her desk and dialled a three-digit number. Jack watched and listened, his impatience and concern growing by the second, while she notified the doctor of his presence.

After putting the phone down, the woman came round from behind her desk. She led Jack to the room she had pointed at and opened the door, nodding at him to go inside. Jack felt her hand on his shoulder before she closed the door between them.

Roisin must have been injured in some way, Jack rationalised to himself. *But how and in what way? Was it related to the shooting of the soldier? Had there been some sort of attack in the hospital itself? Was she ill in some way?* He had no idea.

The door opened again and Dr Prescott, so Jack assumed, entered. He was slim and had short grey hair. Smartly dressed, his immaculate white coat complemented his red striped tie and polished black shoes.

'Dr Prescott?' Jack wasted no time. 'Can you tell me what's happened to Nurse O'Malley? She was supposed to meet me last night, but she never turned up. I know she often can't get away exactly on time, but she normally manages to get a message to me at least.' Jack realised he was gabbling.

'Please sit down, Jack.' The doctor pulled a seat around for Jack and another for himself. They both sat down facing each other.

There were a few seconds of silence as the doctor seemed to compose himself before speaking. Jack's heart was in his mouth.

'I have some bad news, Jack. Some very bad news. Nurse O'Malley died yesterday evening at 9:37 precisely. She had just finished her shift and was walking near the football stadium when she was struck by several bullets fired by an unknown gunman. It has been established that the gunman was aiming at a nearby soldier on foot patrol. The nature of her wounds suggests she would have died instantly.' He paused, watching Jack's reaction.

Jack couldn't speak. He couldn't move. He just stared at the doctor. It was as if a thunderbolt had struck him in the chest. All the air had gone from his lungs.

His first thought was that Dr Prescott had confused Roisin with another nurse from the hospital. It had all been a terrible mistake. Then he experienced a playback of the statement the doctor had made and Roisin's beautiful face, her lovely smile, suddenly appeared before him.

Then he began to tremble. Physically tremble. He wondered if the doctor had noticed it. His body shook involuntarily, and yet his thoughts all seemed coherent.

He became distantly aware that the doctor was talking to him again. He had to focus on what was being said.

'I'm so sorry for your loss, Jack. This news must come as a huge shock. She was a fine nurse and was doing a wonderful job here in the hospital.'

Jack's trembling was morphing into a powerful tensing of every muscle in his body. His fists were tightening. A combination of emotions – shock, intense anger and disbelief.

'Sad and upset, you say Dr Prescott?' There was true venom in Jack's voice. 'This fucking sick joke backwater of the UK with its senseless violence and thick, belligerent and nasty population. No, sad and upset, would not be the words I'd choose.'

As the words came out of his mouth, he knew they were wrong, but he couldn't help himself. A part of him wanted to apologise to Dr Prescott, another wanted to punch him, and yet another wanted to cry like a baby. He wanted to feel Roisin's breath on his face again, to hear her voice.

The doctor seemed to understand and said nothing further for a minute or so. He just sat there, waiting for Jack's next reaction or comment.

Jack was somewhere between disbelief and horror. This was his Roisin. This was his beautiful, funny, loving and caring Roisin. This was the woman who had transformed his life and whom he adored. She couldn't be dead.

And yet, this is what he'd had explained to him.

A stream of reason came to Jack. He needed to understand more. He took a deep breath.

'I'm very sorry about my outburst just now. That was unfair. You said she'd have died instantly Dr Prescott?'

Dr Prescott smiled and waved his hand, signalling that he understood.

'How exactly did she die? Can you explain?'

'She was hit by two bullets. One in the chest and one in her stomach. Death would have been in seconds. I know that for a fact, as I was the one who examined her when they got her back here. I've seen many such wounds and blood loss is very fast.'

Jack listened and tried to imagine her last few seconds of life. She would have known what was going to happen to her. She would have known she was dying.

'Oh, dear god,' Jack began to sob. *Roisin. What did they do to you? Why for Christ's sake?*

He leant forward with his head in his hands and sobbed uncontrollably for what seemed an age. The doctor said nothing, just put his hand on Jack's shoulders trying to comfort him.

Jack's rational brain was trying to break through the devastation he felt emotionally. He sat up and faced Dr Prescott again.

'Please excuse me, doctor, but I have to know more. How is the soldier who was the original target?'

'Still on the critical list. He suffered a serious neck wound. He's lost a lot of blood too. It's too soon to say if he'll make it.'

At least he had a fighting chance of life. Roisin didn't.

'The sniper got away, I'm afraid,' Dr Prescott added. 'These incidents are all over in seconds, and the escape route is well planned.' Jack remembered what Roisin had explained to him.

Another massive wave of sadness swept over Jack. As it passed, he asked another question.

'Has someone informed her parents? They live in Newcastle. They'll want to be here.'

'Apparently, they were visiting their son in Dublin these last few days. Yes, they have been informed, in the early hours of this morning by the Irish Garda Police. They arrived here a few hours ago. Do you know them?'

'She's their only daughter.' A vision of the happy family in

Newcastle came into his mind. 'They're going to be devastated.' He looked up at the doctor. 'If it's OK with you, can I see Roisin please?'

The doctor breathed deeply, and his answer rocked Jack. 'I'm very sorry, Jack, but Roisin is with her mother and father at the moment. They will need some time.'

It wasn't the reply he wanted, but something deep inside respected the doctor's answer. Family always had the first call in such circumstances. He knew that Siobhan and Seamus would need time. Just as he did.

Dr Prescott got up and moved to the door. He turned back to Jack.

'I'll let her parents know you're here. I'm sure they'll want to see you soon. Can I get you anything? A drink perhaps?'

Jack looked blankly at him and shook his head. Dr Prescott left the room and closed the door behind him.

Chapter 21

He had no idea how long he'd been alone in the room when the door opened once again, and Siobhan came in. She looked as white as a sheet and had been crying. Jack immediately stood up and went to her with open arms. She embraced him and they hugged each other tightly for a long time without talking.

She gently edged herself backwards and looked him in the eyes.

'Oh, Jack. This must be very hard on you. How are you?'

That was typical of the woman he thought. Asking him how he was when she was devastated herself.

'I honestly don't know Siobhan.' He became aware of the tears running down his cheeks. 'They've killed Roisin. What do we do?'

Then he remembered her grief too. 'How are you and Seamus?'

'He's upstairs and won't leave her side. He's inconsolable. She was always his "wee girl", and he adored her.'

Jack nodded. He had seen that for himself.

'Thanks for coming down to see me, Siobhan. You probably would have preferred to be with her yourself.' Jack's tears were still falling as he spoke the words.

'It's OK, Jack.' She hugged him again, and her arms patted his back. 'I've said goodbye to her. I'm OK at the moment although I'm aware it will come and go. The grief that is.'

She paused, and they continued to hold each other. He needed it and so, he suspected, did she.

They were still holding each other when Dr Prescott came back in. He waited a few seconds, and they both turned to face him.

'I'm so sorry to disturb you again, but your husband wanted you to know that he's gone out for a walk in the hospital grounds. He wanted to get some air. He said he thought you would understand.'

Siobhan nodded.

'Come on, Jack. You'll want to have some time with her, I'm sure. I'll take you and then go find Seamus. That's OK, isn't it doctor? She and Jack here were very close.' The doctor nodded.

She took Jack's arm and led him out of the room. He lifted his head and looked around. It was the first time for a while that he'd done so, and it made him feel marginally better, more in control. Hospital life was continuing, and people were getting on with their lives. He had to find a way to do so himself, at least for the moment.

Siobhan led him down a long corridor and then up a flight of steps to the floor above. Another corridor, a much quieter one, and then to a windowed door halfway along. Even without going in, he could see her lying on the bed. Only her face, shoulders and arms were exposed. As they went in, his legs began to tremble, and he needed to will them to carry him forward.

There she was, eyes closed and still. She was still beautiful.

He became aware of Siobhan gently sobbing just behind him. Even at this moment, his heart went out to her. She'd just lost her only daughter. How could she ever get past this? How could he?

Siobhan smiled at him through her tears. 'Go you on, Jack. I'm going to leave you two together for a while. She would have wanted that. She loved you very much, you know. She told me that and how happy you made her.'

With that, she backed out of the room and closed the door behind her. Jack turned back to Roisin. He reached for her hand and gently placed his on top. It was a habit they'd developed over time. She'd turn her hand and slip her fingers through his until their hands were locked. But this time, her hand didn't respond.

A crushing ache of grief and despair almost overwhelmed him. Involuntarily he sucked in a huge gasp of air. He would have to live the rest of his life without hearing her voice again, or seeing her smile, or holding her.

At that moment, he didn't think he could go on.

He became aware that the door had opened and a nurse had entered the room.

'I'm so sorry.' The nurse was looking at him. He recognised her but couldn't remember her name. 'We met briefly a month or so ago in the Bot.'

Jack turned and looked at her. She had obviously been crying too. He did remember her. She and Roisin had come into the bar, both laughing at something that had happened at the hospital. He remembered now.

'It's Mary.' She sensed he'd forgotten her name.

'Mary,' he muttered. 'Oh, yes.'

She put a hand on his shoulder. 'Oh, how she loved you Jack. She was always talking about you – how her Jack was so different to the men around here. She liked that.' Jack smiled briefly, remembering Roisin's comments about selfish, chauvinistic Ulstermen. 'She'll be missed by a lot of people. She knew you loved her. You made her very happy.' Her words were comforting to Jack, and at this moment, it was a welcome relief.

'Thanks, Mary. That means a lot.'

'This is my shift,' Mary said quietly. 'I'll look after her.'

The tears started to roll down his cheeks again.

'Thank you.'

He was more grateful for this than he could articulate. He'd seen her, touched her, spoken with her, and now it was time to leave her.

He lifted his head, took her hand and gazing at her beautiful face one final time, bent forward and kissed her. He whispered so only she would hear.

'I'm going to miss you, Roisin. I love you. I have from the first moment I saw you and I always will.'

He laid her hand back down on the bed, slowly turned from the bed and walked out of the room without looking back. His brain was focused on the future and his new purpose in life: to find and execute her killer.

Part 2
Chapter 22
December 1976

Roisin's funeral had been the week before Christmas and the Catholic church in Newcastle had been full. Siobhan had insisted he sat with the family, at the front. He hadn't argued. His preference would have been to sit at the back somewhere and lose himself in the anonymity of the congregation, but he knew that she and Seamus wanted him with them.

Ever since he'd walked away from her in the hospital, anger had raged within. No one would ever have known. To the rest of the world, he simply looked sad and silent. He spoke to people when they spoke to him but didn't start or continue conversations. He was on autopilot.

The dialogue in his head was a different matter altogether. He was determined to channel his energy into fighting the forces that called themselves paramilitaries. It was *they* that chose to inflict the hatred and violence on the rest of the population, and it was one of *them* that had killed his Roisin and in turn ripped out his heart.

He kept his tears to himself. He cried a lot but only in private and at those times, he sobbed, aching to see her smile, to touch her, to smell her. It could never be.

The funeral service itself had passed in a blur. He'd shaken hands, smiled and nodded as people flooded the family with messages of their sorrow. At one point, Conor leant along the pew and put a hand on his shoulder, gently squeezing it. It was a genuine brotherly gesture from someone who recognised Jack's pain as well as his own. He appreciated the gesture, but it made no difference. Roisin was gone.

The actual burial was the hardest. The rain was heavy and swept down remorselessly from the Mourne Mountains. The winds were icy. Jack looked around at the crowd surrounding the coffin and the grave that had been dug.

Part of him was aware of the priest saying the words and then the undertakers slowing lowering the coffin. He became aware of Seamus, a few feet away, almost collapsing with grief as the casket reached the bottom of the trench. He moved forward to support the grieving father only to find Rory had responded more quickly. He stepped back rapidly when he saw the glare Rory gave him.

Roisin's housemates, Jenny and Mary, had flown over for the funeral and after paying their respects to the family, had both wanted to check that Jack was bearing up.

'We're so sad. For you, for her family and for us,' Jenny said quietly as tears welled in her eyes. Mary put her arm around her shoulder and looked at Jack.

'What are your plans? I guess you'll be coming back to England soon. No point staying here anymore I presume. You came here to be near her, and now she's gone.'

Jack was silent for a few seconds. Then he spoke.

'Actually, I don't know whether to stay here and complete my studies or go back to England and do something else.'

'Oh, for Christ's sake, Jack,' Jenny retorted, struggling to keep her voice low. 'You can't be serious! This place is barbaric. Why would you want to stay here and witness more senseless violence?'

'But I have nothing to go back to England for now,' Jack replied quietly.

Mary looked up, her eyes bloodshot.

'I get that, Jack. By staying here you'll at least be near her. Nearer than you would be if you were back in England.'

Jenny shrugged. 'I suppose you're right, but I'd never choose to live here.'

Jack nodded at her.

'I've lived here a few months now and made some friends. Funnily enough, it's not that bad a place. Most people are kind; they hate the violence. Maybe for Roisin's sake I should give it a try at least. I haven't decided yet.'

The story made sense to him. It wasn't the truth, but it seemed sensible to be seen to be keeping his options open. Inside however, he knew he could never return to England permanently – not while Roisin's killer was still alive.

Jane had got a message to him shortly after Roisin's death, telling him to stand-down from his duties and to go home for Christmas. She also made it clear that she would contact him in early January when he was back at Queen's to discuss next steps.

Chapter 23

Christmas and New Year went in a blur. Jack took himself for long walks, talking to no one. His parents respected his feelings and gave him the space he needed. He had known they would be supportive, and it had helped.

When he returned to Belfast at the start of January, he found a note from Jane under his door signalling a meeting the following day. He welcomed the opportunity to ask some questions.

As they began their walk the next morning, she said quietly, 'Jack, I'm so sorry for your loss. Roisin was special to you. I know that full well.' She reached out and squeezed his hand briefly. No one else would have seen it. He realised it was a genuine gesture and his eyes filled with tears. He looked down so she wouldn't see.

'Thanks Jane. I appreciate that. I won't lie, these last few weeks have been very hard.'

'Yes,' was all she said. He sensed from that single word that she did indeed understand.

'I'm a lot better now,' he added, trying to sound upbeat.

'Don't be in too much of a hurry, Jack. These things take time. Healing is very slow.'

They walked on in silence for another minute or so. In that time, he composed himself, wiping away the moisture from his eyes with the back of his hands.

'So, is there any word on the hunt for the gunman?'

Jane glanced over at him obviously surprised at the line of enquiry.

'Jack, you've been in Belfast long enough to know that tracking these bastards down is one thing and – even assuming we catch them – it's incredibly difficult to pin anything on them. They live and operate in areas of West Belfast where they're protected by the community and given alibis that make prosecution impossible.'

'Yes, but the RUC will have a shortlist of possible suspects. I know that.'

'Yeah, we do. As I said though, we can't do too much with the intel.' Her pace slowed and Jack sensed a change in her body language as she turned to him. He wondered what she was about to divulge.

'You know how the IRA has started to use small active service units operating independently in their local areas? Well, our information is that the ASU responsible for Roisin's death was the one operating from the Falls Road. The commanding officer is Declan McGill but in the RUC he's known as the Weasel.'

'Why?' Jack asked.

'Weasels are killing machines and we know McGill is responsible for too many deaths now. He's also a sneaky bastard – just like them. We almost got him a few months ago when he and his team tried to take out an army patrol close to the Falls Road. The soldiers returned fire and were sure they got him in the leg, but even so they lost him. The housing estates around there have so many passageways and cut-throughs, it's like a maze. There are kids too, who operate as lookouts; whistles and dustbin lids banging. It gives men like McGill a huge advantage in avoiding capture.'

Jack appreciated the fact she was sharing confidential information with him but wanted to know more.

'How many are in his ASU?'

'He has four men under his command. We have files on all of them but linking any of them to specific attacks is another matter. As I said, these people are well protected by their communities. Anyone who is suspected of being a tout is killed or kneecapped as a message to deter others. It works.'

Jack took a breath before asking as casually as he could, 'So how do you know McGill was responsible the night of Roisin's death?'

'He was spotted near the hospital earlier that day but again, true to form, he slipped away before they could close in. They knew it was him; he's easy to recognise apparently. Blond hair worn short for a start, but this time he was also moving with a limp. It all makes sense.'

At that moment, Jack could have hugged her. He knew he needed to remain calm – at least as far as she was concerned – but here was the critical information he wanted and needed.

Declan McGill.

The man who led the ASU that murdered Roisin.

He found himself repeating the information to himself, again and again, all the time imagining what he would say to the filthy bastard when – and there was no doubt in his mind it would be *when* – they finally met face-to-face.

He turned with an impassive look towards Jane.

'I hope you manage to get him.'

She looked at him and for a moment he wondered if she might be able to read his mind.

He was relieved when she finally said, 'We'll certainly do our best. Now, you told me you wanted my help to set up a meeting with the top brass. Tell me a bit more.'

Chapter 24

Jack wasn't surprised when he was told it was Lieutenant Colonel Turner himself who had agreed to talk with him. Turner, Jane informed him, had suggested a meeting at a hotel in the centre of Belfast. Ever since he'd been back, the return to thorough searching before entering pubs and hotels irritated Jack. It reminded him just how different Northern Ireland was to England.

'How are you, Jack?' Turner's voice was sombre and serious as they shook hands. 'These last few weeks must have been tough for you. I'm sorry for your loss.' He looked different, his smart military uniform replaced by an open-necked shirt and casual slacks.

'Thank you, sir.' Jack's reply was polite but terse. 'And thanks for agreeing to meet me. There's something I want to discuss.'

'I assumed that was the case. Let's talk over dinner in the hotel restaurant. I've booked a quiet table away from anyone else.'

They ordered from the menu and as soon as the waiter disappeared into the kitchen, Turner began.

'Well Jack, since we last met, you've done well. My contacts tell me you have provided significant intel to the security team and that you've developed a good working relationship with your handler over here.'

'That's good to know, sir. I don't always know the significance of the information I provide, but yes, Jane and I have a good relationship.'

He paused for a moment. *No point in wasting time.*

'Sir, I want to widen my contribution.'

Turner sat back, his body language changing. When he spoke, his tone was more formal.

'That can't happen, Jack, and for a number of reasons.' He appeared to be studying the younger man's face, looking for a reaction. 'Please hear me out.'

Jack nodded again. He had anticipated this reaction.

'You're still badly affected by Roisin's death. There can be no doubt about that. You need more time – time to get your thinking straight.'

Jack took a deep breath to suppress his annoyance, knowing he had to remain calm and collected.

'Go on, sir. You said there were a number of reasons.'

'You're not in a position to *widen your contribution*,' Turner continued. 'You're an English student studying for a degree at Queen's University. Occasionally you pass on snippets of information from your student circle. Sorry Jack, I don't want to diminish your contribution, but that's the truth of it. Yes, you have provided some useful intel, and there's no doubt activities at Queen's are clearer these days, but you must remember it was for that, and that alone, that we brought you over here.'

'I thought you'd say that sir, and you're right, that was the original deal. However, things have obviously changed now. I've been thinking about this for weeks and I know I could make it work. I can resume my studies and intel gathering but I could also offer something else.'

'Such as?'

'Well, I think there's a chance I can stay in touch with one of my girlfriend's brothers – the one with nationalist sympathies.'

Turner glanced up.

'I'm assuming you mean Rory O'Malley. He's been on our radar for some time now. From what we can gather, his taxi service is a front that allows him to get about the city and surrounding areas, promoting a nationalist agenda. He's popped up in some very dubious places and certainly associates with known terrorists, but intelligence reports to date haven't been able to connect him to anything more.'

'My point exactly, sir,' replied Jack. 'I don't know him very well, but perhaps I could exploit the relationship. It's an obvious opportunity.'

Turner's face gave nothing away.

'You don't agree?' Jack reminded himself again not to let his emotions get the better of him. *Stay professional!*

Turner let out a sigh and leant forward.

'Listen to me, Jack. I anticipated all of this and to an extent I agree that your relationship with Rory is one that could be developed, but you are simply not experienced enough to get involved – not at this stage at least.'

He paused and Jack thought he detected a slight shift in body language.

'I have a suggestion, however.' Turner spoke slowly, looking directly at him. 'It is non-negotiable and the only offer on the table.'

Jack hung on every word.

'You're right. Taking O'Malley off the streets is certainly an attractive option. We're pretty sure he's been supplying guns to contacts in West Belfast, but we've never caught him in the act.

He's a slippery customer. However, we think it's possible he can lead us to bigger fish.'

Jack was taken aback. He knew Rory had some dubious friends but to hear he was responsible for supplying weapons to people was another matter.

'Is it possible that O'Malley supplied the weapons involved in Roisin's death then?' he asked as calmly as he could.

Turner nodded. 'Very probable.'

Jack felt his stomach turn. *Stay calm!*

Seemingly unaware of Jack's emotions, Turner continued.

'We're increasingly aware of more guns on the streets and we believe the IRA is beginning to step up their imports. If O'Malley is involved, as we think he is, it would be useful to have someone on the inside to find out more about his contacts.'

'And that's where I can help.'

'Yes, but we both know that O'Malley's associates wouldn't hesitate to put a bullet in your head if they even thought you were an informer. We wouldn't be able to protect you, Jack. You'd be on your own. If you were caught, we wouldn't be able to get to you. Controlled intel on student matters at Queen's is one thing, undercover surveillance with the likes of O'Malley and his people is another thing entirely – and extremely dangerous.'

'Then train me,' Jack said without a moment's hesitation. 'Give me the tools to do the job. My student cover is secure. And this opportunity is too good to miss.'

'Listen Jack. Based on your work in the last few months at Queen's we are prepared to train you, but we need you trained properly. You need to know how to look after yourself.'

Turner leaned forward again, his eyes never leaving Jack's.

'This is what I propose. Here in the province, we have a dedicated force of highly trained plain-clothes surveillance operatives – all very unofficial of course. They work under the command of the SAS and liaise with the authorities, particularly the RUC. They perform what's called "close target reconnaissance" and the information they provide is essential in preventing the war against terror.'

Jack was taken aback. The official British government line was that the SAS were not deployed in Northern Ireland and yet here was Turner explaining the importance of their role in the conflict. Was he suggesting Jack become a part of this?

'Given your RAF association, your proven track record and this unique opportunity with O'Malley, we could facilitate your application to undertake full-time training. It would take six to nine months overall and it's tough. There is no guarantee that you would pass and if you don't, then you would be out completely. Understand?'

'Yes, sir. I understand that completely. What about my studies here in Belfast?'

'Don't worry about that. The story would be that you have asked to defer your studies, resuming in September. That would be perfect timing. Given the recent circumstances, everyone would understand your decision. Furthermore, you would explain to anyone who asked, that you plan to take a temporary job somewhere back in the UK over the next few months. We will provide the official alibi.'

Jack had been listening intently but needed one final assurance.

'Sir, I need to be clear. If I do this, can you guarantee I'd be involved in other, wider operations?'

'For Christ's sake Jack, listen to me. If you choose to take up this offer and manage to complete the training, you will be part of 14 Intelligence Company, trained by the SAS and active undercover in Northern Ireland. You'll be right in the centre of things.'

He paused and took a sip of water, watching Jack's face intently before continuing.

'It's not a done deal though, the selection procedure is hard. I can, and will, make a positive representation on your behalf which should get you into the assessment process – but that is all. If you fail that first assessment day, that's it, they won't take you any further.'

Jack nodded.

'Assuming you make it through that, you'll attend an eight-week course to build your fitness and teach you basic skills. They look for a combination of personal attributes, observational qualities, stamina, the ability to think under stress. You get the idea?'

Jack nodded again, wanting Turner to continue. He could feel the blood pumping through his veins.

'If you survive that – and I have to tell you most don't – you embark upon an intensive six-month programme of what is called "selection by training". You will be taught specialist skills and can only continue if you pass each stage. There's no roll back or second chances.

'It's gruelling, Jack. Physically and mentally. I know you're keen at this moment in time, but the standards are incredibly high and therefore your chances of success are low. You'll be up against military professionals with a lot of practical experience already.'

'What then, sir? If I do get through that is?'

Turner smiled.

'If you get that far, then we'll consider your next role. In your case I'd suggest you're based at Queen's, making use of your existing cover, rather than at one of four military detachments.'

He sat back in his chair, glass in hand.

'Like I said a few minutes ago, this is non-negotiable. You will not continue in Northern Ireland without this training. That is the bottom line. Do you understand that?'

'I do, sir, and I'm grateful to you for your offer of getting me to the assessment phase. I understand the rest is up to me.'

He felt elated.

'That's it then. I'll make the necessary arrangements.' Turner placed his empty glass back on the table and leaned in towards Jack. 'Before I leave, I have a piece of advice for you.'

Jack wondered what was coming.

'I know you are still in pain at the moment, but you must come to terms with the fact that Roisin is dead. Nothing can bring her back. If anyone picks up that this is something personal to you, you'll be out on your ear. Personal stuff will get you, and maybe your colleagues, killed. This job needs clarity of thought. Emotion has no place. Understood?'

Jack felt Turner was trying to look into his soul. Could he know his inner thoughts?

'I understand and completely agree, sir,' he lied. 'Nothing can bring Roisin back. I've come to terms with that.'

It seemed to work.

'I have immense faith in you, Jack, and wish you every success over the next few months. You'll need to approach this period with a steely resolve. Be prepared for anything and everything.'

'That's appreciated, sir. I will do as you suggest.'

'OK then. I'll get the ball rolling. You'll hear from someone soon.'

'Thank you, sir.' The words came easily. 'Would you mind if I suggest something more?'

It was clear from Turner's expression that he hadn't anticipated anything else.

'Go on.'

'It's to do with O'Malley. You obviously know I've met his family. They like me and they've been very kind to me. I propose I phone the family occasionally, and maybe Rory himself, whilst I'm in England. I think Roisin's parents would expect that – maybe Rory would as well. But more importantly it would keep the contact going so that when I go back in September, I can easily pick things up with him.'

Turner thought it through.

'Yes, keep a link with O'Malley. What you've said makes sense. Keep the contact going.'

'Yes, sir.'

The next day, he called in to the Student Union building. He waited a few minutes for a phone booth in the foyer to become vacant. Going inside he closed the door behind him and dialled the Newcastle home number of the O'Malley family.

'Hello, Siobhan speaking.'

Jack was momentarily taken aback – she sounded so like Roisin. He took a deep breath and regained his composure.

'Hi Siobhan. It's Jack here.'

'Oh Jack, it's so lovely to hear from you. How was Christmas for you over in England? And how are you in yourself?'

'I'm OK thanks. I have my moments as I'm sure you do. How about all of you?'

'The same Jack. The house isn't the same without her. Seamus is still inconsolable; he's taking it very hard – as we all are. But my friends and other parts of the family have been very good. They're all rallying round.'

Jack sensed her forced optimism. He felt the same.

'Siobhan, I've called because I've decided to go back to England for a few months. I'm going to get a temporary job and see how I feel then about coming back to resume my studies in September. I can't make that decision at the moment.'

The lie came more easily to Jack than he thought it would.

'Well, that sounds a really good idea, Jack. Give yourself the space you need and make the decision when you're in a better place. Will you have time to come and see us all before you go back?'

'I'm afraid not. I go back tomorrow on the ferry. I just wanted you to know. We'll get together when I'm back in September.'

'You look after yourself ma wee man. Feel free to phone or write anytime.'

'I will Siobhan. You too. Give my best wishes to Seamus and your lads.' He paused and took a breath. 'Actually, talking about the boys, I wonder if you could get a message to Rory for me. I don't have his contact details.'

'Of course. What is it?'

'Well, Roisin was always keen for the two of us to stay in contact as we were both based in Belfast. She suggested that we maybe meet for a few drinks or a meal together sometimes and keep the contact going. I thought for her sake that he and I should do that. She would have wanted it.'

'I'd like that too, Jack. It would be good for him to have a nice friend like you, a friend of the family, to associate with sometimes.'

'What's the best way to get hold of him?' Do you have his work number, or should I call you to pass the message on?'

'Best to call me, Jack. He's always very busy working and I usually end up leaving a message for him. He calls me back or pops in by.'

Then I'll do it that way Siobhan. I'll give you both as much notice as possible. Look after yourself.'

'Bye, Jack.'

He heard the click at her end of the line and replaced his receiver on the hook.

He smiled to himself. *Foundation laid.*

Chapter 25

He arrived back at his parents' house in England to find a letter inviting him to a one-day selection event at an army base in the south of England the following week. He had explained to them that he was exploring the idea of a job in the administrative service of the RAF up near Manchester and that he would decide if he wanted to return to university over the next few months. He was relieved they didn't press him for more information.

Arriving at the army base, he found he was one of over forty candidates to be put through a combination of physical training exercises, IQ tests and convoluted interviews where he was asked what he thought could be involved if he were successful. He had no idea if he had given them the answers they wanted. He was examined physically by an army medic and only found out later that if he'd had any distinguishing scars, birthmarks or tattoos, he would have been rejected.

He returned home a little perplexed, but it was only two days later that a letter arrived informing him that he had been found 'suitable to undergo further selection'. More joining instructions were attached, this time inviting him to a venue in the rural West Midlands. The duration would be eight weeks and he had to arrive in two days' time for a 6 pm start. He was to arrive with no more than two holdalls containing two changes of lightweight military working clothes, his physical training kit and one set of scruffy civilian clothes plus a washbag. He remembered Turner's advice as he packed. He was of course apprehensive, but his excitement far outweighed that.

His dad had let him borrow his second car, an old Morris Minor that he was always tinkering on, with the promise that he didn't do more than 60mph in it and treated it with respect. Jack had agreed, laughing. He and his mum knew that the car was his father's other child.

The late afternoon sun was disappearing quickly as he approached the place, close to the Shropshire and Staffordshire border, marked on his joining instructions. The AA roadmap beside him on the passenger seat showed only small villages within a radius of about ten miles. He was not surprised. As he came closer, he could see what appeared to be a dilapidated army camp.

He drove up to the barrier at the perimeter fence decked ominously in barbed wire and manned by a solitary MOD policeman.

'Evening, sir,' the man said as Jack wound down the passenger window. 'Name please.'

'Jack McLaughlan.'

The policeman looked at the clipboard in his hand.

'Thank you, sir. Yes, you are expected. When I open the barrier, drive through and follow the road for a few hundred yards. You'll see signs for the Reception Car Park. When you get there, find a parking space and wait in your car please.'

Jack nodded and wound up his window. The barrier rose and Jack drove through.

In the fading light, he could just about make out playing fields, a large structure that looked like a gymnasium, and various military-looking buildings. Canvas-covered army trucks and minibuses were parked beside some of them.

When he got to the car park, he found a space and noticed that there were quite a few other cars parked there. He glanced at his watch. It was 17:40.

A sharp tap on the car window made him jump. He turned to face a man dressed in boots, khaki trousers and a dark green sweatshirt. Jack quickly wound down his window.

'Get your bags out of the car, lock it and follow me on the double,' the man said. 'From this point on you address me and all my colleagues as staff.'

Jack quickly wound his window up, jumped out of the car and went to the boot to retrieve his two bags. As he locked the car door, the man turned and ran off in the direction of what was presumably the reception building. Jack grabbed a bag in each hand and began running after him. His eight weeks initial selection process had started.

Jack was allocated the number 35 and photographed holding a card with 35 on it. He was handed two smaller cards with safety pins on the back also showing 35. Another staff member leaned into his face and spoke slowly and carefully.

'You are number 35 now. For the duration of your stay here – however long or short that may be – you will use only that number in all communications. You will not disclose your name or anything about yourself unless expressly asked. Do you understand?'

Jack nodded.

He was then made to run to the accommodation block and up a flight of stairs where he deposited his bags on a bed pointed out by the staff member. Many of the other beds were covered with bags too. He concluded that others had arrived before him although he'd seen no sign of them so far. Each bed – he estimated twenty in total, ten on each side of the barrack room – had a neat pile of sheets, blankets and pillows sitting on it. Next to each bed, a single wooden wardrobe and a bedside cabinet stood on the polished grey floor.

Cosy. Maybe not? thought Jack.

'35, there's a communal washroom just there and next door is the drying room.' The man's hand pointed briefly to two doors. 'Be in the lecture theatre opposite this building in five minutes. Wear your lightweights, boots and top.'

With that he turned and ran off, his boots clattering on the wooden stairs. Jack surveyed his new surroundings for a few seconds and began to change clothes quickly. He was just lacing up his second boot when he witnessed the same procedure repeated, this time with the number 38. The man was breathing heavily and as the staff member ran off, Jack smiled.

'Hi 38, I'm 35. Nice to meet you.'

Number 38 was taller than Jack, slightly heavier and it appeared not as fit. All he could mutter as he changed was, 'Fuck! What a start!' He winked at Jack as he spoke.

The sparse camp lighting made the buildings look eerie as they both doubled between the buildings. The lecture room was brightly lit and pretty full by the time they both entered. Each person was sitting at an old wooden desk on a foldable wooden chair. On each desk was a stack of A4 lined paper, a pencil, an eraser and a pencil sharpener. Jack and 38 sat down at unoccupied desks. A small contingent of what were obviously staff members, sat on the same foldable wooden chairs at one side of the room watching everyone in the room intently but remaining silent. None of them had any sort of rank insignia.

After two more candidates entered the room and found desks, one of the staff members, a lean angular man with short-cropped hair at the front stood up and faced the room.

'Right then. With the materials in front of you, you are to write a detailed account of your journey here today. Five full pages as a minimum. Thirty minutes. Go.'

Jack picked up his pencil. Turner's words ringing in his ears. *Unusual techniques.* His listening and watching role back at Queen's had heightened his abilities to absorb and retain information in his head. The opportunity to write things down was a welcome change. He took his mind to the moment he had hugged his parents as he'd set off earlier that morning and began writing. It seemed to him only a few minutes later that the man in charge spoke again.

'Put your pencils down. Time is up. Make sure your number is shown clearly on each page and hand your work forward to the next person.'

Jack looked down in front of him and realised that he'd completed seven pages. He glanced around him for comparison and felt reasonably satisfied.

A member of staff collected the papers from the front desks and as soon as that was done an older man with an obvious military bearing made his way deliberately to the front of the room. Jack watched him pass by his desk. There was no indication which of the three services he was from or indeed what rank he held. The man stepped up onto an elevated podium so he could be seen clearly by everyone in the room and turned to face the assembly. There was silence.

'Welcome ladies and gentlemen. I have good and bad news for you. The bad first. We have extremely high standards here and it is very likely that many of you will not attain them. That's no disgrace but we need to find out quickly and efficiently who can succeed so we can release you back to your units and the useful jobs that need to be done in the rest of the armed forces. We have very particular requirements here so please don't take a decision to end your time with us personally.'

He paused before resuming.

'The good news is that a lot of you will voluntarily choose to leave in the coming weeks and you will be very free to do so at any time. In fact, you will be encouraged to do so at every opportunity if you have any doubts. Simply make your decision known to any of my staff team.'

He raised his arm to indicate where his team were in the room as if anyone had any doubt. 'Any questions?' He looked around. No one spoke. 'OK then. Chief Instructor. Carry on please.'

With that he walked to the door he had entered from and was gone in seconds. The Chief Instructor, a lean, muscular, and serious looking man in his early forties stood up and addressed the room.

'OK everyone. The rest of this evening begins with a short PT session starting in ten minutes on the parade ground. Then a shower and your evening meal. How does that sound?'

Jack looked around the room and saw a few people were smiling. He chose not to smile. He was preparing himself for what he knew intuitively was going to be a very hard personal challenge over the next eight weeks. He was determined not to be one of those choosing to leave or even worse, being invited to do so. His mind was entirely focused on coming face-to-face with Declan McGill at some point in the not-too-distant future. To do that, he had to deal successfully with whatever was thrown at him in the coming weeks. That was his motivation. The words that came to him seemed a little trite, but they were true.

Failure is not an option.

Chapter 26

The next eight weeks proved far tougher than Jack had imagined.

He understood the end point but the intervening challenges – each requiring huge physical and mental effort – did not always make it clear at the time. The seemingly pointless written tests and endless stripping and reassembling of rifles, machine guns and pistols wore him down. They were expected to do everything to the highest standard and in the shortest amount of time.

He had never felt so tired in all his life. Many times Jack felt he had only just fallen asleep when he was jerked awake by shouting and yelling. The first time it happened had been a real shock.

'OK ladies and gentlemen! You've had more than enough sleep for now! Up you get and into your light PE kit. Meet me downstairs in five minutes ready to rock 'n' roll!'

Jack had thought the words were part of a dream and turned over to go back to sleep.

'That means you too 35!' the instructor bellowed in his ears.

Coming to his senses, Jack rolled groggily out of bed and grabbed his PE shorts from his locker.

People were staring at each other through half-open eyes as if everyone around them was deranged.

'What the fuck, you lot! MOVE! Wake yourselves up! We need people who can function well on far less sleep than you've had! Get downstairs!'

The group began to anticipate the disruption and constant turmoil. Jack learnt to exist on shorter periods of sleep and yet found his instincts became sharper and more attuned to the circumstances around him. Despite the pain, he realised his body was toughening up internally and externally.

Friendships weren't encouraged, but he found he and 38 began to develop a good relationship. There were a few occasions when they encouraged each other as things got tough. Most times just a quick smile, or a thumbs-up or a raised eyebrow but always with perfect timing and always welcome.

The level of dropouts from the course was constant. Sometimes people simply couldn't go on and a staff member briskly marched them away never to be seen again. On other occasions staff made the call, leading poor performers away. After the first four weeks, more than half of the original group had removed themselves or been removed.

The second month saw a new development. Jack had grown accustomed to lengthy runs at any hour of the day or night, but when the Chief Instructor assembled them on the parade square early one morning, he sensed something different.

'OK everyone we've finished your gentle introduction to physical fitness. Now we start some serious training. We'll call it the stretcher phase.'

Jack glanced at the stretchers laid out to the side of the square, each with a six-foot long railway sleeper lashed to the canvas. A wooden pole had been inserted through canvas loops either side.

'You will be required to carry your injured "colleague" to safety in time for them to receive medical attention. Four to a stretcher. GO!'

The recruits ran over to the stretchers.

'Fuck this!' 38 muttered as he grabbed the end of one of the poles. 'They could at least have given us a live body – that would have been easier than this.'

'They'd never have allowed that,' Jack laughed grimly. 'Whoever it was could have slept!'

They picked up the stretcher and started on their way, the instructor yelling at them as they passed by.

'Come on you lazy fuckers! Your patient is dying! He won't make it unless you speed up. 35 and 38, this is not some gentle stroll you know. You're slowing the others down! You'll be the reason you're kicked off this programme.'

The stretcher run became their regular exercise. The terrain or the weather conditions didn't matter – they ran. Staff were beside them constantly, shouting insults, sometimes encouragement, and always urging more speed.

On one occasion Jack slipped on a rock beside a stream and somehow fell under the stretcher swallowing mouthfuls of freezing water. As he gasped for air, a strong hand pulled him out of the water. The welcome face of 38 greeted him.

'For fuck's sake 35, this is no time to take a drink. The rest of us need you to help carry this fucking stretcher.'

Jack managed a knowing grunt of appreciation and in seconds was back on his feet, running once more. He desperately hoped the instructor wouldn't count it against him.

There was never time to relax or even recover. After a quick shower they would be straight into the next exercise. Following the stretcher run it was a boxing session.

'Get your gloves on,' said the instructor as he moved them into pairs of roughly the same physique. 'You have three minutes to batter the hell out of your partner. Don't let up. Keep the punches flowing.'

Jack had thought it would be easy, after all three minutes didn't seem that long. He soon discovered how wrong he was. When the bell finally rang, he fell to his knees, battered, bruised and out of breath. He wasn't the only one.

That evening, in a rare few minutes before lights out, Jack turned to 38. 'My arms feel like lead. I couldn't punch my way out of a wet paper bag right now and as for carrying another stretcher …' His voice tailed off before he added wearily, 'Three minutes is an age, isn't it?'

'Yeah. I suppose the idea is to get us to carry on even when we think we can't,' 38 replied. 'It's the cuts and bruises I object to. How will I pull women looking like Henry Cooper after a bad night in the ring?'

The physicality of the course continued unabated and whilst Jack's body always protested, his brain stayed focused. It needed to. In one exercise, immediately following a timed five-mile run, he was taken, hooded, into a building. When the hood was pulled off, he found himself in a brightly lit hangar facing a large Portakabin door. The lights blinded him momentarily. Before he could say anything, one of the staff quickly opened the door and shoved him inside. The door was slammed shut behind him. Still breathing heavily from the run, he found himself in complete darkness. As his eyes tried to adjust, a harsh voice shouted through the darkness.

'35! You must exit this room by the door on the far side.'

Where the fuck is that?

'You must not make any noise and must stay on your feet throughout! GO!'

Jack guessed he was being watched by one of the staff, presumably using night-vision goggles. He also assumed the room was rigged with trip wires that would set off alarms, or piles of tin cans waiting to be knocked over. He began to slowly feel his way in the direction he sensed was forward and where he hoped the other door would be. *Stay calm.*

He strained with his eyes but there was not a single shaft of light from anywhere. He quickly assessed what he had to do. *Move in one direction. Feel for clues. Keep moving!*

He estimated it took him about ten minutes to reach what he assumed was the exit door. His hands gently pushed the handle downwards and the door opened a crack, light pouring in. As his eyes adjusted, he found himself face-to-face with another staff member.

'Fuck 35, you took your time, didn't you? If that had been a house in Belfast, the fucking boyyos would be waiting outside ready to shoot you dead. You think you should quit this course and make way for faster people? I'll happily take you to sign the release papers.'

'No staff, I don't intend to quit,' Jack replied angrily. 'That was my first time. I'll be faster next time. I'll show you.'

The man gave a hint of a smile.

'That's the spirit 35. More of that. I've seen worse attempts. Off you go and take a shower, you smell like shit.'

'Thanks staff.'

Chapter 27

A few days after his experience in the darkened Portakabin, the staff instructors told the remains of the group to meet in the lecture theatre immediately after dinner. Although they all expected a briefing for yet another exercise, no one could be sure. They had grown accustomed to expect the unexpected.

Jack counted eleven of the original starters from his course sitting around him, about a fifth of the original group. *Well, they got the estimated final numbers right,* he thought. He noticed that 38 had lost weight and his clothes were now baggy. He gave the slightest of nods to his mate, and it was returned with a brief smile. Jack smiled to himself. 38 was probably thinking the same thing about Jack's clothes.

At that moment, the camp commander entered the room and walked to the podium. Again, the room was silent as he began speaking.

'Well done ladies and gentlemen. I have the dubious pleasure of confirming you have been successful in completing the training here at Camp One. My staff advise me that you in this room are the few that have the skills and qualities required to progress to more advanced training for the specialised counter-terrorist role in Northern Ireland.'

Jack felt a wave of relief flood through him. *Another step closer, McGill.*

'Whilst the last eight weeks have been hard, you'd be very much mistaken if you think the next six months will be easier. They will be different but no easier. Some of you sitting here won't make it all the way but at least we've given you a fighting chance and that was our intention. With the meal tonight, I've provided a few beers for you to enjoy. First thing tomorrow, you are to start a week's leave before reporting to Camp Two. Details will be handed out tomorrow before you leave.'

The news was beginning to sink in. Jack looked around the room and saw the smiles break out as the group began to realise Camp One was finally over.

∞

The abundant supply of beer definitely had an effect on Jack's head in the morning. A couple of aspirin from his washbag cleared the cobwebs and by the time he'd had breakfast in the canteen with everyone else, he felt good again. The instructions were to have his bags packed and dropped at the back of the lecture theatre and be waiting seated at 08:00 sharp.

A few minutes before the allotted time he made his way to the lecture theatre with his bags. Staff were already there and as Jack entered the door, he was handed his personal possessions, which consisted of his car keys and his wallet. His car keys had a little brown tag attached to them with a piece of string. The number 35 had been neatly written on it. He smiled to himself.

Even on the last day here I'm still just number 35.

At exactly 08:00, the briefing began.

'Ladies and gentlemen, the next stage of your training begins a week today, 12th March. The location is rural North Wales, map reference 148642. On OS maps it is merely marked as MOD property. You are to report no later than 14:00 hours. If you choose to arrive earlier, lunch will be provided. Clothing requirements are different to here. Civvies only and definitely not smart. No uniform of any description to be brought with you. Any questions?' He paused but no one spoke.

'OK then. You know not to disclose anything about the last eight weeks to anyone. My staff and I wish you all the best of luck.'

Jack said his goodbyes, shook hands with the staff members and grabbed his bags before making his way to the car park. He needed to catch up with how things were in Newcastle and see if he could make contact with Rory.

He called the O'Malley's number from a phone box on the way home. Siobhan was her normal welcoming self.

'Well hello Jack, so good that you called. How are you?'

'I'm fine, thanks. How's the O'Malley clan?'

'We're OK, Jack. Seamus and I were thinking about you just this morning. We went down to Roisin's grave to refresh the flowers there. Some lovely roses. She loved roses.'

'I remember. She did indeed. So have you seen much of the boys over the last couple of months?'

'No, not really. Well not much of Neil or Conor although they do phone to check in with us. They're good lads. As for Rory, he sometimes has business near here, you know, fares from Belfast mainly he tells us, so we see him now and then.'

Yeah, I bet that's the story he tells them, thought Jack.

Siobhan continued.

'I've reminded him a few times that you said you'd like to meet up if and when you're back in Belfast for your studies. Have you decided anything yet Jack?'

'I'm pretty sure that I will come back in September, Siobhan. Working as a labourer on a building site doesn't really do it for me but at least I'm fitter than I was. Carrying bricks up and down ladders all day does that for you. Plus, I've had a few calls from some of my mates at Queen's. They all say that I should go back so I've reserved my place at the same hall of residence just in case.'

'Sure, that's a sensible decision Jack. Keep all your options open for as long as possible. I'll update Rory on your news. He'll like that.'

I bet he fucking will. Jack remembered Rory's hateful stare at the funeral in January. It seemed years ago.

'Thanks, Siobhan. Remind him that he promised to show me around some of the more distinctive parts of Northern Ireland.'

'I'll be sure to mention it again next time I talk to Rory. I'd like the two of you to get on.'

'Thanks Siobhan. I'll call you again in a while. When things become more definite.'

'Take care of yourself Jack and we'll see you again soon.'

He replaced the receiver feeling fairly confident that with Siobhan's help, he would be meeting up with Rory on his return to Belfast.

After that of course it would be his job to get Rory to provide the information Turner wanted and more importantly the information he, himself, needed.

Watch out, McGill. You don't know what's heading your way, he thought to himself as he got back into the car and headed home.

Chapter 28

Camp Two was situated in rural west Wales. The Ordnance Survey map simply referred to it as 'MOD Property' and it was miles from the nearest village.

Jack wanted to arrive as early as he was allowed and, again in his father's Morris Minor, he approached the heavily guarded gates at 12:15. A handful of his Camp One associates had already arrived and were having lunch in the canteen as he entered.

'Hi 35. Good to see you again,' a familiar voice quipped as he joined the group with his tray of sausages and chips and can of Coke.

'Good to see you too 38. Nice to know we're in this together.' Jack smiled and looked round the room. 'Quite a few new faces here.'

'Yeah, I think there must have been other camps over the weeks and Camp Two doesn't start until there are enough candidates in the pipeline.'

'Makes sense,' Jack replied. He turned to shake hands with his friend. 'Let me introduce myself properly. I'm Jack McLaughlan. RAF. I am not a number, I am a free man.'

38 laughed, clearly getting the reference.

'And I'm Joe Robinson. Royal Tank Regiment.' He took another bite of his sausage. 'I'm told this next stint of training is even harder. Can you believe that?'

'Yeah, I can believe that,' Jack replied as he wondered how on earth they could make things more difficult than they already had been.

With lunch consumed, they were given instructions where to find their accommodation, told to drop their gear there and be ready for the briefing in the large single-storey building in the centre of the camp. The barracks were smaller than at Camp One. Only six people per room and there were gentler touches such as lampshades and softer pillows on the beds.

The briefing began at 14:00 on the dot. The building was obviously used for a variety of purposes. It was kitted out with briefing and training materials including a screen and projection equipment. It also appeared to double as some form of recreational room. Joe nudged him in the ribs.

'Looks like there's a bar over there. Maybe this won't be so bad after all.'

Jack laughed. If they were even half as tired as they had been on Camp One, he knew he'd prefer to get some sleep rather than down a few pints.

The briefing was led by a woman who introduced herself as Brenda. She explained she was one of the advanced driving instructors who would be training them all over the next few weeks.

'You lot need to be able to drive fast and effectively in all types of weather, all reconnaissance scenarios and all combat conditions.

Your reflexes need to be fast and seamless. If they are not, you will probably be killed, injured or taken prisoner. You will learn what we need to carry in our vehicles for our jobs and our safety. There may be times when you have to go in and rescue some of our own and for this you will need these skills to a very high standard. I cannot stand people who think they are god's gift to driving. They're the ones that usually fail this stage of the selection at Camp Two. Do I make myself clear?'

Everyone nodded. Jack was impressed by her confident and professional aura.

'Be ready to go at 09:00 tomorrow morning outside this building. Wear loose-fitting clothes. No need for jumpers or coats as my team will keep you warm enough. Any questions?'

One of Jack's colleagues asked what vehicles they would be using.

'There are a few. All are kept in great condition by our motor pool team although I can tell you they don't look sexy. They're not meant to. On the streets of Belfast, Derry or Newry, we want them to look as unobtrusive as possible. We'll introduce you to our babies in the morning. Anything else?'

There was silence. Jack was excited. He loved all things mechanical. A hand down from his dad.

'This afternoon and early evening we have some initial weapons familiarisation sessions for you. That will be led by my colleague Nick.' She turned to the small group of instructors sitting together at the back.

A squat, balding man stood up and walked to the front of the room. He turned and smiled at Jack and his colleagues as Brenda and three men took their cue and left the room. Jack assumed that was the team of driving instructors.

'OK everyone. Make yourselves comfortable as I have the delightful job of introducing you to the weapons currently used by us *good guys* and most unfortunately by the *bad guys*, also known as terrorists, be they nationalist or loyalist supporters. You will get a lot of practice in firing them over the next few months as we have them all in our armoury but for now the objective is to recognise them quickly and know what they can do.'

The rest of the afternoon disappeared in a blur for Jack. After Camp One, he thought he knew a bit about guns, but he had absolutely no idea of the vast array of weapons used in the conflict in Northern Ireland. It was mesmerising.

They began by learning the various properties of handguns, pistols and revolvers, before moving onto rifles and shotguns, and finally the machine guns.

'We'll get to the lesser-known ones in due course chaps,' Nick said. 'Plus the explosives, the mortars, the grenade launchers and a few anti-tank specialties from various gunrunners and overseas military regimes.'

By the time the evening mealtime arrived, Jack's head was full of images of the weapons introduced during the session.

'I had no idea all these were used on the streets,' he said to Joe as they walked back to the canteen.

'Those bastards will take anything they can get their hands on. It means we have to respond with the like. It's a vicious cycle.'

It made Jack wonder what weapons McGill's ASU had access to.

'I can't help being a bit excited about firing some of them,' Jack confided.

'Yeah, you'll enjoy that – in the safety of the camp. Very different on active service. Me? I'm more interested in the driving.'

Jack agreed. The fact that he was going to be taught to drive at huge speeds in demanding conditions appealed enormously to him.

The next day didn't disappoint. Brenda and her team of instructors were the best drivers Jack had ever seen. There were three candidates and an instructor in each car. Brenda announced the teams and Jack was with her. The cars were scruffy and dirty with enough scratches to really give them street cred. Two Ford Escorts, one black and one grey, one red Honda Civic and one blue Hillman Avenger. All four cars were parked neatly next to one another about a car's width apart, all facing the exit to the parade square which today was a car park.

'OK Jack, you're in the front passenger seat and you two, Dave and Gareth, are in the back to start with. Chop chop, we haven't got all day.' She pointed to the black Escort. Jack and the other two ran to the car and climbed in. Jack heard her shout to her instructors who were issuing similar instructions to the others.

'OK lads. This is their first experience of real driving so make sure it's a good one.' Jack noted the wicked smiles on the instructor's face as she sprinted to the driver's door of the Escort.

'Gentlemen,' she said loudly. 'Watch and learn. I'll explain as we go. This morning I do the demos. This afternoon it's your turn. Ask as many questions as you like as we go. We do everything for a reason. Remember that.'

She turned the ignition key and the engine roared into life. Her hands moved quickly between the steering wheel, the gear stick and the handbrake and in a split second they were accelerating towards the camp barrier gate which Jack noticed was being rapidly raised by the military policeman there. The four cars sped out of the camp in single procession and Jack was reminded of the iconic Minis that led the getaway in the film *The Italian Job*.

As soon as the cars got onto the open road, the fun really began. Brenda drove at high speed almost all of the time, overtaking cars and lorries with the engine screaming at high revs. The other cars soon turned off at other junctions.

'Always keep your revs high and select a low gear, gentlemen, it makes the car far more responsive. Always look as far ahead as possible, not just the next few cars. You need to be scanning the scene ahead, looking for anything that might impede your progress. A tractor, a slow driver, a patch of wet road or a potential ambush. Anything in fact. The car needs to become part of you. It must do your bidding instantly. Don't worry about damaging the engine. As I said yesterday, these cars might look shabby, but they are maintained brilliantly, and any damage is rectified immediately.

We have an unofficial motto here. *Drive as fast as possible.* Remember that your own life might well depend on you getting away from any danger as fast as you can, or you might need to get somewhere fast to rescue a hostage or a colleague. Time is always critical so never piss about. Get it?'

They all nodded.

The next few weeks continued at the same relentless pace. Every day was spent either driving or navigating, or occasionally being sick due to the gravitational forces involved. Jack was relieved to find that he was the least affected by the motion sickness. There was no foul-smelling rubber mask clamped over his nose and mouth in this situation.

New skills were constantly taught and reinforced through repetition. Driving backwards at speed as part of counter-ambush manoeuvres together with techniques to get the car pointing in the best direction for a quick getaway.

Evenings, if not spent driving rapidly in the dark on roads or through woods and forests on dirt tracks, were spent on vehicle recognition and learning techniques to remember vehicle plates or significant features. No time was ever wasted.

After a month, Brenda scheduled a meeting in the operations room. Jack sensed that this wasn't going to be the usual briefing. He noted that as well as the driving team being present, Nick the weapons instructor was also there. As the meeting started, Jack was aware that the group was two people short. Brenda's opening remarks explained the discrepancy.

'You will have noticed that two of your colleagues are not here this evening. Unfortunately, Colin and Pete were not up to the required standard for this part of the training. They were told a few hours ago and have already gone. So that leaves you lot who are deemed worthy of progressing to the next stage. More of that in a few moments, but don't think for a second that this is the end of your advanced driver training. This is a cumulative training programme and there will be frequent assessments to demonstrate that you've forgotten nothing and can still perform to the required standard. Understand?'

He was not surprised that his two colleagues had gone. He had seen them in operation too and had also thought their responses were simply not fast enough.

'But now you have other skills to master,' Brenda continued. 'Nick tells me you've done well getting to know your weapons but it's time for things to get more interesting.'

She turned and smiled as she made a little welcoming gesture to Nick with her hand and withdrew. Nick returned the smile, stood up and came to the front of the group.

'Well, everyone, I promised that you'd get your chance to start firing these weapons and tomorrow we do just that. Meet at the firing range at 08:00 tomorrow morning. Until then, your time is your own so make the most of it.'

Chapter 29

Although Jack had looked forward to the weaponry segment of the training, it turned out he found it very challenging. Most of his fellow trainees came from the army or marines and were familiar with handling and firing weapons, but Jack had limited experience. He took longer to feel relaxed with whatever gun he was holding and struggled with each weapon's distinctive features. He began to doubt himself and occasionally made stupid errors. He desperately hoped the staff wouldn't notice.

Two days into the training, they attended a morning briefing with Nick.

'Right you lot. We've got you familiar with a range of weapons but today I'm going to introduce you to what is to become your best friend.' He held up what Jack recognised to be a 9mm Browning pistol. 'Each of you will be issued with your very own 9mm Browning for use on active service. You will be expected to carry it with you at all times. It needs to become part of your undercover attire. We'll issue you a shoulder holster for now, but in many situations, you won't be able to use it. You'll need to learn how to disguise the fact that you are carrying it. We'll help you with that,' he added with a slight smile.

Jack was surprised at the excitement he felt about having his own gun. When he was given it, he held it in his hand, feeling the weight. He knew at once that this was the weapon for him and couldn't help wondering if it was *this* gun that would be responsible for McGill's death.

Nick must have read his mind.

'We'll head to the firing range and see if we can't score a few points against the *bad guys*. Follow me.'

Jack followed the group to an area where human-shaped cut-outs were lined up, each with targets on the chest and head.

'First things first,' said the firing instructor. 'You'll notice where these targets are placed. It's for a reason. In our line of work we shoot to kill. There is no point in trying to wound your opponent. Your safety and the safety of anyone with you is the overriding factor. Never take chances. Now, let's see how you do.'

The recruits spread themselves along a line approximately twenty feet away from the cut-out targets.

'In your own time, gentlemen,' called the instructor. Jack watched as he saw everyone around him assume a side-on position and support their firing arm with their other arm. He copied them as best he could, took aim and pulled the trigger. To his disappointment, he missed the target completely. His second and third attempts weren't much better.

'You've not done this much, have you?'

Jack turned to find the instructor standing behind him.

'No, sir.'

'Well, there's a first time for everyone. See how they're all standing? That's called the Weaver position. Side-on so your body is smaller, weight on your front foot for stability and the shooting arm supported. Give it a go.'

Jack did as he was told.

'Now the secret is in the breathing. Control it. Breathe in and out and watch the gun barrel rise. Now inhale and pause. Exhale and pause. Exhale again and squeeze the trigger.'

Jack did his best to slow his breathing down, looking straight down the barrel of his Browning towards the human shape. He gently squeezed the trigger and felt the recoil.

'Not bad. Certainly better than your previous attempts.'

Jack lowered the gun and was pleased to see he had clipped the edge of the chest target.

'Keep practising, Jack. We'll make a marksman of you yet,' the instructor said with a wry smile.

Over the next few days Jack spent as much time as he could at the firing range. He didn't think he would ever be called upon as a sniper, but his marksmanship improved as the days progressed. He even managed to execute the 'double tap' – two shots fired at the same target point in a split second to increase the certainty of the kill.

The mantra from the instructors was always '*learn and apply*' and Jack did his best to do so. He knew he was making progress, but for the first time, he watched nervously as more and more of his colleagues were quietly and efficiently dropped from the training to return to their former military units.

He breathed a huge sigh of relief a few weeks later when Nick told them they would be moving onto a new skill segment.

'Gentlemen, we've taught you what you need to know with firearms. Do not become complacent. Use the remaining time at this camp to refine your skills. I expect to see you regularly at the firing range. But for now, I hand you over to the surveillance team. You will be delighted to know that once you have the necessary technical know-how, you will have the joy of some night flights in the Lynx helicopter taking photographs at high speed and low altitude.'

As he turned to leave, Nick walked towards Jack.

'You've impressed us with your determination Jack. We've seen the progress you've made. Make sure you continue with the practice sessions.'

The surveillance segment of the training came easier to Jack. He had always enjoyed tinkering with mechanical things so found it easy to remember the facts he needed to memorise about cameras and radios – he had great fun fitting a hidden radio into one of the camp's cars. *Dad would be proud of me*, he thought to himself.

They were taught how to look as unobtrusive as possible. Advice was given on appropriate clothing and haircuts were banished to ensure they would leave the camp with longer hair.

'Look at me,' Joe laughed as he walked around in a set of scruffy clothes. 'I match that old car over there.'

'You may laugh now,' said Michael, one of the actors coaching them on disguises, 'but it may well save you somewhere down the line.'

Jack understood that. He also understood why they were being coached on different accents.

'To be honest any accent will be OK,' Michael told them. 'Northern Irish, Southern Irish, Scottish, American. Anything. Just not English.'

Jack had no problem with the accents and gained a few laughs along the way with his knowledge of Northern Irish phrases. It all helped relieve the growing pressure felt by everyone as they neared the final stages of training. No one wanted to be removed at this point.

Chapter 30

As they moved into the final month, the pace of events seemed to increase exponentially. Jack found it increasingly difficult to fit in regular firearms practice in amongst the new skills they were being taught.

'I had no idea how much there was to learn,' he commented to Joe as they watched a first aid demonstration on how to save someone's life from a knife wound.

'I'm still recovering from this morning's unarmed combat session. I thought the boxing was bad enough at Camp One,' Joe replied.

Jack rolled his eyes as he remembered the instructor's advice that morning: 'When someone's coming at you with a gun you've got to deflect the gun or stop them pulling the trigger. Don't think. Act. Gouge his fucking eyes. Grab his balls and twist 'em hard. Anything to gain additional seconds in which to decide the next move.'

The information had come thick and fast, and he had encouraged them to think laterally about how items such as keys, beer glasses and bottles, even coins and pens could be used to disable an opponent in the absence of a gun.

The final part of the session had become very real as they tried out the techniques they had been shown. Several of them walked away with cuts and bruises added to their already aching limbs.

'Maybe that's why they timetabled first aid for this afternoon,' Jack muttered.

With the final week looming, Jack realised he now understood the true purpose of 14 Co. They were expected, by whatever means, to provide the best possible intelligence to enable the army or the RUC to approach and apprehend the enemy. Sometimes it could mean working undercover amongst the enemy, sometimes it meant watching and waiting from a distance.

'Setting up an observation post is an art in itself,' their reconnaissance instructor explained. 'You may have to operate from an OP for days on end. Planning your route and the placement of the OP is essential. On the streets of Northern Ireland any stranger or unexpected activity is treated with suspicion. You can't let your guard down. Even if you think you are alone, remember the surveillance tricks we've taught you. Stay unobtrusive.'

Jack absorbed everything. He studied the street maps of Belfast and committed them to memory as he was taught to. He knew it could save his life at some time in the near future. *Don't get fucking complacent,* he thought. *Stay focused and alert.*

With one week to go, the group were called to another briefing. The lead instructors stood in front of them. Brenda spoke first.

'Well, you've made it to the final test. And we've saved the best till last. This is a week-long exercise in which you will be expected to apply all you have learned in the past few months.'

Jack felt his pulse increase. The end was near, and he was ready for anything that came his way. It had been tough, relentless and exhausting but he had made it through. The naïve student from England was no more.

'You are required to prevent a simulated terrorist attack on a RUC police station. These sorts of attacks happen regularly around the province as you know. SAS troopers will act as the terrorists so you will be up against experienced opposition. You'll be tested to your limits, and we'll be watching you at all times. You will be judged, both individually and as a team, on your ability to apply the skills we have taught you.'

Nick stepped forward.

'Don't forget that your objective is not to get into a firefight with these guys. It is to frustrate their plans by providing quality intel ahead of time. The role of 14 Co is to try to avoid violence. You've all been trained to use force only as a last resort.'

The instructor's words were clear.

With one exception, thought Jack.

They ate silently that evening. Like Jack, they all knew what was at stake; one slip-up could jeopardise their place in 14 Co. Jack looked around at his colleagues. He sometimes wondered what their motivation was for being there. He assumed he would never know. What he did know was that his own resolve to seek out and eliminate the man who had killed Roisin had driven him on through the most difficult tests and it would see him through this final week.

He was correct. The team worked well together and in the final de-brief were congratulated by their instructors and the SAS troopers combined.

'Congratulations gentlemen. You did what was asked of you. If this had been a real situation, you would have succeeded in saving lives and prevented these bastards,' Nick nodded with a grin towards the SAS troopers 'from doing any more harm. You did good!'

'Well done, everyone,' Brenda added. 'I know the first thing you'll want is a shower and possibly some sleep, but the bar will be open tonight and I hope you'll manage to join us for at least one drink.'

Jack would have cheered, but he was so exhausted all he could think of was his bed. *Fuck the shower,* he thought to himself.

Chapter 31

The following morning, they were called to the operations room. The camp commander rose to his feet and immediately all eyes focused on him.

'I have some good news, some bad news and some information for you.' He paused for effect. Jack thought he could have heard a pin drop.

'The good news is that all of you in this room have successfully passed the training and will be invited to take up operational roles in Northern Ireland in the coming months.'

A few smiles were exchanged amongst the group. Jack didn't join in. He was waiting for the bad news.

'The bad news is that the beer this evening is not free, you have to pay for it yourselves. You've already cost the British taxpayer a huge amount.' He smiled.

The room erupted into cheers, handshakes and back-slapping. Tonight, they really could enjoy a drink.

'Excuse me everyone. I haven't quite finished.' The CO raised his voice, and the room went quiet again.

'The following is an overview of what's been happening in Northern Ireland since you began your training. Things have moved on apace while you've been cooped up here. The paramilitary campaigns of terror have continued; the IRA has continued to detonate bombs in London and elsewhere and more of your military colleagues and police officers have been shot and killed around the province. Recently, three business leaders were assassinated in the province; one in Derry and two in Belfast.'

There were a few looks between the group, but most eyes were locked firmly on the CO.

'IRA sectarian violence has been matched by equally savage Protestant paramilitary UVF and UDA activity. Civilians have been randomly killed and mutilated, instilling terror and fear everywhere. There is also talk of a region-wide strike to be organised by the United Unionist Action Council. They want a more stringent security response from the British government.'

He paused to survey the faces in the room.

'In essence, things over there are even more dangerous than before. We know of at least one of our own having been abducted and almost certainly killed somewhere in County Armagh or just over the border. So, my message to you is very clear. Your role going forward is critical. It's dangerous and dirty but the intel you guys in 14 Co provide will be the difference between winning and losing this war. It's now guerrilla warfare. Take nothing for granted, be prepared for anything, and look after each other. Good luck all of you.' He saluted and left the room.

'Nothing vague about that message, then,' Joe muttered.

Jack was about to respond when they were interrupted by

another officer. He apologised to Joe and gently pulled Jack to one side, away from the rest of the group.

'McLaughlan, a colleague of mine, Lieutenant Colonel Turner, told me to tell you that your operational placement will be different to your colleagues. He said that you'd know what he was talking about.'

'Yes sir, I do. Thank you.'

'He wants you to call him as soon as possible. Here's the number.' He handed Jack a folded piece of paper. 'You're welcome to use my office phone.'

'Thank you, sir. I'll do that immediately.'

On the call, Turner confirmed Jack would return to Queen's, and his room at Alanbrooke. He was to resume his studies and continue to use his student alias. The one disappointing piece of news was that he was not going to be allowed to carry his Browning.

'We simply can't risk it, Jack,' Turner had said. 'If you were based out of one of the 14 Co locations it would of course be different. But we can't risk you having a weapon on University property.'

Jack knew Turner too well to argue the point at this stage. He kept his council while Turner went on to explain that he should phone the O'Malley household to let them know he was back in Belfast. He was to wait for Rory to contact him. If he did, Jack was then to build the relationship.

'Things are escalating, Jack, and given the recent assassinations of prominent businessmen in the province, we can only surmise that they're going to aim higher. Increasingly our sources talk of a "spectacular" – something big that will send out shock waves and give the organisation increased publicity. We thought it might be the Queen's visit in June as part of her Jubilee celebrations – security for the event was huge. But in the end, there were only peaceful demonstrations in some nationalist areas and the visit passed off safely. It was probably too high profile, even for the IRA. We think it's far more likely they'll target a senior politician, possibly Ian Paisley at one of his political gatherings or maybe the

Secretary of State, Roy Mason, on one of his visits over here. My money is on the latter.'

Jack nodded. He wasn't surprised. Turner continued.

'Our sources tell us Mason's name is being mentioned more and more often. He is considered by many in the IRA – and its splinter factions – to be responsible for the tougher role taken by the police and military recently, especially covert operations. In reality Jack, they're right – your own training and deployment bears testimony to that.'

Jack followed the logic. A successful attack on Mason would be seen as a victory for the IRA.

'All ministerial visits over here are kept under wraps for obvious reasons, but we're looking into what may be on the cards in the next few weeks and months. In the meantime, we simply have to know more about the location of these arms shipments. They are paramount to the success of any *spectacular*. That's where you come in. If we locate the shipment, we eliminate the problem.'

Jack agreed. He just had to hope Siobhan would do her part in getting the process underway.

Chapter 32

Jack was surprised at the intensity of emotion he felt when walking back into his room at Alanbrooke. He could almost sense Roisin's presence.

'I'm back, Roisin,' he said quietly to the empty room. 'And now, finally, I'm ready. I'm going to get the bastard who took you away from me.' He sat down on the bed, his mind filled with thoughts of happier times when the room had been filled with laughter and he had been able to feel her body close to his.

It was mid-afternoon, two days later, when the hall porter knocked on his door.

'Phone call for you. Someone called Rory. A friend of yours? He said he'd wait for me to see if you were here.'

Bingo. Well done Siobhan.

Jack picked up his room key and followed the porter to the waiting booth.

The accent and intonation were unmistakable.

'My Ma told me a few times that you called her. What do you want, Jack?' The tone was cold. The accent harsh.

Jack took a deep breath.

'You once offered to give me a proper introduction to other parts of Northern Ireland, and I said I'd take you up on the offer. Well, here I am.' Jack kept his tone neutral.

A few moments of silence followed, then Rory spoke.

'That was before my sister was killed instead of that fucking soldier.' Jack could hear the anger building in Rory's voice. 'Surely you don't still want to have a beer with me, knowing my views on the fucking British army do ya? Catch yerself on!'

Stay calm, Jack thought. *You've prepared yourself for this conversation.*

'Actually, it was more that I thought Roisin would like us to stay in contact,' he said quietly. 'Even if it's just for the sake of her memory.' He hoped his answer would put Rory on the back foot. It seemed to work. Nothing was said for a few seconds. Jack was sure he could hear him breathing deeply.

'OK,' Rory said finally. 'I'll meet ya for a drink. We'll take it from there. Where and when?'

'How about I meet you at The Crown in the centre? Tomorrow? 7 pm? We can stay there or go somewhere else if you prefer.' He tried to insert some false bonhomie in his voice.

'I'll see ya there.' There was a click at the end of the line. He had gone.

Jack knew what he had to do. As a first step, he needed to find Conor Butler.

Jack and Conor had become mates. He was a nice, amiable Irishman who liked a few pints and was sensible enough to keep his views on Northern Irish politics to himself. He had also opted for another year in Alanbrooke to keep his life simple. Jack knocked on his door, half expecting him not to be there.

It opened, and Conor's beaming face appeared from behind it.

'Jack McLaughlan, so it is indeed! How have you been these last few months?'

'I'm OK, thanks for asking.'

'Whenever I see you, I associate you with a pint. Fancy one or maybe a couple? I was just trying to finish up a bit of work but I'm not in studying mode. You're a nice distraction so you are.'

'You read my mind. Anyone else we could rope in?'

'I'll go and rustle up a couple of new guys from the next corridor. They're like you and me. Always have a thirst,' he laughed. 'Give me two minutes and I'll be back. Make yourself comfortable.' He pulled Jack into his room.

'I see your room is even more untidy than usual,' Jack laughed in return.

'Aye, it is that. I was never known for being tidy. My Ma always complains.' He went out of the door, closing it behind him.

Jack surveyed the room. There was an assortment of empty crisp packets, screwed up pieces of lined A4 paper, textbooks and other discarded items. He glanced at the half-open drawer immediately under the desktop and thought he saw what he was looking for. Conor's Irish passport had been tossed in there along with notepads and biros. The burgundy front cover with the harp emblem gave it away immediately. Jack lifted the passport and slipped it into the back pocket of his jeans. He pushed the drawer in a little more, covering the space where the passport had been. He knew that Conor wouldn't miss it for a few hours and that was all he needed.

Chapter 33

Jack stood at the bar of The Crown. It was 7 pm. The bar was rapidly filling up, but there was no sign of Rory.

He sipped his beer, gazing occasionally at the main door.

At seven minutes past seven a voice from behind startled him.

'So, Jack, you made it then.' Jack spun round to find Rory standing there. 'Another drink?'

'I didn't notice you come in,' replied Jack, managing a smile.

'That's for sure then. Maybe you were elsewhere in your head.'

Jack felt uneasy. He should have noticed him. He downed the rest of his drink and put the glass on the bar.

'Another beer would be great.'

'So how have you been keeping in England?'

'OK thanks. I needed some time to get my head together after what happened.'

Rory didn't reply. Jack watched him scan the people in the pub.

'I can't stay long – I'm busy tonight – but let's find a quiet spot,' he suggested and nodded towards an empty booth. They walked over and sat down. Rory continued to scan the immediate environment before sitting down.

'So, Jack. Tell me. Why are you back here?' The hostile tone was there as always.

Jack was prepared.

'Nothing will bring Roisin back, Rory. *Use his name.* But I'd started to make a life over here. I've made some good friends and was really enjoying the course. I thought I'd give it a while longer at least. See how it goes.'

'What do you know about her death?' Rory asked abruptly.

'The reports said caught in the crossfire. An attack on an army foot patrol. IRA, they think.'

Rory remained silent. He was watching Jack intently. He took a slow, deliberate sip of beer, his eyes never straying.

Jack continued.

'I was told that she was in the wrong place at the wrong time. That much is clear. I don't blame anyone, Rory.' *Keep it personal.*

The last comment stuck in his throat. It was a huge lie. He blamed the IRA. He blamed Rory and he particularly blamed Declan McGill.

Rory continued to stare at him.

'Aye. A sad mistake. My sister dead.' He took a deep breath.

Jack had no idea if it was a genuine reaction. He suspected not.

'Tell me, Rory,' he asked. 'Does that happen often? Innocent people killed by mistake?'

'Aye, it does.' Rory kept his voice very low. 'Collateral damage is inevitable. The British army and the English establishment are to blame. They shouldn't be over here. They are an army of occupation and are not welcome. They should be made to go crawling back to

England. If that soldier hadn't been on our streets, my sister would be alive now, so she would.' The last comment was in the usual combative tone.

Jack could barely control his temper. *You've just described your sister's death as collateral damage!* He tried hard to maintain his composure and took a silent deep breath to help him think more clearly.

'It's hard for me, Rory, and no doubt for you too. We've both lost her. It'll take time for us to get used to her not being here, but I get what you say about it being a war, and how in a war, there is collateral damage.'

He looked at Rory with what he hoped was a neutral look on his face and thought he saw Rory's eyes momentarily fill up with tears. Then again, maybe it was the smoke in the bar that had caused it. Whatever the reason, Rory seemed to momentarily lose his antagonism towards Jack.

'So, you said you wanted to see the real Northern Ireland? I'll show you. Can't do it now and evenings are generally busy for me, but I'll get a message to you at Alanbrooke, and I'll give you a tour in the next few days. Maybe we'll take in a few bars in my part of Belfast. Roisin would have wanted that. I'll be in touch.'

Rory drained his glass and stood quickly, smiling briefly at Jack before walking briskly out of the bar.

Jack was surprised at how brief their drink had been. He watched Rory go through the main door, pause, and then head right, onto Great Victoria Street. If his assumptions were correct, Rory would soon be heading west towards the Falls Road and the relative safety of the Republican strongholds beyond it. Jack knew his instructions were to play things gently, cultivate the friendship and at no point take any risks that could jeopardise the main source of intel on the arms shipments. He also knew that would not help him deal with his own problem – McGill.

Sod it.

He downed the remains of his pint and made his way to the door. Once outside, his eyes immediately picked up Rory's black bomber jacket about ninety yards along the road in front. He was walking at quite a pace. Jack scanned around him. Both sides of the road were busy with people. That would make his job a little easier.

He set off in pursuit, being careful to stay as close to the buildings as possible, his eyes never wavering from the bomber jacket.

He maintained a set distance so that Rory, even if he glanced back, was too far in front to make him out amongst the other pedestrians. Every now and again, he'd stop momentarily and look into a shop window or doorway, just in case.

He needn't have worried. Rory didn't look back once and seemed to have no idea he was being followed. Jack's hunch seemed to be correct. He stuck to Grosvenor Road, the most direct and fastest route to the Falls Road. Jack had walked it many times before, since it took him right past the Royal Victoria Hospital where Roisin had been based. He wondered if that same thought had crossed her brother's mind.

As he reached Dunville Park, he saw Rory turn left along the Falls Road, as expected. Jack had studied the street configuration of the area they now entered but had never been there himself. He recalled Roisin's warnings of how dangerous it was.

To continue was risky, he knew that, but he also knew he needed to get a better idea of Rory's destination. He hastened his pace to get to the road junction and glanced in front of him as he turned the corner. His pulse was high. He was relieved to see the bomber jacket heading southwest along the Falls Road. *Where's he going?*

Jack knew the buildings to his left were part of the hospital and on the right was the convent school but beyond that, on both sides of the Falls, were a multitude of little streets. Rory could disappear into any of them and unless Jack shortened the distance between them, he stood a good chance of losing him.

He had just decided going in closer would be too risky, when he noticed Rory slow down and stop at the entrance of a pub. Jack could just make out its name: The Red Devil.

He moved into the shadows of the buildings while continuing

to watch, grateful again for the number of people on the street. He noticed another man, half hidden by Rory, move towards him from the opposite direction. He must have said something as he neared the pub, for Jack saw Rory turn and move towards him. They met, shook hands, and more words were exchanged. The man was shorter than Rory, but Jack couldn't make much else out. He wished he could move in closer.

The two men stood together on the pavement outside the pub for a few seconds more before entering and at that point Jack got his first proper sight of the stranger. He felt his stomach turn. Even from this distance the blond hair was unmissable.

Jack weighed up his options. He knew that the clientele of The Red Devil would be exclusively Catholic and that a stranger would be viewed with suspicion. But he also knew this opportunity would almost certainly not come again.

All his training led him to believe this was a safe meeting place for IRA sympathisers and volunteers; situated in a strongly Republican enclave amidst a maze of small streets, there could be no mistake. He decided to sit it out and see what might happen. He was confident that no one would suspect him, at least for a while.

As he waited, a plan began to form in his head. He calculated his odds: He assumed there would be exits at the back of the pub that could be used in emergencies, but he also knew he had no backup, no radio, no transport and most importantly no weapon. Of course, he had known all that when planning to follow Rory but had taken a calculated risk.

His patience was rewarded about half an hour later when he saw Rory leave the pub and head further down the Falls Road in the direction of the Upper Falls. He was alone.

Jack waited until Rory was out of sight before putting his plan into action. He'd spotted a young woman pushing a pram down the opposite side of the road. If he was quick, he'd catch her just as she passed the pub entrance. He made his move, smiling broadly and doing his best to look unthreatening. Even so, he noted the look of apprehension on her face as he came closer.

'Have ya the right time please? My watch is going slow.' His southern Irish accent was perfect. Her face relaxed.

'Sure.' She looked at her wristwatch. 'It's ten past eight.'

'You're a wee star, so you are,' Jack beamed back. He began crossing the road towards the pub's entrance half turning to her and waving as he did so. Jack couldn't help smile as he saw her wave back. *Perfect*. He was just another young man leaving his girlfriend in order to down a few pints.

His bravado as he entered the pub was just as convincing. He deliberately stood to one side and held the door open for another man who was leaving the pub.

'Top of the day to ya. Come you on first.' The man said something that Jack couldn't make out, but it didn't matter. What mattered was there had been some communication between the two of them.

'You're more than welcome so you are,' Jack added, just to be sure.

This time, as he spoke, quite a few faces turned in his direction and he smiled back, looking around as if he was looking for someone. That part was easy. He was. He got to the bar and again his Southern Irish accent was perfect.

'A pint of Guinness please.'

He reached into the back pocket of his jeans and his hand emerged with a five-pound note. He made sure that as he did so, the passport in his pocket came out and fell to the floor. He pretended not to notice and waved the money at a barman while moving along the bar, supposedly trying to get closer to the pump. All the time he was looking for the blond hair of the man who had been with Rory.

A man's voice suddenly spoke from behind him. The Belfast accent was harsh.

'Hey friend. Think you've lost something. You'll be needing it I suspect. Conor Butler it says. Not from around here are ya?'

Jack turned and found he was facing a short, stout man in his mid-fifties. The man was holding the burgundy-coloured passport between his fingers. There was no trace of friendliness on his face.

Jack feigned surprise, patted his jeans back pocket and then breathed an audible sigh of relief.

'That's kind of you, so it is. And now you know who I am. Yes, Conor Butler. That's what my parents christened me in County Wexford.'

Jack realised in an instant that the man appeared to have swallowed the bait, hook, line and sinker. Irish passport, Irish name. The noisy buzz of the pub had returned. Jack had been labelled. Catholic. Southern Irish. Safe.

'I was supposed to meet a university mate of mine here. He said they serve a nice pint of Guinness here. Do you know him? His name is Sean O'Driscoll. From Donegal.'

'No sorry, I don't know any students,' the stout man replied. 'Here, take your ID. You should be more careful you know.' He handed the passport to Jack and turned away to walk back to the table where he'd been sitting with a few of his middle-aged mates.

'I certainly will be more careful with it and thanks be to Jesus that you saw it on the floor. I'm very grateful to ye. Can I get you and your friends a drink to say thanks?'

The man turned briefly.

'No need for that. Glad to help. Just be sure that young fellas like you look after their documents. Around here, you never know when you'll need to identify yourself.'

Jack's Guinness had been put on the bar in front of him and the barman took his money giving him his change. He leant against the bar and took a few large sips, subtly gazing around the pub. It was full and very smoky. He couldn't immediately see the blond-haired man but there were lots of groups sitting and drinking at tables. He was considering his options once again when there was movement at one of the tables near the window. A man was getting to his feet and as he stood, Jack saw that it was *his* man. No doubt.

Short, blond hair. He took a few steps away from the table and Jack had the final confirmation – the limp was unmistakable. He watched as the man made his way through the bar, noting his small stature and wiry physique. It was clear to Jack it was the right knee that had sustained the injury. It was also clear that he was headed to the toilet.

Perfect.

He watched McGill go through the door before making his own way over to it. He was carrying his now half-empty pint glass. This was to be his weapon. Easy to break and immediately ready to thrust. He'd drag the jagged edge across the Weasel's throat so fast he wouldn't have a clue what was happening. The blood loss would be considerable and fast; he would be dead in less than a minute. No noise and Jack could be out of the toilet and the pub in seconds. The only variable that he couldn't control was that McGill needed to be on his own in there. If he wasn't it would complicate matters. He couldn't afford to leave any witnesses.

He pushed the door open, looking and listening for others. There was a man next to McGill at the urinals but the two cubicles were empty. McGill was still pissing when the other man finished and started to do up his zip.

It was all going so well.

Jack turned the hand carrying his glass to one side and let the remaining black liquid run out onto the floor. He felt both fists clench. He was ready.

As the man started to walk past him in the confined space of the toilet he nodded to Jack. Jack found himself nodding back, aware that McGill had finished and was beginning to zip up his flies.

At that exact second, the toilet door burst open, and two men quickly came inside, one knocking into Jack.

'Sorry man. I just need a piss urgently. Hey, hurry the fuck up Declan will you. It's your round so it is and we're all waiting on you.'

Suddenly the toilet was full of five men. Jack calculated the odds.

Even if he could get to McGill, his exit was blocked and whilst he might be able to take out McGill and one of his buddies, he knew he couldn't deal with the other, and there was the fourth man to contend with as well. If nothing else, the commotion would alert the rest of the pub. He knew if that happened, he was a dead man. That fact didn't worry him but if he was killed or taken prisoner, Turner's operation would be put at risk. Jack knew his role was pivotal there.

Fuck! he said to himself.

At that second, McGill turned towards him. Their faces were less than a foot apart. His breath smelt of stale tobacco and beer.

'Excuse me friend,' he muttered. His eyes locked on Jack's eyes for a second.

Jack made his decision.

He stepped to one side and as he did so, allowed McGill to walk past him. Pulling the door open, McGill called back.

'Alright you bastards, I'll get another round in.'

Jack put his empty glass on the window ledge above the urinals and pretended to pee.

So fucking close!

He spat into the urinal, before doing up his zip and leaving the pub.

Chapter 34

Rory got a message to him a couple of days later suggesting they meet again that evening in The Crown. This time Rory was waiting for him in a booth and had got Jack a pint. He beckoned him over with a smile. Jack took it as a positive sign.

'So, I've arranged for us to visit a few bars in my part of town. I think you Brits would call it a mini pub crawl.' Rory seemed pleased.

'Sounds great,' Jack smiled, as he sat down beside his pint. 'I love a good pub crawl.'

'There's a few ground rules before we kick off.' Rory looked serious. 'Remember, it's West Belfast we're going to. It's not like the city centre. It's entirely Catholic, mostly Republican, and entirely anti-Brit. Even the army and the RUC stay away unless they have to go in and when they *do* go in, they go in mob-handed. There's the odd sectarian attack from the Shankill direction too. I'm not too sure Roisin would have approved of me taking you to this area but, hey, you asked and if you're with me you'll be OK. Understand?'

Jack nodded. *As long as we don't go near The Red Devil.*

'As soon as you open your mouth, people will realise you're a Brit. They'll be suspicious. For all they know you could be undercover military or police. A few have been caught in recent years; tortured, shot and bodies dumped. To be safe, I've vouched for you in advance and explained you were my sister's boyfriend. But just in case, take your cue from me, say as little as you can and be fucking careful. Don't rile anybody or make any wise cracks.'

Jack's mind went back to his time in Larne with Steve. Same dangers, different political alliances.

'I've lined up a couple of bars in Andersonstown. There's tight security everywhere there. You'll be unlucky if something kicks off.'

'Fantastic.' Jack felt relief wash over him. He knew Andersonstown was quite a way beyond the end of the Falls Road so The Red Devil probably wouldn't be on the agenda. There was still a long shot McGill might make an appearance; that part of Belfast was his turf after all, but he would be ready for that. If another opportunity presented himself, so much the better.

Rory's voice snapped him back into the moment.

'You ready then? It's a wee walk but we're both fit young fellas so we are.'

'Lead on! I'm looking forward to it.' He wasn't lying. From all Rory had said it seemed their relationship was beginning to move in the right direction. Turner would be pleased.

With Rory as his guarantor, the evening progressed exactly the way Jack had hoped. Pint after pint. He offered to buy his round when it was his turn but always someone in Rory's crowd insisted that he was their guest and to keep his money in his pocket. Conscious that he needed to keep his wits about him, Jack often took his pint with him to the toilet and poured at least half away when the chance arose. Nobody noticed. He followed Rory's ground rules to the letter and only spoke when he was spoken to. He raised his glass to Republican toasts, smiled and laughed when necessary and over the course of the evening the 'edge' associated with being the lone Brit lessened. He was accepted as the boyfriend of Rory's dead sister. He sensed too that Rory was beginning to warm to him.

At the end of the evening, when they were on their own and just about to make the journey home, Rory leaned forward into Jack's face and put his hand on his shoulder. He paused and whispered drunkenly, 'Jack. Just tell me you understand the reality over here. You do understand it, don't you?'

It was a question. A plea. He waited for a reply, looking dazed, his eyes struggling to focus. Jack chose his words carefully.

'Rory, Roisin explained what happened over here in the last decade or so. I get it. I understand.'

He studied Rory's face, looking for a reaction. He got it a few seconds later as Rory lifted his head and slowly said, 'You're a good man Jack McLaughlan. You might be a Brit, but you were ma wee sister's Brit and she loved you.'

Rory paused and for a moment Jack thought there was more to come, but instead he pushed back his chair and rose unsteadily to his feet.

'C'mon Jackie boy. Time to go. I'll walk back with you to the Royal. You'll be safe from that point on.'

Jack smiled to himself as they staggered back into the relative safety of the city centre. It seemed he had Rory on side now.

∞

Late the next morning, that hunch was confirmed when Rory phoned.

'Hope your head's OK today, Jack. We had a bit of a skinful last night, so we did. Good evening though.'

'It was Rory. Yeah, my head is a bit thick today. Thanks again though. Great evening. We'll have to do it again sometime.'

'Well, that's why I'm calling. How'd you like to come to a party next weekend? It's at a friend's house in Dungannon, the other side of Loch Neagh. I've known him and his girlfriend, Maggie, for years. Maggie knew Roisin pretty well too, so you'll have something in common there, so you will.'

'Sounds great.' His response was quick and easy.

'A couple of other mates will be coming too. There'll be room to sleep somewhere so it means we can all have a few drinks as well. Just bring a sleeping bag. All the food and drink will be taken care of. Liam's a generous guy. The craic will be great.' Rory laughed.

'I'll look forward to it. When would we leave?'

'I'm driving, so I'll pick you up next Friday at 6 pm outside Alanbrooke. It'll take us about an hour to get there. More if we must go through roadblocks – there are usually a few around there. Be ready. OK?'

'I will. Thanks Rory.' A click ended the call from the other side.

Jack replaced the receiver. Things were moving and Turner needed to be brought up to speed on developments.

McGill would have to wait a few days longer.

Chapter 35

Another meeting was set up at RAF Aldergrove the next morning. Jane drove and he noticed she took a slightly different route to before. It was a different car too. His mind went back to his training: *vary your routine, your journeys, where you drink and where you shop.*

As they left the outskirts of the city, Jack filled her in on his summer in England. When the conversation ran dry, Jane said quietly, 'Jack, I shouldn't really tell you this, but I think you deserve to know. We've got a lead on McGill.'

Jack tried to disguise his shock. He waited a moment before replying as calmly as he could.

'Yeah? That's good news. How'd that happen?' He knew he had to be composed or she'd suspect something.

'We have reliable intel that he's holed up in a safe house somewhere in Andersonstown. We have an informer who lives in the area, and they've told us that he's seen McGill around the Falls Road a few times recently. The safe house will probably be close by somewhere. Anyway, I'm letting you know as I thought you'd be pleased. It's only a matter of time before we find out more about the exact location and when we do, we'll most likely arrange to arrest McGill and hopefully one or more of his ASU members.'

'That's good news. Thanks for letting me know.'

He looked out of the car window, feigning interest in the surroundings. His mind was racing. What if McGill was apprehended? What would happen then? Did he want McGill to simply end up in prison? Jack knew that wasn't enough for him. It never would be. He needed to know McGill would be stopped permanently.

As he continued to stare out of the window, he realised he had to act fast. He still had time to get to McGill before the authorities did.

His mind was still racing when the car pulled up in front of a building in the well-protected military part of Aldergrove airport.

They were the last to enter the room and Turner wasted no time in getting the meeting started.

'Jack, this party you tell us you've been invited to. It will undoubtedly expose you to Rory's associates from different parts of the province. I have no doubt that at least a few of the guests will be IRA or those with Republican leanings. We must assume that. Do you know where it will be? Do you have an address?'

'No sir. Inappropriate to ask.'

Everyone nodded.

'And his mates? Those going with you in the car. Do you know their identities?'

Jack shook his head. 'Same response, sir. Inappropriate to ask.'

'We can assume it is to be held at a private house though; in or near Dungannon? And you'll be brought back to Belfast sometime later in the weekend?'

'That's what I presume.'

'What do you think?' Turner turned to face Jane as he spoke.

'It's dangerous. We don't know what O'Malley knows about Jack or even if he really likes him. They've only met a couple of times. If it all goes south, we won't know where he is. Extraction would be impossible.'

'Well, that's the official RUC perspective, Jack. What's your view?'

He felt their eyes bearing down on him.

'Dangerous? Certainly. And Rory? Of course, I can't be certain, although at this point, he seems genuine enough. But if not now, then when? You say yourself, sir, that things are escalating. If there are enough sources that say a major attack is imminent then we can't afford to wait. We have no option but to take this chance, dangerous though it may be. In my view, Rory believes I'm simply a student at Queen's. I'd argue that from his perspective, I'm just an innocent wee Englishman who dated his sister and he's making good on a promise to me to show me the real Northern Ireland.'

He forced a smile before continuing. 'He will feel a need, I believe, to protect me from anyone who questions me. He already has. I understand your concerns, but *I'm* the one who's had the conversations with him, and *I'm* the one who's looked him in the eyes. You haven't.'

He paused, letting his words sink in before carrying on.

'As for the location being unknown and extraction impossible, I know the risks. The first real opportunity was always going to be tough. But surely the more I don't know, as far as Rory is concerned, the safer I am. That's logical, isn't it?' He gazed around the room. 'Think of what information could emerge, sir. It must be worth the risk.'

'You could be right, Jack. We've had reliable intel that a large consignment of weapons and explosives from the US is to be delivered by boat somewhere on the Irish coast in the next few weeks. Based on previous experience, if it gets unloaded the consignment will be broken up within a day or so and distributed successfully by a multitude of IRA supporters in the south, to hidden caches near the border.'

He paused and glanced at some papers in front of him before resuming.

'The timing of that would seem to coincide closely with a visit to Stormont by the Secretary of State on 21st November.'

'So it appears your hunch may be correct, sir.' Jack said. 'It could be Mason.'

'There's no doubt a high-profile attack on Stormont whilst Roy Mason is there would cause chaos back in London,' Jane added.

Turner nodded once again.

'It would prove the IRA can successfully mobilise their forces against us in a planned, pre-emptive way. I can assure you, that if this attack goes ahead, all hell will break loose.'

'So, like I said, time is of the essence.' The frustration in Jack's voice was apparent. 'We can't afford to wait.'

'I agree,' said Jane. 'With this additional information, we simply have to take the risk.'

Turner nodded.

'Agreed. We need to unearth something quickly. Do your best, Jack. But for God's sake be careful. We want you back here in one piece.'

Chapter 36

On Friday, Jack was ready at the front of Alanbrooke. Beside him on the road sat his small holdall and a rolled sleeping bag tied up with an old leather belt.

His pulse was racing. Had he bitten off more than he could chew? He knew at least that he looked the part. Unshaven for three days, his dark hair now over his ears and down to his blue wrangler jacket collar. Faded blue jeans and grey tee shirt. Scruffy student. Perfect.

An old black Ford Escort approached. Rory was grinning and waving to him as he stopped the car a few yards away. Jack noticed another man in the passenger seat and thought he could see someone else in the back. As he approached the car, Rory got out and led him to the back of the vehicle. He opened the boot.

'Stick your gear in here Jack, and we'll get going.'

As Jack dropped his bags into the boot, the man in the front seat got out and came round to the back of the car. He was shorter than both Jack and Rory, with uncombed longish blond hair. He was wearing a black bomber jacket and grey jeans. Jack took an instinctive dislike to him for reasons he couldn't explain.

'You must be Jack,' the man said in a strong Belfast accent. 'Rory tells me you're a student here and that you knew his sister; that you were going out together. I'm Pat.' He made no attempt to offer a handshake.

'That's right,' Jack replied smiling. 'Good to meet you.'

Rory slammed the boot closed.

'You're in the back, Jack.'

The back window was open, cigarette smoke emerging. Jack paused a second or so to let it clear and then leaned in. The smell of stale tobacco was immediate.

'Get in then, man. It's a fair drive, and we should get on the road.' The man's accent was again Northern Irish but had a different burr to it.

Not Belfast, Jack thought to himself but couldn't place it.

He climbed into the back seat and pulled the door closed behind him. The man beside him was older than all three of them. In his mid-thirties, Jack estimated, with curly brown hair to his collar. He wore a brown and orange striped tank top and held a nearly finished cigarette in one hand.

Jack took the initiative and offered his free hand.

'Hi there, Jack.'

The other man took it, with a very firm grip.

'And I'm Donal.' He casually wound his own window down and tossed out the remains of his cigarette. 'Come on, Rory lad, let's get going.'

The car accelerated away.

None of the occupants noticed a cleaning woman, carrying a

bucket and cloths, entering the hall of residence about thirty yards away.

Once the vehicle had disappeared, the woman checked there was no one else about and whispered into her collar microphone.

'Black Ford Escort. Registration UDZ 7717. Just left Alanbrooke. On my way in now.'

Jane walked through the entrance of the hall of residence and towards the door marked 'Cleaning Staff Only'. Once inside and alone, she changed out of her cleaning uniform and into her civilian coat. She then removed the small camera from under some polishing cloths in the bucket and put it into her shoulder bag.

The black Ford Escort soon left the lights of Belfast, heading towards the south of Lough Neagh. Jack had familiarised himself with the probable route and tried to read the road signs as opportunities presented themselves, which wasn't often. His primary job was to assure Rory's friends that he was just a student. He had no doubt that they would be suspicious of him to start with.

'So why transfer to Queen's from an English college?' Pat probed. Jack retold his story.

'So, you're a *right-footer* then?' chirped in Donal.

'Not really any footer,' replied Jack

'But presumably, brought up as a Protestant?'

'Why the question?'

He knew the answer though.

'Just curious. That's all,' replied Donal with a wry smile. A few seconds of silence elapsed before he added, 'You're right Jack my boy. Just 'cos it's a major topic of conversation in these parts doesn't mean that's so back over the water.'

Jack smiled.

'What's the view of the Troubles over in England then?' It was Pat who asked, looking over his shoulder.

Jack turned and looked at the man in the front seat before answering.

'Political or other?' replied Jack.

'Other. Most of us know the political.'

'Most people don't really spend too much time thinking about it or discussing it if I'm honest.' Jack was bending the truth. 'I think that other than the odd bomb, most people think it's an Irish problem.'

He tried to read their faces as he continued.

'Most ordinary English people think that Ireland is Ireland. That it's an Irish issue that needs to be sorted by the Irish.'

He paused, waiting for the reaction he expected. His peripheral vision allowed him to see the three of them exchanging glances, and he thought he could see very slight head nods between them.

It was Rory who spoke next.

'Come on, you two bastards. Stop the interrogation. I told you Jack was alright. He and my sister were the real thing. We had a few drinks in Andersonstown a few days ago and he enjoyed it. Didn't ya Jack?'

'Very different to English pubs.' Jack smiled.

Pat and Donal laughed.

'Yeah, you're right. If you vouch for him Rory my lad, he must be OK. And he's even beginning to speak with a Belfast accent, so he is there.'

Jack's senses were on full alert. He noted that it was the second time Rory had had the term 'lad' used with his name. Did it indicate a lower rank in their organisation?

As the car drove on, he saw a road sign for Armagh.

Rory turned on the car radio, and the journey continued with traditional Irish music filling the air. He recognised the band. The Dubliners. Roisin had been a fan and had introduced him to them back in Ormskirk.

It was getting increasingly dark outside. Jack was aware they were on country roads, the only light coming from the occasional farmhouse or tiny villages,

Suddenly Rory turned off the radio.

'Fuck boys. Army roadblock. Get yourselves ready. Jack, say nothing and only speak if you're spoken to. OK?'

Red lights were swinging in the middle of the road in front of them and Jack could just make out, or so he thought, soldiers with berets and rifles about a hundred yards in front of the car. He also saw a barbed-wire barrier across the road. Rory slowed the car, winding down his passenger window as he did so. The car stopped in front of the barrier and in a split second, a soldier appeared from the darkness, a foot or so away from Rory's open window.

Jack became aware that the car was surrounded by about five soldiers, all armed with automatic rifles.

'Good evening, gentlemen.' The soldier at Rory's window had a clear accent. *Unmistakable. Scouse,* thought Jack. 'Can I see some ID please?' Not a hint of a smile. His rank was that of corporal.

'Sure. No problem.' Rory grinned his best smile. 'C'mon you three, pass me your ID please.' Pat, Donal and Jack duly obliged, and the soldier took the bundle, passing them to a colleague standing beside him.

'Check these out.'

The soldier leant in a little closer and shone a torch at each of the occupants in turn, while another soldier talked into his radio while scanning the identity papers he'd been given. Jack couldn't hear exactly what was being said, but concluded that their details, and that of the car, were being checked against some sort of database.

He was blinded momentarily as the torch was aimed at his face. He blinked. Rory had told him not to speak, so he just turned his head slightly to the side to diminish the piercing brightness.

Still a little blinded, he heard the second soldier say to the man with the torch.

'It's OK Corp. Their papers check out. All from Belfast. All legit.'

Jack felt the tension in the car dissipate.

'So, gentlemen,' the Scouse corporal continued. 'Where are you all going this fine Friday evening may I ask?'

'A party in Dungannon. Friend of mine from years back,' Rory replied. The official spokesman.

'Do you mind if we look in your boot and under your bonnet?' It wasn't a question. Rory's smile didn't change.

'Of course.' He turned the ignition key and the engine died. The headlights continued to illuminate the road and barrier ahead. He got out and walked with the soldier to the back of the car. Jack could hear materials being moved about behind his seat.

Donal spoke quietly.

'Don't worry. Normal stop-and-search procedure. They won't find anything because there's nothing to find.'

Jack nodded. He knew a lot about stop-and-search procedures.

The boot lid was closed with a thump, and the soldier moved to the front of the car. Rory bent forward to activate the catch and the bonnet jumped open a couple of inches. He lifted it up and held it aloft. Jack's view was obscured by the open bonnet, but he saw glimpses of a torch beam examining the engine cavity. After a few seconds, the bonnet was lowered, and Rory engaged the safety catch with a firm downwards pressure with his hand. As he did so, he deliberately winked at the car's three occupants. Jack was sure none of the soldiers noticed.

'OK, then gentlemen. You're free to go. Thanks for your cooperation. Enjoy your party. Looks like you have enough beer to last you a few hours.'

The soldier stepped back gesticulating to two more of the patrol who were standing beside the roadblock itself. They grabbed the barrier and dragged it to the side of the road. He gestured with his hand for Rory to guide the car past his colleagues. Rory raised his own hand up to acknowledge the order and gently accelerated away. As the car pulled away, Jack noticed every soldier's eye burning into the car and its occupants. Not a flicker of a smile from any of them. He wondered to himself what they were thinking.

No one in the car said anything until the darkness of the road had enveloped them again.

'Fucking army bastards.' Donal's tone was menacing. 'They think they own the fucking place.'

'Aye, they do,' Pat chipped in. 'But they're happy we're just partygoers. The check didn't take long just then, did it.'

Jack listened and took it all in. At the next T-junction, Rory turned the car right towards signposted Dungannon and away from Armagh. *Still going the right way*, thought Jack. *Southwest of Lough Neagh* he estimated.

Back at the roadblock, the Scouse soldier spoke into the microphone of his armoured Land Rover.

'Yes, sir. It was them. Number plate confirmed and your man was a passenger in the back. We've ID'd the unknown passengers, and they're known IRA men. The vehicle is still on route for Dungannon.'

'Thank you.' Turner's voice was clear at the other end of the line.

Chapter 37

It was another thirty minutes or so before they arrived at a driveway on the outskirts of the town. Rory had clearly been here before, as he confidently made a right turn into a housing estate.

After that, he made a couple more smaller turns and parked outside a large, detached house at the end of a cul-de-sac. Even with the car windows closed, Jack could hear the loud music blasting out of the house. He smiled to himself at the track playing – 'Belfast' by Boney M.

'We won't need our bags till later, but we'll take the beers in now,' Rory directed.

Jack went to the back of the car with the others, and as the boot opened, Rory reached inside and began handing out some plastic carrier bags. Jack took one and glanced in. It was full of cans of beer.

'One each,' Rory said, as he leaned in and grabbed them in turn before handing one to Pat and Donal. He kept one for himself.

'OK, let's go and join the fucking party. We've got a bit of catching up to do in the beer stakes. The Boys from Belfast are here!' Rory shouted the words as if they were a call to arms and led the way up the front path with the blaring music getting louder with each step.

Jack followed the other three. Through the front windows he could see the house was full of people either dancing or gulping mouthfuls of beer from cans. Some were managing to do both. Jack was pleased it wasn't his house – there was every chance it was going to be trashed this evening.

As they went through the front door, Rory, Pat and Donal were each embraced by a dark-haired man in his mid-twenties and a very attractive, auburn-haired woman.

'Pat, when you're ready, you can bring in the bags and drop them upstairs in the spare room to the left of the bathroom.' The host pointed up the stairs. 'And you, Donal, take the beer into the kitchen. Put it on the kitchen table.' He pointed along the hall corridor towards the back of the house. Pat and Donal happily did as they were told.

More hierarchy? wondered Jack.

'Now then. You must be Rory's friend.' The man offered his hand to Jack. 'I'm Liam. Welcome to my home. Any friend of Rory is a friend of ours. This is my girlfriend, Marguerite – or Maggie, to her friends.' He turned and nodded towards the woman who had been hugging Rory and his friends a few moments before.

'You're Jack, aren't you?' she said, smiling, and before he could answer added, 'You were Roisin's boyfriend, weren't you? I'm so sorry about what happened. A real tragedy.'

She reached forward and hugged him very hard. Jack was not expecting it, and just for a moment, he was disorientated. He pulled back so he could study her: green eyes, short dark-auburn hair and large, sparkling earrings that complemented her beautiful face. He warmed to her immediately.

'Thanks. Did you know Roisin?'

The woman took his hand, saying, 'Time enough for that. Let's get you a drink first. You must be parched after your journey.'

Pat had returned from upstairs, and she led the three of them along the hall towards the crowded and very noisy kitchen. She did not release Jack's hand, and he found it slightly embarrassing to be led by the hand down the hallway. Roisin used to hold his hand like this. He glanced at his host, but he didn't seem to mind and seemed more concerned with talking to Rory and Pat.

As they entered the crowded kitchen and nudged their way past all the partygoers, Donal came towards them smiling. He pushed a can of Tennent's into Jack's free hand. '*Sláinte!*' he shouted, taking a slug from his own can as he did so.

Jack smiled. '*Sláinte* yourself, Donal. Thanks.' He raised his can and took a big gulp. Donal slipped past him and made his way back towards the rooms at the front of the house.

Marguerite finally let go of his hand and poured herself a glass of wine. She turned to Jack and looked up at him. He noticed she was about the same height as Roisin, and despite her dark hair, there were strong similarities between her and Roisin. She spoke in a similar way, the same intonation, and the same accent. She also had the same sparkling look in her eyes.

'It's a bit loud in here,' she shouted. 'Follow me out to the back garden, and I'll explain how I knew Roisin.' She led the way, closing the kitchen door behind them. The noise lessened considerably, and she turned to face him again.

'I knew Roisin, and her whole family really, while growing up in Newcastle. We went to the convent school together for a few years until my dad got a job nearer to Dungannon and we moved here. Rory and Liam were close too. Still are. I was very fond of her, and when I found out what had happened to her, I was devastated. I'm so sorry, Jack.'

'Thanks. It's been hard these last nine months or so but it's getting less painful as the days go by.'

He liked her. He really liked her.

'That's great to hear, Jack. Now let's get back inside and enjoy the party. It's great to meet you in person. Make sure you relax this evening. The last few months must have been hard for you.'

They went back into the kitchen and found Liam and Rory talking in earnest over their beers in the kitchen. She politely excused herself and left Jack near the two men. He was aware that as he approached, their body language changed subtly. As he moved within earshot, the words were about football. He followed his instinct not to hang around them for too long and after a few minutes of idle chat, decided to explore the other rooms of the house. He'd been trained to look and listen for anything.

The music continued and the beer flowed freely. Jack nodded to anyone who looked at him, smiling and holding up his beer can in friendly acknowledgement. A couple of times, he took visits to the toilet, flushing away a large proportion of the beer in his can. At one point he passed an upstairs room where several people were smoking pot. He nodded at a few of them through the door, continuing to sip his beer but decided to return downstairs where more seemed to be happening. He got to the top of the stairs and gazed down to find a couple kissing on the lowest step. They'd obviously picked the quieter spot, away from the crowds and the music in the living room. They were clearly engrossed in each other, and Jack felt bad knowing he'd have to interrupt them to make his way down. He started down the stairs hoping they'd sense his footsteps. He was wrong, this embrace was a passionate one and they were oblivious to everything around them. Jack didn't mind. He was sure that he and Roisin had behaved like that in their first few months.

He paused, wondering if he should simply give them a few more minutes and continue wandering upstairs. As he did so, he thought he heard Rory's voice coming from the hall. He was talking to someone.

Jack gently backed up to the landing and stood out of sight, listening hard. He could just about make out the conversation above the music. It was definitely Rory.

'… essentially he's OK. You know these student types. But Roisin really liked him, and I feel sorry for him in a way. Hasn't got over her death yet. You still OK he's here?'

'Aye. Let him enjoy the craic.' Jack recognised Liam's voice. 'He might be of use to us going forward. I'll give it some thought. Keep the contact with him.'

Jack leant against the stairwell, trying to look as casual as he could in case someone else wanted to use the stairs. Good news. He was not under suspicion.

The conversation continued.

'And what's the latest on Declan?'

'I saw him a few days ago,' replied Rory. 'All's good. Looking out on Milltown Cemetery works for him – easy getaway options.'

'Glen …'

They were interrupted by a woman's voice.

'Hey you two. Where's Jack? You seem to have deserted him.'

'I saw him go upstairs about ten minutes ago. Probably availing himself of some weed. I'm not his keeper, Maggie.'

'Well, if you don't care about the poor wee man, Liam, I'll go and find him myself. Show him we're not all antisocial jerks. Go and mingle both of you please.' She sounded annoyed.

Jack took his cue and quietly walked back to the room he'd seen before where the chilled pot smokers were sitting on the floor. He sat down beside them, smiling and took the half-finished joint he was offered.

When Marguerite entered the room. He looked up at her.

'You OK Jack?' she asked.

He returned her smile, handed the joint back to his new friends, and got to his feet.

'Sure, I am Marguerite. Never been better.'

'I can see that, Jack. Half pissed and half stoned,' she smiled. 'Come back downstairs with me will ya? I'd like to introduce you to some other friends. I think they'll like you.'

Jack followed her downstairs. The kissing pair had moved and so had Rory and Liam.

As the evening moved on, and people began to leave, the numbers in the house thinned considerably. Marguerite asked him to dance, as did some of her friends, but he politely declined. In macho Northern Ireland, men didn't dance, preferring to talk in little groups with each other and leeringly stare at the women dancing. He didn't want to stand out.

It was just before midnight when Rory approached him.

'Sorry to leave you to your own devices so much, but Liam and I had quite a few things to catch up on – fishing mainly.'

He laughed and so did Jack.

'We don't see each other that often what with me based in Belfast and him out here.'

'Ah, no problem, Rory,' Jack replied, with a deliberate slight slur to his words. I've enjoyed myself, and it's good to get away from Belfast for a change. People have been friendly; the beer has flowed. A tiny bit of weed. All good. Thanks for the invite.'

'You're welcome. There's something Liam wants to run past you. He's in the kitchen. Come on through.'

Jack followed him into the kitchen and found Liam leaning against the countertop with a drink in his hand.

'There you are, Jack. I see that you've been enjoying yourself. That's great.' He put an arm on Jack's shoulder. 'I thought you might like to come to the club with me and the boys.'

What club?

'Sounds great. Where is it? Will it still be open at this time of night?' Jack tried hard to maintain his increasingly drunken persona. Inside, his senses were again on high alert.

'You'll see for yourself. Rory and his Belfast mates say you're OK so that'll do for me. Let's go. You don't mind, do you pet?' He was talking to Marguerite who was listening nearby.

'Please yourself,' she retorted. 'I'm not sure you should take Jack, though. It's not his scene.'

'Any chance for more beer and I'll take it,' Jack slurred.

Liam shrugged. 'You worry too much, Maggie. We'll look after him. The night is young. Go to bed and we'll be back in a few hours. Don't worry your little head.'

The condescension obviously annoyed Marguerite. She said nothing but glared at him before walking out of the kitchen, back to the music in the front room.

'She'll get over it.' Liam wasn't bothered by his girlfriend's comments it seemed.

'I'll drive,' volunteered Donal.

As they left the house, Jack glanced into the front room and saw Marguerite standing near the door. Their eyes met, and she silently mouthed, 'Be careful.'

Chapter 38

Jack was squeezed into the back seat between Pat and Rory. Liam sat in the front and acted as navigator. The darkness was total; Jack had no idea which direction they were travelling in.

'Are you OK back there, Jack?' Liam called over his shoulder. 'We're not going far. Five minutes or so.'

'All good here.' To maintain his pissed appearance, Jack gave the men either side of him a nudge. No one responded and the journey continued in silence. Inside Jack's head, the sound of blood pulsing was deafening.

The car slowed to a gentle stop. As far as Jack could make out, they seemed to be in a large, concreted car park. About one hundred yards away, in the corner of the car park, he thought he could make out the outline of a single-storey building. There was the faintest chink of light emanating from what could have been a doorway, but he couldn't be sure.

'C'mon boys.' Liam led the way.

They walked towards the building, and as they did so, Jack became aware of a muffled thumping sound. His body tensed immediately as a man emerged from the shadows and stood in their way. He was carrying a handgun. Jack immediately recognised it as a Luger. Its distinctive shape was a giveaway. Old, obviously. Probably World War Two. A favourite of German officers.

'It's Liam Connelly with some friends,' Liam said in a low voice.

'I can see that Liam. Who's with you?' The tone was assertive and no-nonsense.

'Rory, Pat and Donal from Belfast. And a friend of Rory's from Belfast as well. Jack. Rory and me both vouch for him.'

Jack held his breath, realising that he was on the threshold of something significant. The security man stared in turn at each of them without speaking. His face came close to Jack's. Neither man said anything. A few seconds elapsed before he spoke.

'OK, go you on then, the lot of you.' The man nodded at what seemed to be a door about twenty feet in front of them. He then disappeared into the darkness. As they neared the door, the thumping sound became louder.

Liam approached the door and banged hard on it with the side of his clenched fist. From the sound created, Jack could tell the door was thick metal. They waited. Suddenly a small eye-level slit was pulled back with a snap, and bright white light shone out followed by just a set of peering eyes.

'Who is it?' a voice growled.

'Liam Connelly with some friends. We've just identified ourselves to Mick.'

'OK. Hold on,' continued the voice.

The sound of four separate bolts being withdrawn was heard before the door opened. The sudden brightness made them all blink momentarily. The unmistakable sound of Irish music blared from inside: pipes, whistles, fiddles, bagpipes and the driving beat of the bodhran. Fast, stirring and exciting. They went quickly inside, and the door was quickly closed and bolted again. Jack realised they were in the entrance area of some sort of clubhouse.

'Are you guys carrying?' The owner of the voice was a large gorilla of a man. His accent thick and deep.

'No,' Liam replied simply. 'But go ahead.' As he spoke, he raised his hands above his head and allowed the doorkeeper to search him. This was repeated with all of them. Jack the last.

'OK – you're all good then. On you go there.' *Strong accent but not Belfast*, Jack thought.

Irish tricolour flags pinned to the walls alongside small, assorted murals, most featuring the letters IRA and other nationalist and Republican slogans that Jack immediately recognised. He knew *Tiocfaidh ár lá* meant 'Our time will come'.

The music was much louder now. Jack's senses were on automatic. He was inside the inner sanctum of a Republican IRA stronghold. *Incredible.*

The huge bar area was heaving with people. There were no windows, and the walls and ceiling were covered with more Irish flags. The noise was incredible, a combination of the music and people laughing and shouting.

'Jack, will you get the drinks in? Five pints of Guinness.' It sounded more like an order from Liam. Jack nodded. He was skilled at getting to the front of bar and pub queues. It only took him a few seconds more to identify a slim bargirl wearing a tight-fitting white singlet. Tattoos covered both her arms, and multiple rings in both her nose and ears identified her as a punk. He raised his arm when he judged the moment was right and she looked up and nodded at him. He was next.

She placed the last pint of beer in front of Jack's neighbour at the bar and turned to face him. She smiled. The message was clear.

'Five pints of Guinness please.' Jack tried to speak over the noise. She turned her head slightly away from him so he could see her ear. It was festooned with a variety of piercings. He shouted it the second time.

She froze and lots of heads swivelled round and looked at him. It was like dominoes being knocked down, the movement cascading in every direction and the noise level dropping to a total silence within a few seconds. The music had stopped too. What had been a cacophony of vibrating noise and movement a few seconds before now became a deafening silence and stillness.

Fuck! thought Jack. He realised in that instant that an English accent would be completely out of place here and would set alarm bells ringing around him. They knew he wasn't Northern Irish. As far as they all were concerned, he could be an English soldier in plain clothes. His nerves were taut, adrenaline was pumping through his veins and his mouth was dry. He realised that his options were not good. In that same second, he heard Liam shout from the other side of the room.

'It's all right lads. He's with me.' He was smiling.

A few people began to laugh and that led to others doing the same and within only a few seconds more, people had turned away from Jack and had resumed their conversations. The band started playing again and the whole club returned to the noise and animation of before. It was as if nothing had happened. The bar girl had begun pouring his drinks. Normality resumed. Jack began to breathe again.

He realised immediately that he'd been set up by Liam. Of course, there'd be no other English accent in the club. Any guest allowed in would have to have been 'approved' by a member first. Liam and the others must have been laughing at his expense in those few moments. Jack forced a smile as Rory came towards him to help carry the pints of Guinness.

'Fuck, that was funny.' Rory still had tears of laughter in his eyes.

'Yeah, I suppose so.' Jack resisted the urge to punch him, and instead, followed him back to the rest of the group. Liam was still laughing.

'Couldn't resist it,' he grinned.

'I'll remember that and get my own back one day,' Jack managed to grin in return.

They had a few more drinks, and as the alcohol increasingly took its effect, Jack became less tense as people around him seemed to accept his presence. His cover was intact.

So far, so good.

They stayed a couple more hours before Liam herded them all back to the car and they drove back to the now deserted and darkened house. He was relieved when everyone headed upstairs and climbed into their sleeping bags.

As he lay there marshalling his thoughts, Jack hoped that more useful intel on the arms movements would present itself in the coming days and weeks. Establishing his credibility as a clueless and often pissed student was one thing. Hard data that could be useful to the military and RUC to foil an attack on Stormont and Mason was another. The information on McGill was priceless though. More pieces of the jigsaw had been provided.

Chapter 39

It had been a quieter journey back to Belfast since all of them had hangovers, but he had noticed the other three seemed less cautious in what they said to each other in front of him.

He had put his head against the window feigning sleep to encourage their conversation. It was Donal's voice he'd heard first.

'So, we're all set for a couple of weeks then?'

'Yeah, we've agreed a time and place,' Rory confirmed.

'Great. It's a mixed consignment.' Jack's ears had pricked up at the mention of 'consignment'. There was no mistake. This was about weapons.

Pat stopped him saying more. 'Change the subject, Donal.'

Again, Jack had felt eyes on him. He kept his eyes closed. The talking stopped and the radio was turned on.

It was not until early afternoon that they arrived back in Belfast and dropped Jack off at Alanbrooke. As he opened the door to his room, he found a message from Jane lying on the floor.

> *If you fancy a walk along the riverbank tomorrow, I'll meet you at the usual place at 10:00.*
>
> *Jane*

The pick-up the next morning at 10:00 was executed impeccably. Again, a different car with Jane at the wheel. The journey to Aldergrove was by yet another route, and both checked regularly to ensure they weren't followed.

At Aldergrove, three other men had joined Turner. Two plain-clothed men, introduced as senior RUC Special Branch officers, and a third who was a young Royal Navy Lieutenant called Seb Ayling. Jack assumed that their roles would become clear during the meeting.

Turner started the meeting.

'Thanks everyone for your time today. Jack, everyone here is aware of your role and the Dungannon trip.'

Jack glanced at each person in the room and nodded. *No wasted time,* he thought.

Turner continued, 'Bring us up to speed please.'

Jack composed himself and started.

'I'm sure that all three men I travelled with are members of the IRA.'

'I can confirm that, Jack. The army roadblock you encountered called in their details. Go on.'

Jack recounted the essentials of his experience at the house and what he'd heard from the top of the stairs, the visit to the Republican club and the conversation in the car on the return to Belfast. The only part he omitted was the reference to McGill. That was a separate matter.

When he finished, it was Ayling, the Royal Navy Lieutenant, who responded.

'It makes sense. When the shipments arrive, they'll be distributed, covertly, to their destination near the border, ready for immediate deployment.'

Turner paused again and took a sip of water.

'So, let's summarise what we know. Firstly, that Liam Connelly and Rory O'Malley go back some years. They grew up together in Newcastle. From what Jack has surmised, Connelly has seniority of rank and Rory is a low-level volunteer. Doherty and Byrne are associates of both, and like Rory are based in Belfast. The party on Friday night was obviously an opportunity to meet and advance their plans – whatever they may be. They chose not to carry any weapons in the car on the journey to Dungannon for fear that they'd be arrested. The army roadblock you encountered confirmed that to us, but I'd bet my life on it that there will be guns involved the next time they meet up.'

Turner paused to let the information be digested.

'So, let's consider our options. Option one is that we lift them now and stop whatever it is they are planning. That way we get four men off the streets and degrade one avenue of arms and explosives entering the province for distribution. Option two, let them continue – at least for the foreseeable future – and try to catch them with a consignment of arms in their possession. Jack has eyes and ears on them. He doesn't seem to be regarded as a threat and might therefore be able to get more intel on their operation. Option three is to leave their plans in place long enough to hopefully get better, more strategic information on the bigger issue of the supply of weapons for the planned attack on Stormont in three weeks' time. Do we have any other options?' He gazed around the room.

It was the Naval Lieutenant that broke the silence.

'Those are our options, sir, and there are pros and cons for each, but I favour option three. My sources at the US Coastguard confirm the noise about a big shipment of arms and explosives due to be landed in the next week or so. We still have no idea where though and that's the major concern. We don't have the manpower or the technology to effectively monitor and patrol the whole of the Irish coast. It's about sixteen hundred miles from Derry to Cork and there are literally hundreds of coves, inlets, natural ports and harbours where the arms could be landed. We need to find out more specifics. That much is obvious. The job is made harder as we also don't know the vessel that will be used or its route. The IRA pays US sympathisers well to obscure and falsify details of goods carried across the Atlantic.'

The room was quiet again. Jack knew that his contribution at strategic level was questionable; he was simply too inexperienced. But he agreed with Ayling. If there was a chance of foiling the major arms shipment it should be taken.

'I agree. I suggest I crack on with O'Malley. See if I can find out what they're planning and if it's linked in any way to the larger shipment.'

Heads were nodding.

'OK, then. Decision made,' Turner announced. 'Jack, keep us informed when O'Malley gets in touch. Let's just hope it's soon. Ideally the contact will come from him, but you may have to risk reaching out to him if he goes quiet. That's your call, Jack. In the meantime, we'll keep Connelly in our sights. Anything you get, anything at all, feed it to Jane, and we'll take it from there.' He looked around the room.

'Have we missed anything?' His tone suggested to Jack that he was either frustrated or nervous. The room was silent.

Jack glanced at his watch. It was a few minutes to two in the afternoon and that meant he'd be back at his hall of residence well before three.

The meeting finished; Jane drove him back to the hospital car park.

'He'll be in touch Jack, I'm sure. So be ready. We really need this.'

'Yeah, I know. It's just being patient that's hard, especially with what we know they're planning. Things are getting closer and if

Turner is right about the Stormont target, we're beginning to run out of time.'

She nodded.

'I agree. But the opportunity will present itself.'

'I know.'

His mind was immediately taken back to the moment in The Red Devil when McGill's neck and the pint glass Jack was holding were just a few feet away from each other.

He wouldn't miss the next opportunity.

Chapter 40

Jack heard nothing from Rory for the next few days. The waiting was frustrating. It would have been unbearable if he hadn't been able to fill his time with thoughts of McGill. Time and again he cast his mind back to the conversation he had overheard in Dungannon. He was certain they had been talking about the safehouse in Andersonstown that Jane had mentioned. It made sense, with the reference to Milltown Cemetery. But who was Glen? He replayed all the conversations he'd had with Rory but came no closer to solving the mystery.

On the Tuesday evening, in an effort to take his mind off everything, he went for a few drinks with his mates at the Union bar. He arrived back at Alanbrooke late. It was dark and drizzling in the usual Belfast way and as he approached the entrance a figure stepped out of the shadows. To his surprise it was Rory.

'Hi Jack. Sorry I haven't been in touch for a few days, it's been busy. I need a break, I do. Listen, do you fancy coming over to Dungannon again at the weekend? Just you and me. Liam and Maggie have invited us. They said they'd like to get to know you better and would be happy to extend their hospitality to us.'

Jack could barely conceal his relief. 'That sounds great, Rory.' And it did. *Finally!*

'Maggie has offered to drive you around the area and show you the sights. I said you'd enjoy that, given how you like to see the real Ireland and all. Liam and I will pass on that, we'll go fishing and meet you for a meal and drink in the evening.'

Jack nodded, wondering what Rory and Liam *really* had planned. He was fairly sure it wasn't fishing.

Rory wasn't finished.

'You got time for a quick beer now? You'll surely have a couple in your kitchen fridge. My next job isn't until midnight. I've got a ride from the centre out to Carrickfergus: a businessman back to his hotel after a party.'

Jack sensed this wasn't the whole truth but didn't press the matter. They made their way inside and up to his room.

'I'll get the beers,' he said as he unlocked the door and threw the key onto his desk. He nodded to Rory to go in, while he made his way to the kitchen at the other end of the corridor. He took his two cans of Tennent's out of the fridge and returned to his room, surprised to find the door was locked. He tapped lightly and heard movement the other side. Rory unlocked the door. He was smiling.

'Sorry, must have locked it as habit. Can't be too sure in Belfast.'
Pull the other one.

'No problem.' He handed Rory one of the beers.

'By the way,' Rory added. 'This was on the floor. Couldn't help reading it. It's from a woman called Jane. She wants to see you tomorrow but doesn't say where.' He handed him the note.

Shit!

Jack thought fast.

'Thanks Rory. She's taken a liking to me. I've told her that I'm not interested and explained about Roisin, but she seems to think she can change my mind.' He put the note on the table opposite his bed. Rory sat on the bed, leaving the plastic chair for Jack.

He was watching for a reaction. Any reaction. He was annoyed at his carelessness. If he'd gone into the room first, he'd have seen the note and could have picked it up and pocketed it. Rory would have been none the wiser. Now there was a potential problem.

Rory opened his can and took a long sip of beer.

'Look Jack. I've said before. It's your life. Roisin would want you to be happy, so don't feel as if you have to please me by not seeing other women. You're not a monk.'

Jack said nothing. He didn't know what to say.

Rory continued. 'You know, at the start, when I first met you, I thought you were just another Englishman. No fucking idea of what life over here was really like or what the issues were. I was wrong. You can't help that you're English, but you and my sister were good for each other.' He paused, took another sip of beer and continued. 'But she's dead now, and nothing will bring her back. You have your life to lead. If you want another relationship, you should get on with it. You're a long time dead. Maybe you should cut this wee woman Jane some slack.'

If circumstances had been different, Rory's little outpouring on the philosophy of life might have worked on Jack, but Rory was moving guns about for the IRA. Guns that killed innocent people. Guns that had killed his own sister. Jack saw through his shallow philosophy.

'Thanks, Rory but it's still far too soon. It'll take me a long time to get over her death. I have to deal with that in my own way.'

He was trying to keep his voice constant but felt a surge of sadness as he spoke the words.

'OK, Jack,' replied Rory. 'Message received and understood.

But just so you know, seeing this Jane is OK with me. Seeing any woman is fine.'

Fuck off you callous bastard.

'Thanks, Rory, I'll remember that.' Jack made himself smile and offered up his own can of beer in mock salute before taking a few gulps.

Rory drained his can and stood up.

'Must go mate. Work to do. Thanks for the drink. I'll pick you up on Friday evening as before if that's OK? And no sleeping bags this time – we're proper guests.'

'Sounds great. I'll look forward to it.'

Rory paused as he left the room.

'By the way, I have a job tomorrow late afternoon down near home so I'm planning to pop in have an evening meal with my Ma and Pa. They're bound to ask about you. What do you want me to say?'

Jack thought quickly.

'Can you tell them that I'll arrange to go down and see them in the next few weeks. I can miss a few lectures. It's not a big deal.'

'Will do.'

Jack smiled. In the space of a few minutes things were looking much brighter. Another visit to Dungannon was planned and Rory was going to be out of Belfast. He'd be able to risk another visit to The Red Devil.

They walked downstairs and Jack gave his friend a pat on the back before he walked away. On the way back to his room, he ran over what had just happened.

'Trust your instincts,' one of his instructors had impressed upon the class a few months before.

He closed his eyes and let his mind search his subconscious. Why did Rory close the door when *he'd* left it open? Something didn't add up. Sure, he'd found Jane's note, but that would have taken seconds to read, and it didn't require the door to be closed.

What other reason would there be? He would have known that

Jack would have returned in less than a minute with the beers. He didn't want to be interrupted. That could be the only explanation.

Was he looking for something? Did Rory suspect him, despite what had been said to Liam at the party in Dungannon? Had he found out that Jack was military intelligence and that he knew about Rory's IRA links? Surely a proper search of his room would take longer than the time it had taken to get the beers. What the fuck had happened in that short space of time?

Jack opened his eyes and stood up. He looked around his small bedroom. He looked for anything that might be missing. Nothing was missing. *Be methodical*, he thought. *Take your time and look for anything different.*

He checked his bags under the bed, the books on his bookshelf, his clothes in the drawers and the papers, files and folders on his desk. Nothing.

The only place he hadn't looked was on top of his wardrobe. It was a space of about six inches between the wooden top and the ceiling. It was too small and inaccessible to store anything of real use. *Surely not.*

He gently lifted his plastic chair from under the desk and put it next to the open wardrobe door. He didn't want to risk waking anyone in the adjacent rooms. Carefully he stood on it and reached his hand up to the gap above. Even on the chair he could only reach about a hand's width into the gap. He started a slow sweep of his hand from the right-hand corner of the wardrobe.

All he could feel was the dirt and dust he had known was there. His sweep covered about half of the gap. He stepped down, brushed his hand over his jeans and moved the chair. He stood on it again. He repeated the sweep starting above the centre of the wardrobe and moving towards its left edge and above the door frame.

His fingers met something hard. *What the hell?*

He stretched an inch or so higher, and his fingers explored further. He knew immediately what it was. He had become familiar with handling such objects in recent months.

He carefully withdrew his hand and stepped off the chair before reaching for a sock from his bedside drawer. He slipped it over his hand and stood back on the chair, reaching up simultaneously.

Slowly and carefully, he gripped the gun and pulled it into his view. As he did so, more dust tumbled down onto his head.

He stepped down from the chair and examined the weapon in his hand. It was a Browning HP – and with a full magazine of ammunition. Thirteen rounds; standard military 9mm. Generally regarded as a very efficient killing weapon. A popular handgun, short recoil-operated and easy to source ammunition for.

Jack knew his room in Alanbrooke had been chosen as a safe place to hide a weapon, somewhere it could be recovered with very little effort when it was needed. Was this what Liam had meant when he'd said Jack could be of some use going forwards? At least it removed any lingering doubt that he was anything but a student in Rory's mind.

Then the less rational part of his mind took over. *What a bastard. Wilfully exploiting his dead sister's English boyfriend.*

He replaced the gun, out of sight in the dark and dusty place he had found it. Rory didn't need to know he'd discovered it just yet. He had another thought too. He missed having his own pistol. His Browning. During his training, it had become a good and trusted friend to him. A reliable tool that gave him huge confidence. He'd agreed with Jane and Turner that it was simply too dangerous for him to retain his gun whilst posing as a student. However, he would categorically need a weapon for what he was planning. Now he had one and one he knew very well. Fate was taking over or so it seemed to Jack.

Chapter 41

At their meeting the next morning, Jack filled Jane in on Rory's visit. He chose to omit his discovery of the Browning pistol.

'Something must be happening if Rory is meeting Connelly again so soon,' Jane commented after he had filled her in. 'Do you think Connelly's wife is involved?'

'I don't know. But I think I'm being used as a patsy,' said Jack. 'Having an English student in tow, and one who is a family friend at that, gives them some sort of implied legitimacy. I can be wheeled out as a clueless student who's keen to see the countryside and meet Irish people. It's a good cover story for them.'

'You could be right. We're going to track you this time though. Apparently, the Americans have some new bugs that might be suitable. Tiny, but high quality. Turner has said he'll brief you accordingly in a day or so.'

Jack nodded. New tracking and surveillance technology was always being developed. He admired her thoroughness and professionalism. She was very good at what she did, and he was very glad she always seemed to 'have his back'. He found himself wondering why she had chosen a career in the RUC and particularly Special Branch.

She interrupted his thoughts.

'You'd better get to your lecture, hadn't you? It's *Communications and the Brain* today, isn't it? Professor Watkins? You don't want to be late.'

She even knows my schedule. Why aren't I surprised? He smiled inwardly, as they did their sudden parting of the paths.

Turner had employed the services of a military electronics specialist, and the sergeant in question, a young man in his mid-twenties, obviously knew his stuff.

He carefully picked up a small black rectangular object between his thumb and forefinger and held it in front of his face so that the others in the room could see it.

'This is our latest transmitter. Good for up to two years and sends out an infrared signal every five minutes. It can be secreted easily into the stock or the handle of a rifle, and unless you were the one who put it there, you wouldn't know. It can also be hidden in the handle of most modern handguns, if you know how to do it.'

Jack was impressed.

'So you need prior access to the weapons.'

'Correct.' The army man was concise.

'Once we locate a consignment,' said Turner, 'the trick is to get in, spike a few weapons and get out. Our IRA friends – or the people transporting the weapons – must not know it's been done.'

'That's where my contribution might help,' Ayling added. 'We have informants at docks around the UK and Southern Ireland and a few others based in Europe overseas. If we know where the weapons are, we can plant the transmitters. However, as I've said before, there are thousands of boats and too many places for them to land. We need more of a lead before we can act.'

Jack nodded. He was sure that Rory and Connelly would discuss such matters in the next few days, but he doubted he'd be lucky enough to overhear that conversation.

'What about listening devices? If I'm conveniently out of the way when they're *fishing*, we'll need something like that.'

'We have more of a challenge there,' Turner responded. 'Sergeant Atkins informs me that if we know where they are planning to meet, he could plant reliable devices ahead of time. Do you have any idea where this meet might take place?'

'No,' replied Jack. 'My sense is that I'm not going to be told the specifics and I don't think I should ask. My role is to be a grateful tourist around the Dungannon area. I'll obviously try to find out and get a message to you if I do.'

'Sounds good. Even if you get a rough idea, we can try to stake out a few likely places and set up longer-range listening devices. That's worked in the past.' Turner sounded optimistic.

Jack knew that any intelligence he could provide in advance would increase the team's chances of success.

'So, what suggestions does anyone have for me getting information to you on the Friday evening or Saturday?' Jack was keen to explore ideas.

'Good question. Ideas anyone?' Turner glanced around the room.

It was Jane that spoke first.

'Well, let's run through what we assume will happen and take it from there. Jack and Rory travel up to Dungannon again on Friday evening, the day after tomorrow. They'll probably take a similar route to last time. Rory may, or may not, choose to carry a weapon or have one secreted somewhere in the car, his car. She paused for confirmation and got it with silent nods all around the table.

'They get to the house and have a few drinks and a meal – at the house, most likely. Then maybe off to the Republican club again or another local bar. Or they might simply stay in the house. Marguerite might go too. She might not.'

'Yes. I agree so far,' said Turner.

'So, it will be difficult for Jack to do anything on Friday evening. His best chance might be to get Marguerite talking as early as possible on the Saturday and then pass on the information to one of our people when they go sightseeing. We intend to have a few in the area.'

'We'll be extremely cautious since the town isn't a big one and strangers might arouse suspicion,' Turner reassured him.

'I can provide a bug for your whereabouts,' the army sergeant added. 'Lessens the danger for you, sir, as we'll be able to keep track of you.'

Jack smiled. He wasn't used to being referred to as an officer.

'Have you got anything small enough not to arouse suspicion?'

'I think so, sir. We have these.' The sergeant reached into his tunic breast pocket and withdrew what appeared to be a bank cheque guarantee card. The marking was that of Barclays Bank. 'These are brand new. Early results show them to be effective up to about a mile radius. The tiny one-way transmitter is encased in the plastic so it's invisible and it weighs so little it doesn't add any significant weight to the card. If there's one of our undercover vehicles within distance, the quality of the signal is assured.'

Fuck, that's good, thought Jack.

'Who do you bank with?' Turner asked him.

'NatWest,' replied Jack. 'Do you need my card to adapt it?'

'No, that's OK,' replied the sergeant. 'I'll make you one and make sure it looks appropriately used and scratched. Can I have yours to copy?'

Jack reached into his back pocket and removed first his wallet and then the card from within it. It was the only card he had. Credit cards were a rarity among students who had very little income, but cheque guarantee cards were indispensable when cashing a cheque. He handed the card to the army sergeant.

'Thanks, sir. I'll get your replacement to you in the next twenty-four hours.' He took the card from Jack.

'Sergeant, make that twelve hours. I don't want to risk anything going wrong.' Turner was emphatic.

'Of course, sir. I'll get on it right away.' The sergeant excused himself and left the room.

Turner turned to Jane.

'Jane, perhaps you'd like to continue. How might the rest of the weekend play out?'

'As I said, I think Jack should work on Marguerite – or Maggie as she's known. She was a good friend of Roisin in their school days back in Newcastle, so there's a common link there. At present, Jack thinks that even if she's aware of Connelly's IRA role, she's not an active player herself.'

'I don't know for sure of course,' Jack intervened. 'But I think Connelly keeps most of that stuff away from her. She knew I was being taken to the club that night and went to some trouble to warn me to be careful.'

Jane continued, 'We'll find out soon enough. We must proceed on the basis that she does know they're both IRA and is aware they're planning something. She might or might not know what that is. It's Jack's job to try and unlock that from her.'

'Don't worry. If she knows anything useful, I'll find out.'

Turner turned to the naval man.

'And anything else you get Seb, will be useful. We're looking to join up as many dots as possible and as quickly as possible. We're working on a timescale here. I've had confirmation that the Stormont meeting is still scheduled to go ahead on 27ᵗʰ November. That's less than three weeks from now. Mason and the PM won't change their plans unless they see proof of a credible threat and we don't have that proof at this moment in time. I don't need to tell you how much is at stake here. Intel on arms movements over the border, and how these are distributed by O'Malley and his cronies is essential.'

Before they left, Turner asked if Jane could wait behind for a few minutes. Jack didn't mind. It would give him time to mull over what had been said. He wandered down the corridor, noticing the maps on the walls. He stopped when he came across one of Belfast. His eyes were drawn to Andersonstown and the location of Milltown Cemetery. He replayed the conversation between Liam and Rory once again. *'Looking out on Milltown Cemetery …'*

He spotted the Falls Road, running alongside the cemetery. That made sense. Jane had said the Weasel had been spotted in the Falls Road area. He saw the length of the road and shook his head. No wonder it was taking the RUC so long to find him. *Where could he be hiding?* He let his eyes wander over the area and stopped short as he saw the name of one of the other main roads. His heart began to race.

Of course! How could I have been so stupid?

He peered closer, looking at the smaller streets that led onto the Falls Road near the cemetery. And there it was, in plain sight: Glen Crescent. Overlooking Milltown Cemetery.

Got you!

His thoughts were interrupted as Jane reappeared.

'Sorry about that. Let's go.' She walked off in the direction of the car and Jack followed, still coming to terms with what he had discovered. 'So, it seems it's all kicking off,' Jane said as they walked. 'Don't take any chances Jack. You might be their patsy but remember that you're expendable as far as they are concerned. They won't hesitate to kill you if they suspect anything at all, so be extra vigilant.'

'I will.' He meant it.

'Do you want me to drop you near Alanbrooke?'

Jack's mind was on other things.

'Yes thanks. I'd like to get back sharpish as I've got a few things to do. Some people seem to forget I'm a student, and right now I'm behind in a couple of essays.'

Jane laughed.

The trip back to Belfast and Queen's was a relatively quiet one. Both were locked in their own thoughts. The weather was cold and drizzly, and the windscreen wipers created a slow hypnotic effect.

Jane stopped the car about a ten-minute walk from Alanbrooke.

As he opened the passenger door, she leaned across and said to him, 'By the way, Jack, for what it's worth, I think you've handled things brilliantly since your girlfriend's death. This coming weekend is a critical time. We're so close to cracking this fucking arms cell and you're pivotal to our success. Stay focused and don't let anything distract you.'

Does she know something? Has she sensed something?

'Thanks Jane. I will be totally focused on the Dungannon trip.'

That wasn't a lie. He would be. He just had one thing to do first.

As the car pulled away, Jack pulled up the collar of his denim jacket and turned into the biting wind and rain.

Chapter 42

Jack made sure his door was locked before recovering the Browning from its hiding place above the wardrobe. He checked it over and was pleased to note it was in relatively good condition. The ammunition clip was full and could be inserted and removed easily. The trigger pressure was firm. Rory, or whoever it belonged to, had looked after it. That was good.

He knew he could easily make his way to Milltown Cemetery. It was a massive cemetery and well known in Belfast. He'd made it to The Red Devil on the Falls Road without being challenged and again to bars in Andersonstown, albeit with Rory. He'd walk fast, keep his head down and bluster his way out of any potential problems. The wind and rain would help.

He was confident he'd be able to identify the safe house in the crescent. It had to be one of the first few houses in Glen Crescent if it was to overlook the cemetery. That narrowed things down a lot. There would of course be the possibility of someone, maybe even McGill himself, keeping a lookout through a window but Jack been trained for these eventualities, and it would be dark.

He put all thoughts of Jane's warnings out of his mind. He knew McGill was vulnerable at this time. He also knew this window of opportunity would diminish as the RUC closed its net.

He waited until past 11 pm and slipped quietly out of Alanbrooke. He nodded to a few residents as he passed them on the corridors but said nothing. Late-night drinking was common in university life.

He walked at pace through the rain with his collar turned up and his head down. He had memorised his exact route there and back. There was no hesitancy.

He felt the weight of the pistol in his waistband under his jacket. His senses were on full alert. He felt focused and determined. If McGill was hiding in one of the houses in Glen Crescent, he'd find him. He'd share the reason he was there and then watch the fear in the Weasel's face as he faced his own execution. The added irony that it would be Rory's gun that killed McGill was not lost on him.

He reached the low wall surrounding the cemetery in just under forty-five minutes and followed it for another minute or so until he reached the junction with Glen Crescent. He was breathing heavily. He had seen remarkably few people on the journey. Most sensible people knew to keep off the streets at this time of night. The cold and wet conditions helped too.

He paused for a few seconds to catch his breath. There were no streetlights and no people as far as he could see. Jack realised why McGill would have liked this location. Lots of small, terraced streets around, the open space of the cemetery that would allow a quick getaway between the graves and tall headstones. He would have lots of options.

Most of the houses either side of the road had downstairs lights on and all were curtained. He focused his attention on the first four houses in the street, estimating it was those that had a view of the cemetery. He could see the flickering lights of a TV around the edges of the curtains in a couple of them. The third had upstairs lights on. Again, curtains obscured the view. Only the nearest house, the closest to the Falls Road and the cemetery, appeared to have no lights on.

He crossed the road, keeping in the shadows of the houses on the left-hand side and passed the house. He was right. There was no sign of light escaping through the curtains. Not at the front at least. He carried on walking past six of the terraced houses until he came to a covered alleyway that led, he assumed, to the back of the houses.

Checking once again that no one was around, he made his way along the alleyway to the rear corner of the row of houses. In the darkness he could just make out a six-foot-high brick wall that ran parallel to the houses, marking the rear boundary of the houses' yards. Keeping the wall between him and the six terraced houses, he silently made his way along. He counted five wooden gates and stopped behind the sixth. He put his eyes to a narrow gap in the warped wood to peer through.

As soon as his eye was able to focus on the downstairs kitchen window, he knew he'd hit gold. There were no curtains and inside on a wooden table was a dimly lit Davy lamp. This made sense. He knew McGill would go to any lengths to make the house seem unoccupied; he wouldn't risk using electricity.

He waited and watched. There was no movement of any sort, just the lamp's ghostly glow.

He instinctively reached for the Browning in his waistband and flicked the safety catch off with his right hand. With his left hand he gently put pressure on the gate, and it swung slowly open.

Still no movement from the window.

Staying in the shadows, Jack slowly advanced towards the back door, his gun held out in front, ready to fire. As he approached the back door, he saw it was very slightly ajar.

His brain was working overtime. Was someone inside? Was there more than just McGill? Had he already been seen by someone who was now just waiting for him?

He knew he had no option but to enter the house and find out. He moved closer to the door, placing his back against the door frame and glancing through the open gap. He could see the lamp on the table and strewn around it, what appeared to be takeaway food containers. Jack's nose identified the aroma. Chinese chicken curry.

He lowered the Browning for a few seconds and moved his head from side to side to get as good a view into the kitchen as possible. Nothing. No movement. No sound. Nothing that suggested the presence of a human being.

He decided to go in. Crouching down to minimise the risk if a shot was fired at him, he stepped quietly over the stone entrance step and into the room, immediately raising his gun and arcing from left to right. There was no one there. He listened for sound elsewhere in the house. Nothing. His training had taught him to check a property thoroughly. Room by room, the same procedure in each. Only sparse furniture in each.

When it became apparent that the house was empty, he made his way back downstairs to the kitchen. He looked at the mess on the table. The white lids that had helped to keep the food warm had been removed and lay beside two metal containers. One plastic disposable fork lay there too. None of the food had been touched. A discarded white plastic bag lay under the table with other empty food containers and old newspapers. He extended his hand towards the metal container and put his knuckle against it. It was still lukewarm. It was obvious that something had spooked the person who'd been planning to consume this feast in the dim glow. What had happened to make him leave so suddenly?

Jack felt an anger build inside him. He had no doubt this was McGill's safe house. Everything pointed to it. And he must have been here just an hour or so ago. The Weasel had escaped again. His rage and frustration erupted, and he flung the carton of curry at the wall.

That's twice now you lucky fucker! You can't run from me forever!

He stood, watching the curry sauce run down the kitchen wall and wished with all his heart that it was the Weasel's blood.

Furious and frustrated, he retraced his steps back to Queen's and replaced the pistol in its hiding place. Would another opportunity present itself? He couldn't be sure.

What he was sure of was that McGill was feeling the heat. That at least was a good thing. His empire was eroding. He was much less safe in Belfast than he had been.

Chapter 43

The following day he had lectures and tutorials from nine-thirty to three-thirty. He was tired from his exertions the night before but knew that all had to appear normal. As a young psychology undergraduate he needed to be sociable and attend at least some lectures and tutorials. He'd missed a few in recent weeks with his meetings at Aldergrove and although he could find people who were prepared to help him with missing notes, he didn't want to push his luck too far.

He arrived back at his room just after 4 pm and noticed an envelope on the floor by the door. Jane's modus operandi. In it was a note and a NatWest cheque guarantee card with his name embossed on it:

I hope you have a nice weekend, Jack. Co Armagh is very beautiful. Enjoy your trip. I also found your bank card underneath one of the benches in the launderette downstairs. It must have fallen out of your jacket pocket. You should be more careful. Talk soon, I hope.
Jane

Jack laughed out loud to himself.

He examined the bank card. It was a very fine piece of work. Appropriately scuffed and looking somewhat worn. Perfect. He put it in the breast pocket of his denim jacket.

He assembled his weekend bag ready for the pickup. He also went to the small local supermarket and bought a bottle of wine to take with him. He was ready.

With half an hour to go, he was surprised by a knock on his door. He opened it to find Rory there, holding two bottles of beer.

'One for the road? Thought I should repay your hospitality from the other night.' He walked in and sat down on the bed. 'Have you got a bottle opener?'

Jack was sure he knew what this was about and chose to play along.

'Sure. I'll get it from the kitchen.' He took his time and when he returned, noticed the plastic chair had been pulled out from under the desk. Rory was sitting on it.

'I see you're sorted already,' he commented, looking at Jack's bag. 'Let's neck these down and get going. The sooner we leave, the sooner we get there!'

It was raining heavily as they went out of the main door a few minutes later. Jack hurriedly opened the passenger door and climbed in, dumping his bag by his feet. He put the bottle of wine under his seat.

'All set Jackie boy? Better put your seat belt on. Don't want to be stopped by the RUC, do we?' he grinned.

The journey to Dungannon was uneventful albeit the rain continued to pour. There were no roadblocks this time. The conversation between them was light and easy: football, the weather, Rory's taxi business, Jack's studies. Nothing contentious. Jack left it a while before dropping in a few questions about fishing and where Rory and Liam were planning to go the next day.

Rory was vague.

'Oh, I leave the locations we fish to Liam. He knows the area much better than I do. All I know is that we normally go to places in or around Aughnacloy. He says the trout in that area are bigger than most. There are lots of rivers and streams to fish. Liam is always good at picking the right places.'

'Sounds great,' replied Jack.

He had made it his business to get to know much more about the Northern Irish geography since he first met Roisin and his current intelligence activities had taken that knowledge much further. He knew that Aughnacloy was only a mile or so from the Irish border. It was all coming together. He could feel it.

'Sorry that you're not going to be with us and pulling big fish out of the water tomorrow. You'll have a great time with Maggie, though. Did you know that she was a good mate of Roisin a few years back?'

'Aye, she told me at the party,' Jack replied.

'Our family sort of adopted her some summers,' Rory continued. 'At one time I fancied her but then Liam came on the scene.' He looked a little disappointed as he said it.

Jack didn't reply. He just nodded.

'So where will she take me tomorrow?' he asked, changing the conversation.

'Well, there are a few options. Dungannon Castle, Navan Fort, Armagh itself isn't far. She's very organised and will have it well planned, don't worry.'

They arrived at the house just before seven in the evening. As they drew up, the front door opened, and they could see Liam and Marguerite standing there. Rory opened his door, and they heard Liam's loud shout.

'So, you made it then! Welcome to the both of you. Get yourselves inside out of this rain.'

'Go you in. I'll be right behind you with the bags,' Rory said. Jack ran up the path, shook Liam's hand and was about to do the same with Marguerite when she stepped forward and embraced him.

'So glad to see you again, Jack,' she beamed. 'Come on in, and I'll get yous both a drink.' She tugged his arm and led him along the hallway to the kitchen past yet more fishing gear. They were obviously going to some trouble to deceive him – and possibly her, too. His peripheral vision noticed that Liam had walked down the drive towards Rory and the car. No chance of hearing what they said but he thought he saw Rory nod a response.

A few minutes later, he was sitting at the kitchen table with a can of beer in his hand. The room was pleasantly warm, and the black Aga in the corner was obviously holding their supper as the smell permeated the air. It reminded Jack of the O'Malley kitchen in Newcastle. The heart of the home.

Liam poked his head around the kitchen door.

'Hey love, we're just going to load the car up now before we sit down for supper. The rain has eased a bit. It will save us doing it in the morning and means we can get away promptly at six. That OK?' It was more of a statement than a question.

'Don't take long as we're eating in about five minutes.'

Marguerite wasn't looking at him as she replied. Liam withdrew his head and closed the door behind him.

'Sure, those two are fishing mad,' she said once the door was closed. 'I'm glad I'm going to be spending some time with someone who I can have a sensible conversation with.'

'It's nice of you to offer to show me around, Marguerite,' Jack smiled at her. 'You don't mind?'

'Not at all. And will you not call me Maggie? All my friends do.' She spoke in the same way as Roisin had. The same accent, intonation and phrases. It was somewhat disconcerting.

Surely, she can't be involved in all this.

'We didn't get much chance to talk properly Jack, when you were here for the party. And then of course they took you down to the club later. I wasn't amused – as you probably guessed. You with an English accent and all that. Liam told me he'd played a trick on you as well. He thought it was hilarious. I felt for you.'

'It was funny for him and the others, but yes, I was worried at the time,' Jack replied honestly. 'I did see the funny side afterwards, though.'

They continued to chat while she pottered around the kitchen tending to the cooking. It all seemed so normal.

You're either unaware of Liam's activities, or you're a superb actress, thought Jack.

He heard the front door slam and then steps and voices in the hall. The door opened, and Liam and Rory came in and sat down. Jack noted they all assumed that Maggie would be the one to get them a drink.

When Jack excused himself to go to the toilet, he noticed the fishing tackle in the hallway had gone. Only his bag remained. They had clearly loaded a car but which one?

On his return, Maggie offered each of the men a plate of sliced wheaten bread. The table had been set and looked very welcoming: beef casserole with boiled potatoes and green beans. She was an excellent cook, and the food was delicious. It was the sort of meal Siobhan would have cooked.

The four of them chatted over the food, and as the effects of the drink began to take hold, Jack sensed his opportunity.

'So where are you two going tomorrow to fish then? Is it near here?'

Rory glanced at Liam and waited for him to speak.

'Oh, not far at all, Jack. But it's good to get there early to set up and to get the bait prepared. Trout can't be rushed. You have to be patient. Worth the wait though. Isn't that right, Maggie?'

'Well, when you do bring some home, they are delicious, yes. You missed out the fact that you're not always successful and quite often come back empty-handed.' Jack couldn't quite tell if she was being sarcastic or just honest.

'Oh, that's hardly fair Maggie,' Rory chipped in. 'We're successful more times than we're not. Trout are famously clever. They can lie dormant at the bottom of a lough for hours refusing to take the bait.'

'Sometimes I wonder if it's not easier, and quicker, just to go to the fishmonger in Armagh and buy them there,' Maggie commented.

Jack noticed a guilty glance between the two men.

'Even as a non-fisherman, I get that locating, attracting, hooking and netting a big fish is exciting and gratifying. But isn't knowing where to look the most important skill?'

Liam smiled.

'You see Maggie, Jack's never fished, but he still gets it. It's the chase and capture that's important, and the rivers and streams close to Aughnacloy very rarely disappoint.'

'Do you need a lot of gear then?' Jack continued. 'I get the impression from what I've seen, you do.'

'Yeah, I suppose we do. Rods which are quite complicated these days and come in pieces that slide and lock together, nets and various hooks, bait and flies. Then there's all our gear to stay warm and dry.'

'Plus a few cans of beer and the odd drop of Black Bush or Potcheen to keep us warm,' Rory added.

Jack took his life in his hands. 'Sounds a lot to fit into Rory's car. I'm amazed it all went in!'

'Aye, it did Jack. Plenty of room to spare too. Rory always has good cars with plenty of room. The customers like that.' Liam was on a roll. 'If the wee woman here has done our sandwiches as I've asked, that's the last thing to go in before we leave.'

Marguerite nodded.

'They're done and in the fridge. Don't forget them in the morning as I'm certainly not going to get up at that ungodly hour.'

Liam grunted ungraciously.

Jack's mind was racing. He needed one more piece of information.

'Can I just have your car keys for a minute Rory?' he asked as nonchalantly as he could. 'I brought a bottle of wine with me, but I've left it in the front of the car.'

'You don't need to do that, Jack. We've got plenty to drink here,' said Marguerite.

Jack thought quickly. 'Thanks all the same, but it's the least I can do. I don't mind, honestly. Back where I come from its bad etiquette to arrive empty-handed at someone's house. I should have remembered it earlier.' He held his hand out for the car keys.

Rory pulled them from his pocket.

'I'll just be a minute,' Jack said and jumped up.

'Best put your jacket on,' added Marguerite. 'It's tipping it down out there.' She handed him his denim jacket and he quickly slipped it on.

'Thanks,' he smiled at her.

He opened the front door, and having stepped out onto the doorstep, pulled it almost closed behind him. He then walked towards the gate and Rory's parked car just outside it. His pulse was racing. *No going back now.*

He inserted the key into the driver's side door lock and heard the click. He withdrew the key and opened the door. He didn't know if he was being watched from the house but didn't want to take any chances, so knew he only had seconds. He leaned in over the driver's seat, glancing briefly at the contents of the back seat. It was consistent with what Liam had said a few minutes before. Fishing paraphernalia only.

He reached down for the bottle of wine. As he did so, he pulled the bank card from his breast pocket and pushed it down as far as he could between the edge of the passenger seat and the side of the gear stick housing. Wedged there, he was confident it wouldn't easily be seen, even in daylight. In the same movement, he turned his head to face the dashboard and made a mental note of the mileage showing on the gauge.

It had all taken less than ten seconds. He was pleased.

He hadn't heard anything behind him, but as he stood up and backed away, closing the car door and locking it again, he became aware of a movement behind him. He spun around to find Rory facing him. He was staring straight at Jack with a quizzical look on his face.

'Got it!' Jack held up the bottle of wine triumphantly.

'I just wanted to check that you remembered to lock the car door,' said Rory. 'I wouldn't say it in front of those two, after all they live here, but there are a lot of car thefts around here, and you can never be too sure.'

He reached past Jack and tried the handle. It was locked.

'OK. Let's go back inside, Jack, and get out of this bloody rain!'

Chapter 44

Jack was pleased to have his own room. As was the norm these days, he slept badly. It was increasingly difficult to switch off – his brain was working overtime.

He knew he had to find a way of contacting Jane to tell her the transmitter was now in Rory's car and was determined to do that as early as he could the following morning.

He had sown the seeds already, explaining it was his mother's birthday and she would expect a birthday phone call from him. Liam and Marguerite did not possess a telephone in their house – *for fear of phone tapping?* he'd wondered – so he'd have to find a public call box while out with Maggie.

He'd drifted into a shallow sleep when he was awakened by

noises downstairs. Liam and Rory were getting ready to leave the house.

Fully awake in an instant, he looked at his watch. It was 6:45 am.

He heard the front door shut and footsteps on the path. Seconds later came the sound of car doors and then the car ignition being fired and what he presumed was the car driving away.

He lay there quietly. He needed Marguerite to stir so the day could start, and he could make his call. After what seemed like an eternity, he heard movements in the bathroom a few doors from his room. Finally, footsteps headed down the stairs and into the kitchen.

He quickly dressed and went down himself.

'Oh, hi, Jack. Sorry if I disturbed you, but they made so much noise when they left that they woke me, and I couldn't get back to sleep. Now it looks as if I woke you as well. Cup of tea?'

'Don't worry, Maggie. They woke me as well and yes to a cup of tea, please.' He paused. 'What's on the agenda today then?' He made himself sound as positive as possible.

'I thought I'd take you to Armagh. More to see there. Churches, if you're interested, museums, the observatory and Navan Fort is nearby. We can have lunch together. It'll be much nicer than being the fishing widow I've become these days.'

Jack laughed. She reminded him so much of Roisin.

'And you can tell me more about Roisin in her early years. Would you mind that?'

'I'd be happy to. Roisin and I used to be very close. I think of her often. And the circumstances of her death. I don't get to talk about it much though. Liam and I always end up arguing when we do – he has very strong views.'

She suddenly changed the subject. It was as if she realised that she shouldn't have touched on the subject.

'Finish your tea, help yourself to a shower, and I'll make us some breakfast. We can head off immediately afterwards.'

He had his shower and returned to the kitchen. Twenty more

minutes had passed. Another ten passed while he ate the scrambled egg on toast she had made for him, and they drank another mug of tea. They talked of Roisin, and as much as he wanted to hear all that Maggie had to say, he was conscious of time passing. When she offered him yet another mug of tea, he finally reminded her he needed to call his mother.

'Of course you do. I have an idea. I've got to get a few things from the shops up the road, and there's a phone box right next to them. They'll be open by now. You can call your mum and wish her a happy birthday while I get the shopping. Then both our daily duties will be done. Let me get my shopping bags, and I'm with you.' She rummaged through the cupboard under the sink and emerged with two hessian bags.

It took them about five minutes to drive to the parade of shops. Marguerite parked on the road in front and pointed at the telephone box about fifty yards away.

'You OK for coins?'

'I am thanks, Maggie. I'll be less than ten minutes. See you back here.'

'Don't hurry. I'll wait in the car if I finish first.'

They both got out and headed in different directions.

Jack was pleased that there was no one in the phone box. He went inside, got his pile of coins ready, and dialled the number. It rang four times and a female voice answered. 'Elite Cleaning Services.'

'Hi, Jane. It's Jack. I haven't got long, so listen please. I'm in a phone box near the house in Dungannon.'

'Go ahead.'

'The transmitter is in the car that Rory and Connelly are using for their trip today. I'm pretty sure they won't find it, and in any event, they almost certainly won't smell a rat. They'll just assume I dropped it in the car last night on the way from Belfast.'

'Hope so,' Jane said calmly. 'Leave it to us now. The transmitter is working. Its location is a mile or so from a small town called

Aughnacloy, near the border. It hasn't moved for an hour or so.'

'So, what happens next?' asked Jack.

'They're under surveillance as we speak. I can't tell you anymore, but Turner will make the decision to lift them or to let them leave the site.'

'Good news,' said Jack. 'Marguerite is taking me to Armagh in a few minutes, so I'll be out of contact for the rest of the day.'

'OK,' Jane replied. 'Enjoy your sightseeing.' The phone went dead.

He put the rest of the coins in his pocket and saw that Marguerite was returning to her car with the shopping. *Perfect timing.*

He left the phone box and walked towards her, giving her a thumbs-up. She was smiling. When he got close enough, she asked, 'Was she pleased? Your mum?'

'She was, indeed. Thanks, Maggie. She said she wasn't expecting the call, but I'm sure she was hoping,' Jack smiled back. *Keep it simple. Don't overcomplicate things.*

'We're good souls, you and I,' Maggie replied. 'Our duties are done, so let's head off to Armagh!' she added happily. 'We'll just drop the messages off at home, and we're all set.'

They climbed in and headed back to the house. She insisted he stay in the car while she took the shopping inside. He watched as she put the bags down to get the key from her pocket and unlock the door. Then she picked the bags up again and went inside, leaving the front door open.

Jack fiddled with his seatbelt and looked around him. An old man was walking his collie dog, two children were playing in their front garden about fifty yards away, and he noticed a net curtain twitch a few houses along. *Nosy neighbour*, he thought.

Three minutes passed.

There was no sign of her. All she had to do was put some meat and milk in the fridge, some cans in the cupboard. *It shouldn't take this long.*

He got out of the car and stretched his legs. His senses were on high alert. *Why hasn't she come out yet?* He walked up the path and gently pushed the front door open further.

'Maggie,' he called through the doorway. 'Is everything OK?'

There was no answer.

He called again. 'Maggie. You in there? Is there a problem?'

This time, he heard movement in the kitchen, and a second or so later he heard her say,

'I'm in the kitchen, Jack.'

There was something not quite right with her voice. It sounded different. *Hesitant. Shaky*, he thought.

He stepped through the front door and walked slowly along the hallway towards the kitchen door, which was ajar. He tried to see past the door into the kitchen, but all he could see was the back door which was also open. He knew something was wrong.

He slowly pushed the door open further and stepped inside.

Marguerite was sitting at the kitchen table. Both her hands were on the table in front of her and she was visibly trembling. She looked up at him, her eyes full of terror. Then her eyes darted in the direction of the door to the utility room. Jack followed her gaze.

Rory was standing there, pointing the Browning directly at Jack. His clothes were mud-spattered, and he was breathing heavily.

'Come on in then you British bastard. Take a seat with your girlfriend over there.' He nodded at the chair next to Marguerite.

'Rory, what the fuck has happened?'

'The talking is over,' Rory said coldly. 'How did they know where we were, eh? You thought you were oh so fucking clever, didn't you?'

The words were dripping in loathing.

Jack felt his training kicking in. *Stay calm. Ask questions. Deny everything. Put doubt in his mind.*

'Rory. Stop this for fuck's sake. What are we supposed to have done?'

'Liam is dead, Maggie. It was a setup. An ambush. They were

lying in wait for us. He was shot twice. They got him in the leg, and a few seconds later he took one in the head. Oh fuck, Maggie, they executed him! They shot the others too! I only just got away. Somehow I got to the car and headed back here.' Rory was breathing heavily, but he kept the gun pointing straight at Jack.

Marguerite stared at him open-mouthed as he continued.

'Four shot dead. In seconds. The bullets missed me somehow, though I heard them inches away from my head. It was murder, Maggie. A fucking assassination!' He was shouting.

Jack's eyes glanced between the gun and Rory's face. He was searching for a sign. The gun was pointing straight at him. It crossed his mind to lunge at Rory, but in the split second it would take to rise from his chair and throw himself towards him, Rory could pull the trigger.

'Marguerite and I don't know anything …' he started to say.

'Shut the fuck up, Jack,' Rory interrupted him. 'You must think I'm stupid. All this bullshit nonsense about studying in Belfast, about wanting to see Belfast and Northern Ireland. You bastard! No one else other than Liam, me and the three others this morning knew about the meeting. Only you. And her.'

The Browning momentarily shifted towards Marguerite and then instantly back to Jack.

Marguerite had started sobbing, and Jack instinctively put his hand on top of hers on the table.

'Jack is this true?' she sobbed.

'Of course not, Maggie.' *I need more time*, he thought.

'You fucking British bastard,' Rory snarled. 'You're a fucking liar, and you're gonna die.' His arm brought the revolver up to within about three feet of Jack's face.

'Rory,' said Jack desperately. 'It's obvious you're in trouble, but you've got it all wrong.'

'Shut your fucking mouth!' Rory snarled. 'I know it was you that shopped us.'

'That's insane Rory. I had no idea where you intended going this morning. Maggie and I were just on our way into Armagh. Weren't we, Maggie? You two were fishing. I had no idea where. That's what you told both of us. I saw all the fishing gear in the house last night, remember? You had loads more in your boot. I saw it.' He tried to get some reason back into Rory's head.

It seemed to be working. Rory's eyes seemed to diminish in intensity for a few seconds.

'I don't believe you, Jack. I just don't believe you. You knew enough from what you heard last night.'

Through her tears, Marguerite sobbed, 'Oh Rory. How could you …'

He turned the gun on her again. She leant towards him with an outstretched hand. The room exploded into sound. Her body jerked backwards, falling back across the chair. To his horror, Jack realised Rory had pulled the trigger. He saw the wound in her chest begin to ooze blood and caught a glimpse of her eyes. They were lifeless. She slumped to one side of the chair, her head hanging grotesquely.

Rory stood there, momentarily frozen.

'Oh Jesus Maggie, it was an accident. I didn't mean to …'

The unmistakable sound of a helicopter's rotor blades stopped him saying any more and jerked him into action. He dashed to the kitchen window to see where it was. Jack realised this was his chance to take the initiative.

He launched himself over the kitchen table, his eyes staying focused on the Browning and his hands outstretched to minimise the distance between the two men. Rory turned, swinging the gun back towards Jack. Jack's right hand reached for the barrel of the pistol, and he curled his fingers around it, pulling it to one side, his training kicking in. As he did so, the gun burst into life again and sprayed the kitchen wall opposite with bullets. Plates and ornaments on the wall shattered together with a mirror. The noise was deafening. Jack's grip didn't loosen. He pushed his right arm downwards, and more bullets ripped into the wooden floor, sending splinters in every direction. He felt a sharp pain in his right ankle but was not about to let go of the gun.

Time seemed to slow. He brought his left hand into play. Instinctively it was in a fist, and he used it to punch Rory hard in the side of his head. Rory's head jerked to the side and Jack knew he'd hurt him. The boxing experience kicked in as he continued to punch with his free hand.

Rory seemed to realise that he'd been hit hard, and his eyes turned to Jack. They stared at each other. His eyes conveyed hatred but he still gripped the gun. Jack's job was not over.

'Rory. For fuck's sake, give it up. It's over!' Jack shouted. It seemed to work as Rory paused for a split second, but then he wrenched the gun out of Jack's fingers and brought it sharply across Jack's face, tearing his skin. Through the pain he saw Rory pulling back the Browning to take aim. Instinctively he launched himself again and brought them both tumbling to the floor. He managed to roll on top of Rory and push the hand holding the gun away from them both. Another spray of bullets hit the cupboards housing the sink and there was a sound of metal being punctured.

Then there was silence. The gun wasn't firing any more. Jack took his chance and drove his forehead directly into Rory's face. Rory grunted at the force of the impact and his nose erupted into a bloody volcano. He dropped the pistol and wrestled his arms free from Jack's grasp. He lashed out in a frenzy of blows, but Jack rolled with the punches to lessen the impact. He sensed that Rory was tiring. He raised his right fist in a split second and brought it down with force and accuracy into Rory's solar plexus. All the air from Rory's lungs deserted him and he gasped for breath. The blow was decisive. Rory grasped his chest in a desperate attempt to try and get his breath back. He lay on his back, murmuring and whimpering, unable to move. Jack wasn't interested in what he was trying to say.

He rolled away and got to his knees. The pistol was beside him. His foot was throbbing with pain and his vision was obscured. He started to wipe the blood away from his eyes, trying to take deeper breaths.

At that second, he realised the pair of them were no longer alone.

Through his bloody vision he could just about make out the muzzles of four automatic assault rifles pointing at both of them.

'British Special Forces. Stay very still. Move and you will be shot.'

'Welcome gentlemen,' Jack tried to smile despite the pain. 'I wondered how long you'd take.'

Part 3
Chapter 45

Jack was taken at speed in an unmarked ambulance to a small hospital unit at Aldergrove airport where he had a five-inch shard of wood removed from his ankle, and a variety of cuts and bruises tended to. The doctor also gave him some painkillers before giving him the all-clear.

He'd been told in the ambulance, by an armed soldier sent to accompany him, that Rory was being held separately and was on his way to Belfast Castlereagh Interrogation Centre. Jack had tried to explain in his bruised and bloodied state, that he was sure Marguerite was not involved in anything terrorist related. The soldier simply put his hand on his shoulder.

'The woman is dead. We can sort it all out later mate, when

you've seen the doc and been cleaned up. I've been told to tell you that there'll be a de-briefing in a few hours so all will become clear then. Until then, just relax and wait to get cleaned up. Your injuries will heal quickly.'

He had nodded to an ambulance orderly who was sitting opposite them for confirmation of what he said. The orderly smiled and nodded.

'Looks like you were pistol-whipped. You're lucky; it just missed your eye. You'll have a few bruises that's for sure.'

Jack was not used to hearing English accents but felt reassured that he was in the right hands now.

It was a few minutes before noon when he was ready to leave.

Jane was waiting for him outside the small medical room. She grinned when he emerged.

'So, you're largely OK then?'

'Looks like it. My foot and face are still hurting like hell, but the doc says the painkillers will kick in very soon.'

'Hope so,' she continued. 'We need you alert for the de-brief. It starts in thirty minutes. You hungry? Wanna grab something to eat?'

'No thanks,' he replied. 'I want to get up to speed with developments as soon as I can. I'm also concerned that an innocent woman has been shot dead. I'm sure she had no part in all this. She was in the dark about what Connelly was involved in.'

'You are probably right Jack, but we can't take any chances. What happened in the house? How did she get killed?'

Jack proceeded to fill her in on the events leading up to Marguerite's death. 'It all happened in seconds. She was shot in the chest, accidentally I think, but who knows? I'm pretty sure she died instantly. After that, I just went for him and managed to overcome him. The rest is history.'

'I'm glad it wasn't you that got shot.'

'Me too,' replied Jack. 'So, what happened with the IRA boys?' he added.

'You'll hear the official version from Turner later, but essentially it was a meeting, five of them, near the border – made to look like a fishing trip. Three of them had travelled across the border from the south and met O'Malley and Connelly there. Your transmitter worked a treat in pinpointing the location. We'd never have found them if it weren't for you. A stretch of the riverbank near the town and surrounded by trees. One of our guys managed to get close enough to aim a listening device at them.'

'So, what happened? I thought we were just listening in to get an idea of the bigger plan?'

'Not sure exactly. We'll find out. I just relayed your message to Turner, and he deployed the soldiers. SAS boys I'm told.'

'Something else must have happened. Rory said that all but him were shot dead.'

'From what I can gather, they got spooked by something they heard. Turner made the decision to take them out. It was all over in seconds, but when our guys moved in, it was clear that Rory had escaped to his car somehow and drove away at speed. He obviously knows the back roads well because he made it back to the house in Dungannon and parked behind the house out of sight. The transmitter meant that he could be quickly tracked though. We're unclear why he went back there.'

'I think he thought I'd still be there. He was after me. He'd worked out by then that I was undercover. Wanted his revenge I suspect.'

Jane put her hand gently on his elbow.

'You did well, Jack. Thanks to you, we've eliminated an IRA cell that has been distributing weapons for some time now. With Rory in Castlereagh, who knows what additional intel we'll get. Come on, let's go to the ops room to get the full story.'

He followed her down the corridor. His foot hurt.

Chapter 46

The ops room at Aldergrove was unusually full when they both arrived. As Jack entered, gentle applause rippled around the room. He wondered what was going on before he realised everyone was looking at him.

Turner got up from his chair, walked over to him and shook his hand.

'Well done, Jack. Fine piece of work,' he said loudly and turned to the rest of the room. 'If you weren't already aware, this is Jack McLaughlan. He's the reason we got this group of IRA bastards.'

There were more smiles and handshakes as Turner led him into the room and invited him to sit in a chair next to his. Jane took the remaining spare chair, on the other side of the table. There were eleven people in the room. Turner introduced them all in turn, and Jack realised that a sizeable proportion of Northern Ireland's top security personnel were in attendance.

'Let's start by bringing everyone up to date,' Turner began once the introductions were over. 'Earlier today, a mile or so from Aughnacloy, we engaged a group of five known IRA men. The three from south of the border are all known to have contacts in both the US and Eastern Europe. They have all been associated with the purchase, shipment and distribution of illegal arms into Northern Ireland. Prior to this morning, we were not able to pin anything on them, and all three had disappeared from our radar over the last few days. We now know why. They were making their way, under false identities, to meet with Connelly and O'Malley this morning.'

A few people scribbled on notepads as he spoke, others nodded.

'The area has been cordoned off, and the forensic teams are still there collecting as much evidence as possible. I can tell you though that a substantial consignment of weapons has already been found.'

Turner's voice slowed.

'As you are aware, the operation did not proceed entirely as planned. One of our men was seen and shots were fired. Four of the five suspects were hit. One got away and that man was Rory O'Malley.'

Jack listened as the account of events unfolded.

'The site by the river was made safe and all four men were declared dead within minutes. O'Malley was finally apprehended in the house at Dungannon, our men arriving seconds after Jack had put him out of action.'

The account was emphatic. Four men dead.

'So,' Turner continued, 'although things have not gone entirely to plan, we still have four known IRA men in body bags and a fifth in custody. We've shut down one channel of arms into the province and have taken some existing ones out of circulation. That, ladies and gentlemen, is a fine result.'

Something jarred in Jack's head as Turner spoke. He knew the IRA was a brutal organisation, but he'd always assumed that his own side was less so, that death was the last resort. Surely?

'At this point the press are still in the dark about the incident, and we intend to keep it that way until our men on the ground have completed their search. At that point we will decide what to tell them.' Turner looked around the room. 'Any questions?'

Jane spoke first.

'Do you believe this shipment was the one connected to the Stormont attack?'

'We'll know more once the team on site complete their report. But I have to say, despite this being a significant consignment, my gut feeling is there is more to come.'

Ayling nodded in agreement.

'From what I've heard, I believe the main consignment is still to come. We may have had some success here, but the big one remains out there and at this moment we are no closer to identifying where and when. Time is running out.'

The room was silent.

'I have a question, sir.' Jack looked at Turner.

'Go ahead.'

'What will happen to Rory?'

'Over to you, Roberts.' Turner looked at a tall slim man, dressed in a dark suit, white shirt and tie. 'For those of you who don't know, Inspector Roberts of RUC Special Branch is based at Castlereagh. He has taken responsibility for O'Malley's interrogation which is due to begin very shortly.'

Jack knew of Castlereagh's reputation. Beatings, sleep deprivation and other forms of torture were the norm there. He also knew that the British government turned a blind eye to the methods used to get suspects to confess or give up important information. Their view was that the ends justified the means when fighting terrorists.

Roberts nodded to acknowledge Turner's introduction and referred briefly to his notes before responding. When he spoke,

Jack was aware of a strong Belfast accent.

'Good afternoon gentlemen. Rory O'Malley has been arrested on a variety of charges, including murder, and is currently being held for questioning at the RUC Holding Centre at Castlereagh. If found guilty – and he *will* be found guilty because he *will* confess to his crimes – he stands to serve over thirty years. That will rid us of another piece of vermin on the streets of Belfast.'

Jack stared at Roberts. The last time he'd observed such hatred was at Roisin's funeral. The time that Rory had glared at him beside the grave. He couldn't help but think how Seamus and Siobhan would react to this man's words. Although he had never had much sympathy for Rory, Jack knew at heart he was just an angry young man who had been pulled into dangerous and illegal activities. Now he'd been caught with the big guys. He felt for the family. They were still reeling from the loss of Roisin. Would they cope with losing Rory as well?

As he contemplated this, another thought occurred to him. One that made his gut wrench. If Rory was behind bars, he would lose contact with the one person who was a conduit to McGill. Without Rory, the search for Roisin's murderer would be so much harder. He knew he couldn't afford to let that happen.

'Inspector Roberts, I think I might be able to help.' Jack spoke clearly and deliberately. He paused to gauge the reaction in the room.

Roberts looked at Jack and then at Turner.

'Go ahead. Share your thoughts.'

'O'Malley knows me, and he now knows that I was involved with his arrest. Given what went down earlier, he'll be disorientated and scared. Everyone in this room knows Castlereagh has a tough reputation. Rory will also be very aware of that fact.'

He glanced at Roberts who looked stern faced. It was one thing to know about the reputation of Castlereagh, it was another to vocalise it.

'Go on,' encouraged Turner.

'Well, he clearly knows about IRA gun-running activities north and south of the border. We agreed that some time ago. Maybe not as much as Connelly, but perhaps enough to help us.'

'And your point is?' Roberts' tone was harsh.

'My point is that if the press is still not aware of what has happened, it's also possible the IRA are not fully aware either. They may be thinking something's not right, but they won't yet know the exact details. It may be a slim chance, but I think, if we act fast, we could make this work to our advantage. I could talk to O'Malley and encourage him to shed more light on the larger network. I'd be able to point out the advantages of him doing that.'

'And just what makes you think he'll talk to you?' said Roberts. 'He tried to kill you this morning, and he'll be fully aware of what the IRA does to informers. He won't risk that. With the greatest of respect, you're only recently trained, have no active service to speak of and your specialism is reconnaissance. My team deal with these bastards every day, we know them and our track record to date shows that we get confessions when required. I have no doubt that our proven methods will work with O'Malley.'

Jack noticed a few wry smiles around the room.

'I realise that, Inspector, but it's my link to the family that can make the difference,' Jack explained. 'They're unaware of what he's been doing. I'm sure of that. They detest all violence. They will be devastated when they discover he is actually an active member of the IRA. If I were to be involved in the interrogation process, I could reach out to him and stress what the effects would be on his family. That might encourage him to share more with us.'

'You say *might*, Mr McLaughlan.' Roberts was staring at him. 'The methods we use don't allow for *might*. They always work. These IRA scumbags are cowards at heart. Take the guns and explosives out of their hands and they're not so brave. They're only too keen to talk when they haven't slept for three days or more or have been "encouraged" a little. We get the information we need if given enough time.'

That was Jack's cue.

'That's the point, Inspector. We all know your methods get results, but what happens if it takes longer than you hope to get some useful data from him? You just said, "if we're given enough time". We don't have that time. We're sure that an attack is already planned for the 21st November and we still don't know where and when the weapons for that attack will be landed. Rory almost certainly has that knowledge or at least some of it and we need him to tell us quickly. I think I can get to him and fast.'

He paused, letting his words sink in around the room.

He turned his attention to Turner.

'Knowing the risk to his family, the constant suspicion of being associated with a convicted IRA gunrunner, it might just loosen his tongue and give us stuff we need. Surely that's worth a shot in the circumstances?'

There was a murmur of agreement in the room.

'You don't need to be there for that,' Roberts countered. 'We could make all those points to him – I think I'd rather enjoy that.'

'You could, indeed, Inspector. But you don't *know* his family. I do. You weren't in a serious relationship with his sister. I was. You didn't bury her. I did. You haven't spent time with him recently. I have. I have a personal connection with him. I'm sure that I have a better chance to get into his head and I'd be willing to bet I can do it quicker than you can.' He let the silence hang.

Turner looked at Roberts and nodded. The inspector nodded back.

'You've made your point,' Turner concluded. 'We have everything to gain and very little to lose. Is everyone else here agreed we give Jack a shot with O'Malley?'

Around the table, people nodded their assent.

'OK then Jack. Let's get you to Castlereagh as soon as possible. Roberts, presumably you'll go with him? Someone else will need to be in that meeting.'

Roberts nodded.

'I wouldn't miss it for the world.' He turned to Jack. 'I'll need to brief you properly first. We have a "loosening up" approach that my team and I use. Always works before we start the serious stuff. I'll explain before we get there.'

Jack knew to keep quiet at this point. He'd got himself a face-to-face with Rory and that was the objective.

Chapter 47

The journey to Castlereagh in East Belfast took just under an hour. The pouring rain made driving conditions more challenging. They travelled in the back of a heavily fortified Land Rover and Jack was reminded of the day he'd first seen one for real – when Steve had introduced him to Belfast. It seemed an age ago. A different life.

Their conversation was focused. Who would say what and when; what would happen and when. It was clear that Roberts was skilled at interrogation and must have conducted many in his time. He had stressed the need to follow a game plan and that he, as the experienced interrogator, would lead it. Jack listened intently. Everything made sense – fear, deliberate disorientation, and some unpleasant physical treatment.

'You have to understand, Jack. People who come in here have no real idea of what they'll face. We like it that way. They've heard rumours of course and that is deliberate. Perpetuating the fear helps.'

As the Land Rover swept through the heavily guarded gates and into the compound, Jack shuddered. The place had a sinister feel. Roberts seemed to notice and his demeanour mellowed.

'Been quite a day for you, Jack. And not over yet. How are your wounds?'

'Fine thanks. It could have been a lot worse.'

'I heard that the entire contents of his gun magazine were discharged during your tussle. You were very lucky you weren't hit.'

Marguerite wasn't so lucky, thought Jack.

The vehicle came to a halt outside an ominous looking three-storey building. Grey, dismal and threatening. Jack's sense of apprehension grew.

'Welcome to my world,' Roberts announced as they climbed out of the Land Rover. He nodded towards the second floor. 'He's in there. Remember what I explained before. He'll be sitting in the room, cuffed by both arms and legs to the chair. He can't get at you, so don't worry.'

'I'm not worried,' Jack said calmly and truthfully.

He followed Roberts through the main door, again guarded by armed policemen, most of whom saluted him. They obviously knew the inspector well. Credentials were officially checked, and they both signed in.

'Which room is the suspect in?' asked Roberts of the duty sergeant on the desk.

'Green 162. Second floor,' the sergeant replied.

Roberts led the way. They climbed two flights of stairs and made their way through a set of green double doors. Another armed officer stood beside them.

Room 162 was clearly marked.

'You ready?' Roberts asked Jack.

'Let's do it.'

The inside of the room was just how Roberts had described it. Dark metallic walls, low ceiling and windowless. The temperature was also cold. Jack presumed that the décor and temperature were deliberate. Designed to be intimidating and uncomfortable.

Rory's back was to the door they entered. He was dressed in a grey jumpsuit and was wearing white elasticised plimsolls. He was manacled in the way Roberts had described.

As he became aware of the new entrants to the room, he swivelled the top part of his torso. He registered Roberts, presumably as a man of seniority, and then his eyes widened momentarily as he recognised Jack. He said nothing and turned back round to face the table in front of him.

'So, it's you, you English bastard. I wondered when you'd turn up again.' The hatred in his voice was palpable, but there was something else there as well. Was it fear?

Jack didn't respond. He knew that Roberts had to position his presence there first. *Follow the game plan.*

They walked around the table and sat opposite Rory, facing him. Two chairs had been left there. Jack's eyes never left Rory's. He noticed his face was heavily bruised and there were specks of blood around his nose. He realised it was undoubtedly his own blows that had caused the injuries. A uniformed officer sat at the edge of the desk with a black cassette recorder in front of him. Roberts nodded at him, and he leant forward to switch the machine on. A red recording light appeared.

'I am Inspector Roberts of the RUC Special Branch, and this is Jack McLaughlan, 14th Intelligence Company. Rory O'Malley, you know why you're here.' Rory's eyes dilated at the information, but he said nothing.

'You've been arrested for carrying and distributing illegal weapons and for being an active member of a known terrorist organisation. You are also charged with the murder of Marguerite Gilpin, resisting arrest, and trying to endanger the lives of RUC and other military staff.'

Rory stared defiantly at him.

'I didn't try to resist arrest, and Maggie's death was an accident.'

Jack just stared back. *Let's see how long you keep up the hard IRA man image,* he thought.

'You're a lucky man O'Malley. Jack here thinks you might want to cooperate with us for a lighter sentence.'

'Fuck off. I'm no tout. I'll take what's going.' Another attempt at continued bravado.

Roberts turned to Jack. 'Over to you but I don't think he's ready to listen to you.'

'You're fucking right,' Rory sneered. 'He's the last person I'd listen to.' He turned to Jack. 'I like what I've done to your face by the way. I hope it hurts.'

Jack smiled and let the silence continue for about ten more seconds. He stared at Rory throughout, his face impassive. *Stay with the script.*

'Rory, you need to listen to what I have to say. And listen hard. You don't have to believe it if you don't want to. You don't have to act on it immediately, but you do have to listen.' This time he didn't pause. 'You're done as a terrorist. You're done as a member of the IRA. The police have had your card marked for a long time. They just needed to catch you in the act – and now they have. And they have you on a charge of murder.'

Rory just stared back. Again, Jack sensed the fear behind the stare.

'I don't care what you think of me Rory. I know where I stand, but you? How can you stand tall? You know it was the IRA – your own organisation – that killed Roisin. You can suggest otherwise, but that is the truth, and I know you know it.'

Something in Rory's eyes suggested that Jack had got his attention. He pressed the point home.

'How does it feel to have killed your own sister?'

'Go fuck yourself,' Rory spat out. 'Both Roisin and Maggie were accidents.'

'Tell yourself that if you like,' Jack said quietly, 'but we both know that's a lie. You've been supplying guns for a while now, and it's those same guns that have been responsible for the deaths of so many innocent people. Roisin and Marguerite were just two of them. Ballistics will prove it. Your sister was killed with one of your own guns.' He saw Rory's body tense. 'No one can get you for Roisin's death, but you're going down for Maggie's murder. And you'll have to carry the guilt about Roisin with you to the grave. That will be your punishment. That and explaining to your parents that it was a gun provided by you that killed their daughter. That will be an interesting conversation.'

He was sure he saw panic in Rory's expression.

Roberts twisted the knife in a different direction.

'Mid-twenties now, aren't you? You'll be over sixty when you get out – if you get out. You should think long and hard about that O'Malley.'

Rory appeared to digest the information. When he spoke next, it sounded as if he was reading from a script.

'You might have me, and you can invent stories that see me put away, but the IRA will continue to prosper. People will follow in my footsteps. You'll lose this war one day, and the soldiers and all you other fucking spies, and the whole biased and corrupt police force will be kicked out and made to crawl back to England so that we have a united Ireland.'

Roberts threw his head back and laughed.

'Do you know the number of times that I've heard that little speech? Dozens!'

Then, in an instant, he nodded, and the uniformed officer pressed the pause button. He leaned forward across the table and punched Rory hard in the face. Rory's head recoiled at the blow and his nose and lips began to bleed. He tried to move his arms to protect himself, but the chains became taut and prevented him. It all happened in seconds. The uniformed officer pressed the play button again on the tape recorder. Jack winced inside. He heard the words in his head.

The ends justify the means.

'If you just knew how funny that sounds from where I'm sitting. Look at you,' Roberts continued seamlessly, as if nothing had happened. 'You're going away for a long, long time and all you can do is make stupid political statements.'

Rory tried to spit across the table at Roberts but only blood mixed with saliva dribbled down his chin. He glowered at them both in turn, but his eyes gave the fear away. It was Jack's opportunity to take another tack, letting Roberts' words penetrate.

'Rory, forget the politics. You need to think about your family. What about your parents, and your brothers? What's going to happen to them now?'

He paused for effect. It worked. Rory snapped back.

'Fuck off, Jack. You know full well they're nothing to do with this. It's only me that's involved here. Why bring them into this?'

The fear that Jack had seen in his eyes was amplified.

'Come on, Rory. You know what will happen to them. You know how people think. They'll be seen as a family that has knowingly and actively supported one of their sons being in the IRA.'

He emphasised the words 'knowingly and actively'.

Rory's eyes were portraying confusion as well as fear now.

'They'll be rounded up and arrested themselves, and almost certainly held for quite some time. The Garda in Dublin have already been notified, and Conor is in custody as we speak.'

'You bastards!' Rory shouted and tried to get up from the chair. The chains tightened again and jerked him back down. 'You know they're all innocent, Jack. You were invited into our home! You've betrayed us! All of us!'

Jack's eyes never wavered.

'Interesting concept, betrayal Rory. What will your family think of your gun-running operation and your part in Roisin's death? Who do you really think they will hold accountable?'

'It's you who are the betrayer, O'Malley,' Roberts intervened. 'What happens now is normal procedure at times like this. You know it is. The IRA knows it is. All family and known contacts of anyone we arrest are brought in for questioning. We've got your mates too – Pat and Donal. Do you think they'll stay loyal to you? They're already spilling their guts.'

He turned and nodded to Jack to pick up the baton. It was all unfolding just as he had said it would.

'Rory, get real. It's *your* actions that have led to this. No one else's. Your family will never recover. Nor will you. You'll be in prison for years. Maybe you'll never get out; maybe you'll die in there. Think of your parents. How will your Ma and Da cope with losing a son only months after losing Roisin.'

He leant in closer to emphasise his point. '*You've* done this Rory. You and you only. *You're* the one that has destroyed your family, not me.'

Rory looked as if he was about to face a firing squad. If he had prepared himself for a stint in Castlereagh, it was clear he hadn't thought about the effects on his family. His bravado was fast evaporating, exposing the immature and pitiful aspects of his personality.

Tears began rolling unchecked down his cheeks. His shoulders heaved with the realisation of what was unfolding before him. Jack watched silently. Sitting manacled in front of him was a man who was beginning to realise the impact of his actions. That was the intention.

Roberts glanced at Jack and nodded to the door.

'OK Rory, listen to me.' His tone was menacing. 'We're going to leave you alone awhile to think on things.' Jack heard the click of the pause button again.

'I'll be back to talk soon and will bring another of my colleagues. You'll be keen to know he makes me look like a softie. I'm just a simple old boxer – as you've seen – but this guy, well, he knows how to *really* hurt someone and not leave marks.'

The play button was pressed again.

'Jack, you haven't eaten for a while, have you. Take yourself off to the canteen and get yourself an Ulster fry. I'll give you a shout in a few hours once your friend Rory here has answered a few more questions for us.' He leant in threateningly towards Rory. 'You will answer them, won't you Rory my lad?' Rory was visibly trembling as he finished speaking.

Jack stood up, knowing this was the next stage of the process: time for Rory to be on his own, to reflect under the bright lights, in the cold, with no food or drink and to urinate in his clothes if he needed the toilet. Time with Roberts and his colleague would follow that. He had a good idea what was in store for Rory, and making his way to the door, he almost felt sorry for him – the idealistic lad drawn into a senseless war. He could relate to that.

As he left the room, he heard the pause button click.

He winced again.

Chapter 48

It was several hours before Roberts came to the canteen to find Jack.

'I think you might find your man a little more amenable now,' he said with a wry smile on his face.

Jack had had plenty of time to think how best to get the information he needed from Rory. He raised it with Roberts.

'Is it possible to have some time alone with Rory? Some private time. Just the two of us. With the machine switched off?'

Roberts hesitated before responding. This wasn't part of the plan.

'If you think it will do any good, sure. He'll be aware that there can be lots more *inducement* to talk after your conversation. In fact, it would be great if you could remind him of that while you're in there.' Jack noted the emphasis on the word inducement. 'If you're ready, we'll head back to the interview room.'

That's one way to describe it.

Roberts opened the door and as he did so, Jack noticed that Rory's head was hanging limply on his chest, the trembling was still apparent but this time he could hear quiet sobs as well. Roberts nodded to another man sitting opposite Rory, and to the officer operating the tape machine. They both returned the nod, got up and left the room. Jack looked over at the tape machine. It was switched off. He concluded that not much of the last few hours had been recorded.

Behind Rory's slumped body, Roberts pointed at the chair facing Rory and then offered a silent thumbs-up before leaving the room.

Jack quietly made his way around the sad hunched figure. The table had flecks of blood, saliva and hair all over it and a paper pad and biro in one corner shared the same decoration. Presumably the evidence had been deliberately left there to remind Rory there was more to come. A part of Jack shuddered. Another part reminded him he had a job to do and that it had to be done soon.

He let Rory continue to sob for another twenty seconds or so and then spoke quietly.

'Rory, it doesn't have to be like this. You do have some options.'

Rory slowly raised his head. His face was a bloody and bruised mess, and it was clear that clumps of his hair had been ripped from his head. He looked deflated. The transformation hadn't taken long. Roberts must have seen it many times before.

'Jack, you know my family aren't involved. I don't want them to suffer because of me.'

The brave IRA warrior had gone. Was this a new Rory or just a front?

He chose his words carefully.

'Listen, Rory. I loved Roisin very much. I came to Northern Ireland to be near her. I like your family. I don't want them to be involved either. You can believe me or not on that – I don't care one way or the other. I wasn't a spy as you call it. I got involved when Roisin was killed. I was approached by the security forces when her death linked her to you. I'm planning to go back to England very soon now. My job here is done. You are no longer supplying arms to the IRA and that was my objective. But before I go back, I owe it to Roisin to make things safe for your family. You owe it to them as well.'

Jack realised he was bending the truth but it was necessary. He couldn't tell if what he was saying was sinking in.

'Come on, Rory. Talk to me.'

Rory appeared to be processing it all. Jack noticed his eyes seemed glazed – was he in shock?

After a few seconds, he found his voice.

'What do you have in mind?' The words seemed to be uttered from a broken and frightened man.

'Let me explain. No one other than us knows what happened at Aughnacloy. The press hasn't been informed, and the site at the river is cordoned off. No one can get near it. That means the IRA chiefs can't yet know the details – though I'm sure by now they'll have realised something has gone wrong. The bodies of your associates have been removed, and their identities are still under wraps. If you work with us now, you can be moved out of Northern Ireland. We can keep your parents out of this, your brothers too. I'll vouch for that.'

'But what happens then?' Rory asked. 'If I help you, I'll be a marked man. The IRA doesn't tolerate touts. Touts are killed. That's public knowledge. My family will still be marked.'

'You'll be given a new identity.' He recalled the discussion with Roberts in the Land Rover. 'You'll be listed as dead. All five terrorists shot dead. It's already been agreed in principle. The fifth corpse will be unrecognisable. Shot a couple of times in the face. That will be you. A fresh corpse – same height and weight – will be located and used. No one looks too carefully at corpses anyway.'

'Located to where?'

'No idea at this stage. Could be another part of the UK or could be somewhere else in the world. I'd get a message to your parents to say you're OK but can't be contacted – at least for a few years. It would be a shock to them but better than thinking you were dead.'

Rory was silent again. After a few more seconds, he spoke.

'How do I know you'll keep your word?'

'You don't Rory. Let's face it, you don't. But there are two reasons for you to say yes. Firstly, you're not exactly in a good negotiating position, are you?' Jack nodded at the manacles. 'Look at yourself. Bruised and bloodied and held here at Castlereagh with its record of obtaining confessions from much harder men than you. The longer you're in here, the more chance you'll be regarded as a tout. The RUC will make sure your terrorist mates suspect you've cooperated with the security forces. Your IRA days will be over. No one will ever trust you again. You'll be kneecapped – or worse. There's no way you'll be able to talk your way back into their good books.' He paused and thought he saw a flicker of acknowledgement in Rory's eyes.

'Secondly, you have to trust I'm doing it for Roisin and for your family. Roisin wouldn't have wanted you to go to prison for the rest of your life and I owe it to her memory to do what I can to prevent that. I'll let it be known that the gun went off accidentally and killed Maggie. I was the only other person there, remember. Manslaughter is much better than murder.'

Roberts had stressed to Jack that it all needed to be spelt out. He only hoped Rory was able to take it in.

'This is a once-in-a-lifetime opportunity, Rory, and it finishes in hours. If you fuck up, you know your own fate and that of your family.'

Rory was silent. Was he weighing the options?

After what seemed to be an eternity, he finally looked up.

'I don't know much. I don't know how the weapons are used once I've delivered them, and I don't know where they come from originally. I'm just small fry, Jack.'

Jack tried not to let his irritation show. He knew there was more to come.

'If that's the case, Rory, you have nothing to worry about, do you. You may think of yourself as *small fry*, and that may be true, but the powers that be want the bigger fish and something *you* know may help them.'

He drove home his point.

'By cooperating now, you give yourself a way out. If you don't grasp it quickly, your life is effectively over. They'll put you away and throw away the key. Your family's lives will never be the same again. It's a no-win for anyone.'

The door opened. Inspector Roberts leaned in and made eye contact with Jack.

Jack looked at Rory and thought he saw the slightest nod. He couldn't be sure, and he needed to be.

'Five more minutes,' he said to Roberts, who nodded and withdrew from the doorway, closing the door behind him.

Jack looked back at Rory. *Last part of the dance,* he thought to himself.

'Time is running out, Rory. Make your decision and make it now before your options expire. Think of your family for fuck's sake. Your only loyalty now is to them and to yourself.' He stopped talking. He let the silence hang once more.

After another few seconds, there was a definite change in Rory's body language. He shifted in his chair and took a deep breath.

'So, what do you want to know?'

Jack was ready.

'Two things. Firstly, what do you know about the new arms shipments coming in south of the border? And secondly,' Jack glanced again at the tape machine to check it was off, 'how can I track down Declan McGill? The man behind Roisin's death.'

The look of surprise was apparent on Rory's face.

'I know your mate McGill fired the bullets that killed Roisin. I just need intel on where he is now and how to find him.'

Rory stared at him through bloodshot eyes. Jack continued.

'Tell me what you know on both counts and if I believe you, I'll get Inspector Roberts back in here. You can tell him on the record. Tell me the truth Rory. Anything other than that, anything deliberately missed out that turns out to be crucial, will just make things much worse for you.'

Jack paused, looking directly into the battered face the other side of the table. In the silence that followed, Jack found he was holding his breath. Was this the moment Rory would finally break? Was this the moment he would get closer to avenging Rosin's death?

Rory began to speak.

'OK. I'll tell you what I know, but it isn't much. And you have to give me written assurance that you'll do what you say. In fact, an assurance that *they* will do what they say.'

'I'll do what I can to help you Rory – you and your family – but if you lie at all, that's it. I'll be taken out of the equation. I'm only here because of the connection with Roisin. So, let's start with that shall we? How do I track down McGill?'

After a few more seconds Rory made his choice.

'Declan and his team operated out of two safe houses. One near the Falls and one in Andersonstown.' Jack noted the use of the past tense. 'He kept his weapons separate so that he could take possession of them just before a planned op. Sometimes kids and women took them to pre-arranged drops to be picked up, used and returned after the op.' He paused.

'You said *operated*. Does that mean he's not based at either now? Be very careful about what you're telling me Rory, or this will backfire on you. Understand? Do you want some more Castlereagh hospitality? Inspector Roberts and his boys will happily oblige.'

Rory flinched. His voice trembled.

'He got word from further up the chain that he was getting sloppy with his attacks. Roisin was an example. Too much collateral damage. Too much bad PR in the community.'

There was that expression again. Jack's rage resurfaced as an image of Roisin's dead body at the hospital forced its way into his mind. Here was her brother again using the callous term about his own sister. He felt an overwhelming urge to punch Rory the way Roberts had before, and his fists clenched automatically. A voice inside him, reminded him of his training – the need to stay calm; to make his rational brain work.

'Go on,' was all he could bring himself to say.

'A decision was made to take him out of Belfast – at least for a while – until things calmed down. He told me Brendan O'Doyle, his number two, has been told to hold the fort.'

Jack felt the need to test him.

'The same safe house?'

'Yeah, it was never compromised.'

'You got a location?'

'1 Glen Crescent.'

'You sure?'

'Yeah, I'm fucking sure. I've been there.'

'Good. So, if McGill's been told to get out, where is he now?'

'How the fuck should I know?' Rory snapped back.

'Let's try another tack then.' Jack kept his impatience from view. After all, this was just the start. 'When and where did you last see him?'

'About a week ago. I had to drop off a couple more ArmaLites and some ammunition as his team were running low. Declan told me his rifle had jammed a day or so before and that he couldn't clear it.'

Jack had a sense he was getting closer. He pressed on.

'OK Rory. I'll make it clear to Inspector Roberts that you've helped with McGill but he'll want to know where he is now. He's still dangerous.'

'I don't know! We're only told what we need to know! It's safer that way.'

Jack smiled inwardly. *Well, it didn't help you, did it? And it won't help*

McGill.

'Don't give me that crap Rory. You and he are mates. We've known about your links with him and the IRA for a long time now. You must know where he's gone and one way or another, you'll tell us.' He started to stand up. Rory took his cue, a frightened look on his face.

'It's true! Honestly it is,' Rory implored. 'All he told me the last time I saw him was he'd been told to head south of the border. They knew the authorities were closing in on him.'

Jack stared at Rory, willing him to say more.

'So where is he now?'

'I tell you, I don't know! You have to believe me! I know he's not in Belfast, but I don't know where he is!' The desperation in Rory's voice made Jack think he was telling the truth. He couldn't believe it. He didn't want to believe it. The Weasel was wriggling out of his grasp yet again.

FUCK!

His training kicked in.

'Tell me what you know about the new arms shipments coming in south of the border. Roberts will be back in a few minutes. They need information on that. Reliable information. What you have on McGill isn't enough for a deal. They want info on the bigger stuff. You need to give them something.'

Rory stared back at him, his eyes pleading.

'You've got to promise to help them Jack. To keep my family out of this. They need protection!'

Jack nodded.

'Aye, I'll uphold my end of the bargain if you do the same with yours. I'll get Roberts back in, and he can take it from here. Give him the information he wants, or all deals are off the table. If your intel is good, your family, and you, will be looked after. I guarantee it.'

He stood up to signal the end of the discussion.

As he walked to the door, he heard a barely audible 'Thank you,

Jack' come from the broken body behind him.

Jack couldn't tell if Rory's thanks were genuine or not. He suspected not. He was certain though that Rory now understood he had to turn informer in order to protect his family. The RUC's methods and his own logic about the dangers to Siobhan and Seamus had worked. What would happen from this point on Jack couldn't be sure, but it was clear Rory's active contribution to the violence in Northern Ireland was over. He was a spent force.

'He's all yours,' he said as he passed Roberts in the corridor. 'I think we've got him.'

He walked back towards the canteen, knowing Roberts would be able to extract whatever information Rory had on the arms shipment. Hopefully it would be something of use – unlike the information about Declan McGill. *'Somewhere south of the border,' What use it that?* Jack threw himself into a chair in frustration. He would have to be patient a while longer before he could pick up the trail again, but he knew it would happen. Intelligence on the IRA was increasing all the time and he'd get access to all those files: The movers and shakers, the suspected new turks, the old guard, the middlemen and the headcases. The last eight years, since the Troubles had started, had seen a lot of useful intelligence gained through the work of informers, good police work and captured terrorists. One could question the methods of places like Castlereagh, but the emerging data contributed to an increasingly clear picture of how the IRA, and its splinter factions, worked. Jack was confident that sooner rather than later he would cross paths with McGill. He'd promised that to Roisin.

Chapter 49

In the next few hours, a vast amount of information came pouring forth from Rory. The sluice gates had opened.

Inspector Roberts led the process of collection, and everything Rory uttered was recorded.

Roberts and Turner convened a security briefing back at Aldergrove to discuss the information and next steps. Jack was invited.

Turner began the meeting by summarising developments and the intelligence that Rory had provided.

'O'Malley has been successfully *turned*. Well done everyone. The bodies of the four IRA men have been removed from the scene and all have been successfully identified. Forensics have now finished, and the site has been cleared of evidence.'

That was quick work, thought Jack.

'I have just held a press conference where I stated an operation to seize illegal weapons has been successful. In the operation, five IRA operatives were shot dead, and as a result, we believe this cell has been eliminated. To explain Gilpin's murder, we've put out a story, not too far from the truth, that Gilpin was a known IRA suspect. She resisted arrest, and she too was shot dead.'

'As I've said, sir, I'm pretty sure that the woman wasn't involved herself.' Jack felt duty-bound to speak up for Marguerite.

'Noted but that remains uncertain. This way it adds substance to the story that she was involved too. After all, she was Connelly's partner. Part of the *fog of war.*'

Jack didn't like the answer but facing Turner down in front of everyone in the room was in no one's interests. He also knew that a credible picture had to be painted, and quickly, to allow them to act on the intelligence Rory was providing. He decided to hold any objections until a later time. After all she was dead now.

'Now we come to the information that O'Malley has provided. His decision to cooperate has provided us – and continues to provide us – with important intel. He has been responsible for the collection and distribution of weapons, ammunition and explosives to and from a variety of arms dumps in Northern Ireland. He, personally, never crossed the border as the organisation believed that would simply raise his profile. He has confirmed the existence of a network of active IRA terrorists in the south. This network ensures that weapons smuggled into Ireland from other countries are collected and then conveyed by a variety of specially adapted vehicles over the border into IRA hands. If they are not used immediately, they are stored at secret arms dumps for retrieval later. O'Malley has given us the names of contacts in the south that were known to Connelly and where they are based. That's as far as we've got at the moment.'

Jack could feel the excitement growing in the room.

'One key name he's provided, and not known to us before, is a man called Sean Buckley,' Turner continued. 'We're doing some research on him as we speak, but from what we've found out already, it appears he was living and working in the US until a year or so ago, at which point he returned to Ireland. He bought a small boatyard in County Cork in a little place called Kilmacsimon Quay, about eight miles upriver from the fishing port of Kinsale. His boatyard offers winter lay-ups for smallish vessels as well as boat repairs. In the warmer months, he rents his own boats for fishing and tourist trips. According to O'Malley, one of the men shot at Aughnacloy was a close associate of Buckley.'

Things were falling into place in Jack's mind.

'O'Malley says the boatyard's covert function is to offload and hide weapons that have been smuggled into Kinsale. They're brought in smaller vessels, under cover of darkness, upriver to Buckley's boatyard. Apparently the Aughnacloy meeting was to discuss the arrangements for moving a large shipment of arms and explosives arriving at Kinsale in the next twenty-four hours. Connelly had told O'Malley the weapons were due into Kilmacsimon Quay in the next two days and would leave there one day later bound northwards.' Turner paused and looked around the room. 'Gentlemen, I believe this is the shipment we've been looking for. Mason's Stormont meeting is only a few days away. It all makes sense.'

Jack sat back in his chair with a sigh. It seemed that Rory had come through.

Turner continued. 'Of course, once out of the boatyard, we run the risk of losing the shipment. There is a myriad of routes they could take and any number of locations to hide weapons on the way up. O'Malley hasn't been able to help us on that. We know where they are now, and we need to act fast.'

He stood up and walked over to a map which had been pinned to the wall. He pointed to the southwest coast.

'Kilmacsimon Quay is only a few miles from the N71 at a town called Innishannon. It's well off the beaten track with limited road access to and from the boatyard. If we act quickly, we might be able to nail Buckley with the weapons and hopefully close down his operation for good. That should degrade their plans in the north.'

Seb Ayling was the first to comment.

'It certainly makes sense. But can we be sure that Buckley will suspect nothing given the murder of five of his associates?'

'Good point,' nodded Turner, 'but O'Malley has told us the shipment is already on its way. They'll need to land it somewhere. Given that, and the recent press conference, I believe it's a chance we can take.'

Jack's mind was racing. Turner continued.

'We need someone in or near Kilmacsimon Quay to advise us of Buckley's movements and report back. We want – and need – to catch this bastard. If we get this right, we will be closing down a major weapons route. It'll be a huge blow to the IRA. They'll have no choice but to suspend any planned attacks for some time to come.'

Again, a murmur of assent flooded the room. It was Jack that spoke next.

'I have an idea, sir.' Everyone turned to listen. 'You said Buckley offers boat trips as part of his cover. What if I go to Kilmacsimon Quay and enquire about renting a boat to go up and down the river? Lots of English people holiday in the south of Ireland. I can have a radio with me and can advise you accordingly.'

'After what you've been through in the last twenty-four hours Jack, I would have thought that you fancied a break,' Turner smiled.

'No, hear me out, sir. You need eyes and ears on the ground. That's what I'm trained to do. From the way you've described the location, access in and out of the village is difficult. One minor road in and out alongside the river. Moving of soldiers in the area would arouse suspicion, and we can be sure Buckley will be observing all movements. He'll most likely have the weapons well hidden, probably somewhere on the site. Our best chance to act will be the moment they are loaded onto the transport vehicle and we don't know what that is. It could be a lorry, coach, van or anything like that. We don't even know the size of the shipment or exactly *when* it's happening.'

It was Jane who spoke next.

'I think playing the English tourist card might work very well. Jack's right about tourism in the area, sir. The English do like the south of Ireland. It's just up here they're frightened of.'

There were a few smiles around the room.

'If Jack wasn't on his own but went with a girlfriend, it would look more natural. A young couple enjoying a romantic holiday in the south and enquiring about a boat trip. Very natural.'

'And who might Jack's girlfriend be?' Turner asked. 'Are you volunteering Jane?

She was laughing when she replied.

'Awful job, sir, but someone would have to do it.'

The room erupted into laughter. Jack laughed too.

Turner's eyes rested on him.

'What are your thoughts?'

Jack nodded his approval. McGill was on the back burner and could stay there until this op was over.

'OK everyone, any other suggestions?'

There was silence.

'Right then,' he continued. 'Looks like we have a plan. I'll need to liaise with the Irish military and Garda. It's on their patch and it will be their operation. They'll insist on that. You'll be under their jurisdiction when you're down there. Is that understood? Any intel you get will go to them. Time is of the essence, so we'll fly you both down to the Irish army base just outside Cork and I'll arrange for a vehicle to be ready for you. They'll brief you from there. All we need is good intel right up to the second the Irish Special Forces go in. You know the drill.'

He continued in command mode.

'Seb, will you liaise accordingly with your opposite numbers in the Irish Naval Service at Haulbowline? I'll do the same with my senior army contacts at Collins Barracks. They'll need soldiers close to Kilmacsimon Quay, and they'll also need helicopter support. I'll leave that to them.'

Jack felt a surge of excitement and a flood of adrenaline coursed through his veins, drowning out the aches and pains on his body.

Chapter 50

The helicopter flight was scheduled to take just under two and a half hours. Jack was in his element. It took him back to his time at RAF Woodvale. As they had climbed into the hold, the pilot had handed him a small package.

'I've been instructed to give you this. Turner said you'd be pleased to be reunited.' Jack had guessed what was inside and now, as he sat there, he could feel the familiar shape of his Browning lying comfortably in its shoulder holster. It was a good feeling.

'Special operation then?' the pilot asked him when they'd reached their cruising height and speed of one hundred and twenty-two mph.

'Something like that,' Jack replied. They both knew that they couldn't discuss the details, and that was fine with both of them.

'Cork, from Belfast, puts us towards the far end of our range.' He smiled. 'But this old bird can be relied on to get us there.'

The flight was noisy and uncomfortable, but Jack loved it. No airsickness, just the thrill of flying at speed through the night air over mainland Ireland. Jane, on the other hand, looked nervous and tense.

'You OK?' he asked at one point early in the journey.

'Fine mostly but the turbulence makes my stomach heave. Don't take it personally if I throw up all over you.'

Jack empathised with her.

'Don't worry about it,' he said with a wry smile. 'It happens to the best of people.'

The helicopter landed on schedule at Collins Barracks just north of Cork. After thanking both pilots, he and Jane scrambled out onto a large parade square where the commanding officer introduced himself to them and shook their hands.

'Welcome to Collins Barracks both of you. I'm Brigadier General Byrne, and this is Captain Reynolds, my ops liaison officer,' he shouted under the whirling helicopter rotor blades. 'Come with me. I'll explain everything inside.'

They followed him through a large door in the centre of the austere grey stone building lining the parade ground. The room they walked into was ornate and spotlessly clean. The walls were filled with large portraits of decorated, senior military figures. The main piece of furniture in the room was a large rectangular polished mahogany dining table. Jack couldn't fail to compare it to the starker décor of the operations room he was used to at Aldergrove.

Byrne pointed to four chairs at the corner of the table and nodded for them to be seated at one end. He and Captain Reynolds took the remaining chairs.

'I spoke with Lieutenant Colonel Turner while you were both on your way down here and he's explained the nature of the operation to me. He's impressed on me that speed is of the essence, and you are to be given every assistance. He said you'd need some suitable transport for your cover.'

He sorted through some papers in front of him and produced a sales pamphlet with a picture of an old-looking VW camper van on the front. He pushed it along the table in front of them.

'One of my staff hired it from somewhere in Cork a couple of hours ago. Very popular with tourists it seems. Here are the keys. It has a full tank of petrol, and we've checked it over mechanically. It's in good running order.' He handed Jack a key ring with a green leather fob with the initials VW on it and two keys.

'Inside you'll find all that you need for your cover as tourists: sleeping bags, cooking and eating utensils, some food, a couple of grabs with clothes inside for each of you and a wallet with money – Irish notes. Hidden under the front passenger seat is a small military radio which has already been set to the correct frequency. I've been assured that you both know how to operate such devices.'

Jack looked at the photograph and then to Jane. He wanted to burst out laughing but thought better of it. She smiled back.

'Well, we should certainly pass as tourists.'

'Here's a map of the area, and directions for how to get to Kilmacsimon Quay.' Captain Reynolds handed both to Jack, who smiled and nodded. 'We have one of our helicopters and a small squad of our special operation troops ready to be called into action on your signal. It can be mobilised to wherever you need it within ten to fifteen minutes. Is there anything else you need?'

'I don't think so, sir,' Jack replied, looking at his watch. 'Given the time, we hoped we could stay overnight and set off first thing in the morning.'

'No problem at all,' said Byrne. 'We'd assumed that was an option. Captain Reynolds will take care of that.'

'I have already provisionally allocated two rooms for them in the officers' quarters,' the captain replied.

'Excellent. Thank you,' replied Byrne.

'What time will you leave the barracks, sir?' Reynolds asked Jack.

'Well, it will look a little suspicious if we get there too early, so I suggest 08:00 hours. What do you think, Jane?'

'Sounds about right.'

'OK, then. I suggest breakfast in the officers' mess at 07:00. It's the building adjacent to where you'll be sleeping,' Reynolds offered. 'Be aware we already have the road junction between Innishannon and Kilmacsimon under surveillance – in case they decide to move earlier. Any vehicle joining the main road from Kilmacsimon Quay has to pass there, so we can complete a stop-and-search operation – although that is definitely the poorer option since we can't guarantee Buckley will be with the vehicle.'

'That's great, sir. Many thanks,' said Jack. 'You seem to have things well under control.'

'We try our best,' smiled Byrne. 'An example of excellent Anglo-Irish Army cooperation. Good night both of you and the very best of luck. Welcome to our operation. Rest assured; we'll do our part when the time arrives.'

He stood up and offered his hand to both of them in turn.

'Captain Reynolds will take it from here. He'll show you to your quarters and show you where the van is parked.'

He saluted, then shook each of their hands and left the room.

'Come this way both of you please. I'll show you to your rooms. I didn't know whether you'd eaten and so you'll find some flasks of hot drinks in your room with some sandwiches.'

Chapter 51

Jack awoke at 06:00 the next morning. He'd set the bedside alarm clock provided in his room, and the shrill beeping sound had an immediate effect.

He had dreamed of Roisin, and in those dreams, he had felt her skin next to his, seen her eyes sparkle and look lovingly at him. He hadn't had such a vivid dream for a while now, and it buoyed him.

He showered and dressed and when ready, left the room and knocked on Jane's door.

'I'll be downstairs when you're ready. I want to check the van. You have a preference for who drives?'

'I think you should. Means I can handle the radio and map more easily,' she replied.

'Makes sense. See you whenever you're ready.'

It was about ten minutes later that she joined him outside the building.

'It's strange to see this van in a military environment. They don't seem to go together, do they?'

'Right,' Jack agreed. 'Better than a tank though.'

They both laughed.

They spent the next five minutes assuring themselves that they had everything they needed and then headed into the mess to have breakfast.

'All OK?' said a voice from behind them as they headed back out to the van. They spun around to find an impeccably uniformed Reynolds standing behind them.

'Yes,' replied Jane. 'I believe you've thought of everything. Thanks for all your help, Captain, and please convey my thanks to your C.O. Hopefully, if all goes to plan, we'll be back very soon.'

They shook hands.

'Good luck both of you and if I may, I'd like to share an Irish proverb with you. I feel as if it's appropriate in your circumstances.'

Jack nodded.

'It is better to be a coward for a minute than dead for the rest of your life.' Reynolds spoke slowly and deliberately. 'These are dangerous people. They won't hesitate to kill you in the blink of an eye if they suspect you. Be very careful. Just do your job, get us the info we need, we'll do the rest.'

'Sound advice, Captain. Thank you.' A few seconds elapsed.

'OK, Jane, ready?' Jack moved into decisive mode.

'Let's go,' Jane replied equally decisively.

They climbed into their seats and the camper van burst into life and drew away.

With Jane navigating, the journey to Innishannon took about three-quarters of an hour. Jack found the camper van easy to drive, and they used the time to agree their cover story.

They were five days into a two-week holiday, having sailed on the ferry into Dun Laoghaire. After two nights in Dublin, they had hired the van to drive to County Cork around the coast of Southern Ireland stopping at Wicklow, Wexford and Waterford.

'That's easy to remember,' said Jane. 'Three Ws. Presumably, we've slept in the van since leaving Dublin?'

'Of course. We're an impoverished couple hopelessly in love and living frugally, so we've been using off-the-track places to park overnight.'

'And what's our itinerary for the rest of the trip?'

'No absolute plans, I suggest. Other than stopping where we like in Kerry and Limerick, all the touristy places, and then heading back east across mid-Ireland back to Dun Laoghaire to get the ferry back to Wales. As few specifics as possible. Sound sensible?'

'Yep. Going where the mood takes us, no need to book anywhere in advance and self-sufficient. I'm OK with it all apart from the *hopelessly in love* bit,' she laughed.

'You never know,' he laughed.

'In your dreams, handsome.'

Their laughter took the edge off the danger they knew they were heading into.

Innishannon was quite busy for a small town at that time of the morning, and the traffic along the N71 was slow. Jack glanced at his watch. It was just before nine o'clock. He caught glimpses of the River Bandon behind the various shops and bars on the left-hand side. He'd studied the map in detail the night before and knew that soon after the buildings finished the main road curved to the left and crossed the river via a bridge. The smaller road to Kilmacsimon Quay was immediately after the bridge.

'OK,' he said, 'this is our turn-off coming up. This is where Byrne said he'd place his men.'

As the van drove over the bridge, Jack scanned the scene in front of him. The road to Kilmacsimon was immediately enveloped in deep woodland. He'd seen that on the map too, but the denseness of the trees surprised him. As did the narrowness of the road and the proximity of the river. *No turning back now*, he thought.

He steered the van off the main road and onto the smaller one.

Jane's voice broke his concentration.

'Probably about ten minutes along this road.'

'Yep, we're in no rush,' Jack replied. 'We're tourists after all.'

He slowed the speed of the van to about twenty miles per hour and tried to relax his shoulders. He was aware his hands were gripping the wheel tightly, and his jaw was set tight.

'Beautiful scenery,' announced Jane after a minute or so – more to herself, it seemed to him.

It was beautiful. The morning sunshine broke through the trees intermittently, highlighting the many shades of green leaves and the tumbling white water. The air smelt fresh and sweet. It had taken Jane's observation to remind Jack that the Irish countryside, south and north, was invariably natural and unspoiled and very different in so many ways to England.

They drove on past a few isolated houses set back from the road, and he wondered what kind of people lived in them and what jobs they did. Did they travel into Cork city every day, or were they local to the smaller towns in the area, Innishannon or Bandon? He had no idea.

His thoughts were interrupted again by Jane's voice beside him.

'Think we go left here.'

They had come to a fork in the road. The river swept away to the left, and it was logical that they followed it. Jack realised he'd been in a world of his own for the last few minutes.

'Yeah, sorry, Jane. I was somewhere else in my head.'

'Well boyfriend, you'd better concentrate on the job in hand, or we'll be in trouble.' Jack couldn't immediately tell if she was being sarcastic or was mildly angry. His confusion ended when she added, 'You're supposed to only have eyes for me remember? Hopelessly in love and all that.' Her smile reappeared, and she blew him an imaginary kiss. 'Now, let's go and try to book our riverboat with Mr Sean Buckley.' She sounded determined and positive.

Jack pulled the steering wheel to the left and they drove on for a few more minutes before seeing a sign for the hamlet of Kilmacsimon Quay. He slowed the camper van down as the narrow road swung to the right, and the first set of cottages appeared. They were tiny two-up, two-down dwellings that were built together in a row. It seemed to him that not much had changed for a hundred years or so.

The bar, as they approached it, consisted of what seemed to be the back door of a house and the only thing that suggested alcohol was sold there was a faded metal Guinness sign. There were no people about.

'Let's park here,' Jack suggested, indicating a space next to the cottages where the road was a little wider.

They got out of the van, and he locked both doors; the radio and the Brownings were uppermost in his mind as he did so.

They could see the gates of the boatyard where it seemed that the road ended. Wire mesh metallic gates with a large sign on the right-hand gate which read 'Kilmacsimon Boatyard' in large black letters. Underneath in slightly smaller letters were the words 'Private Property'. Under those it said 'Proprietor – S. Buckley. Opening hours – 10 am to 4 pm'. A telephone number followed it.

The gates were locked together with a heavy-duty chain and a large padlock. Through the wire mesh, Jack could see dozens of boats in varying positions. Some were left on metal towing gear as if waiting to be collected or having just been dropped off. Some were suspended in the air by large canvas straps that were attached to side metal supports, and many others simply seemed to be balanced upright on their keels and propped up either side by wooden supports.

'Look beyond the boats,' Jane nodded past the gates towards the back of the boatyard, cut into the surrounding hill.

Jack focused his eyes and saw what she'd noticed already. A one-storey Portakabin with two windows, one each side of a single door. He assumed it was probably the boatyard office. The windows allowed any occupant to have a good view of the entire boatyard and the entrance gates.

'Look to the right of it,' Jane whispered.

Jack turned his head, but all he could see were boats.

'Where exactly?' he enquired.

'On the perimeter. Just behind that large white boat on the hoist. Next to the green container.'

Jack squinted and managed to see another building. Smaller than the Portakabin and grey in colour.

'I see it. What do you think?'

'Storage of some description. Tools maybe.'

They looked knowingly at each other. As he was about to speak, Jane put her finger to her lips.

A female voice from behind suddenly spoke.

'Well, morning to the both of you. What can I be doing for you now?' The southern Irish lilt was friendly and welcoming.

Jack spun around. The woman facing him was in her mid-fifties and was wearing a dark green duffle coat with a light green scarf neatly wrapped around her neck.

His instinct took over.

'Oh, hi there,' he said, returning her smile. 'My girlfriend and I are on holiday. We're looking to rent a boat for a river trip in the next day or so. Looks like we should come back in an hour or so? Would that be right? To speak to whoever rents the boats?'

The woman looked at them both in turn for a second or so. Her smile never wavered.

'Well, isn't that lovely. Two young English people on holiday. And wanting to enjoy our river. Is that your camper van behind us?' She turned and pointed at the van.

'It is,' said Jane. 'But Jack's the English one. I'm from up on the north coast, Ballycastle, County Antrim. I work in England these days. I'm a nurse. My name's Jane.'

They had prepared and rehearsed their stories. Jack had suggested she be a nurse. Jane had known all about Roisin's background and her training in Ormskirk. It seemed sensible to them both.

Even so, he hadn't heard the cover story verbalised by her before. She told it so naturally and convincingly. He was impressed.

The woman listened and continued to smile and nod.

'Well, my name is Kathleen, and I live in one of the cottages here. I work in Bandon, at the library there. I'm on a half-day today. I don't have to be there until after lunch. Have you been to Bandon yet? You'll need, as you say, to come back after ten, and then you'll be able to speak to Sean.' Jack began to wonder if she would ever take a breath. 'He's the owner and the manager of the place. He's quite new himself but is a nice chap. He's taken over the boatyard and he and his two staff look after the place. They fix and clean the boats. He's brought a bit more life into the village since he took over and more and more people are bringing their boats here for repairs and refurbishment. Isn't that lovely?'

A local woman who likes to talk. Couldn't get much better, thought Jack.

'Would the pair of you like a cup of tea at my house? You'd be very welcome to wait there. Better than having to make it yourselves in that van of yours I suspect.'

Before Jack could answer, Jane smiled and replied, 'Well Kathleen, that's very nice of you, but we don't want to put you to any bother.'

'Oh, that's no bother. No bother at all. It's only common courtesy. You've both come all the way here on holiday, and you deserve to be made welcome. Come on both. Over tea and a bit of toast, if I have enough in the back, I'll fill you both in on this bit of Ireland. I've lived in these parts for forty years.'

She turned and led the way. Jack raised his eyebrows to Jane, and she simply smiled in return, shrugging her shoulders as if to say that they had no choice.

As they followed her, Jack noticed the slipway into the river between the buildings. This was obviously where the boats left and re-entered the river at high tide. He saw Jane make a mental note as well.

'I'm a widow,' she said as she went through the door. 'My

husband, Patrick, died of cancer three years ago, and our three children have all moved away for work. One to Dublin and two to England. I have six grandchildren but don't see them as often as I'd like because of the distance and the cost.'

They both nodded. It was hard to get a word in.

The tea was strong and tasty, and the toast was made from fresh bread. Kathleen continued to talk and talk.

'Yes, Sean has livened up Kilmacsimon Quay a lot since he arrived here. Did I tell you he is a nice man? He came back to Ireland from America. Made his fortune there it seems and bought the boatyard. It had fallen into disrepair really before that. And our bar here, Brian runs that, and he runs it very well too. Not too many customers you understand as we're a bit off the beaten track down here, but there seem to be more and more tourists wanting to come here – fishing you know and sailing and boating generally. He's always taking boats out of the water or putting them in, so business certainly seems to be picking up for him. Sometimes he and his men work late into the night.'

I bet they do, thought Jack.

'I don't go in, you know.' They both looked confused. 'To the bar, you understand. Wouldn't be seemly going in on my own, would it? I did sometimes – when Patrick was alive – but rarely these days.'

She was the human epitome of a machine gun. All Jack could do was smile. She seemed lonely. That much was obvious.

Jane was better at sensing when the pauses were coming than he was. She chose one and asked, 'So, Kathleen, do we go to the office when Sean arrives? To book our boat ride?'

'I'll take you to meet him myself,' Kathleen offered. He'll be here any minute. Usually arrives about this time with his men and opens the gates. We'll hear his car. He drives a Land Rover.'

'That's very kind of you, Kathleen. You've made us very welcome, and we really appreciate that,' Jack said truthfully.

A few minutes later, as if on cue, a large dark vehicle passed by the window.

'That'll be Sean,' she announced. 'I recognise the sound of his car, and in any event, not many people drive down this far so early in the morning. It was your van going past earlier that made me wonder who it was. A bit early for Sean, I said to myself. Leave it a few minutes, and I'll take you up to his office.'

They sat and waited. Jack felt unusually relaxed, and he listened as Jane and Kathleen did all the talking. He noticed how skilfully Jane sidestepped the more detailed questions about nursing, about Ballycastle, about how long she'd known Jack, while at the same time finding out more and more about Kathleen – her life, her family and her interests. She was born to be an undercover police officer, he thought.

Jack looked at his watch. It was about twenty minutes past ten. He was keen to get moving and to meet the famous Sean Buckley. Jane sensed his restlessness. She took the opportunity when Kathleen was putting some more coal on the fire to nod at him. He nodded back, and she spoke up.

'Should we go and speak with Sean now, Kathleen? We'd like to plan our time as there is so much we want to see and do. If we can get out onto the river today, that would be great.' Jane's tone was kind and yet insistent.

'Of course, dear. What was I thinking of? It's just that I don't get to talk with that many people these days. Library work can be very quiet, you know.' She seemed a little deflated. 'Come with me.' She stood up and reached for her duffle coat. Jack took it from her and held it up for her.

'Oh, you've got yourself a good one there, so you have,' she said smilingly to Jane. 'Good looking and with manners. Just like my Patrick. An important quality in a man, don't you agree?' Leaning in closer, she added, 'And very good looking too. Shame about the cuts and bruises.'

Jane smiled. Jack's face reddened.

'I do indeed, Kathleen. Shame he's a boxer,' she replied and then cast a glance at Jack and winked.

'Follow me,' the woman said and led the way out of the front door adding, 'And just pull the door to behind you. We never lock our doors around here.'

Jack was the last one out and did as she requested.

They walked through the now wide-open boatyard gates and towards the Portakabin. Jack absorbed the features around him. The way he'd been trained. Three men were standing just outside it, and a brown Land Rover was parked at one end. He made a mental note of the licence plate. The men were talking and didn't immediately notice the little group coming towards them.

It was the older one that saw them first and turned to face Kathleen. The other two turned a second or two afterwards. They looked impassively at the new arrivals.

The older man stepped forward and said with a smile, 'Well, good morning, Kathleen. How are you this fine day?'

Jack estimated that he was mid-forties with greying hair swept back over his head. He was about five feet ten inches, similar to Jack. He wore black boots, black corduroy trousers, a checkered shirt and a black unbuttoned waistcoat. Slim and with large hands. He was a handsome man without doubt.

'Hi yourself, Sean. I'm great thanks. Haven't seen you for a day or so. You been busy?'

'You know me, Kathleen, always busy these days. Business is good and getting better.' He smiled warmly, but Jack noticed something in the man's eyes. Suspicion he thought.

Kathleen took her cue.

'Well, I'd like to introduce you to two new friends of mine.' She turned and nodded briefly at Jack and Jane in turn. 'They're over here on holiday, from England, and they want to hire a boat from you to see our lovely Bandon River. This is Jack, he's a student, and this is Jane, his girlfriend. She's a nurse.'

Jack stepped forward and offered his hand.

'Nice to meet you, Mr Buckley. We're hoping you can rent us a small motorboat. We'd love to go down to Kinsale and have a look around.'

'Call me Sean, please.' His smile didn't fade for a second. He turned to Jane and offered his hand to her as well. The smile continued.

'Hello, Mr Buckley. Kathleen speaks very highly of you.' Jane's tone was polite and yet warm, as well.

'And nice to meet you too, Miss.' Buckley was very courteous.

He turned to his men and added, 'Well, then, lads. We'll carry on with the schedule for today a bit later. Give me a few minutes with these two fine folk, and I'll come and find you.'

Neither said anything but nodded and went off in the direction of the grey shed that Jane had suggested might be the tool shed.

When they'd gone, Buckley turned back to Kathleen.

'Leave these two with me Kathleen, and I'll sort them out with something in the next day or so. As you like them, I might give them a discount on the price.' His accent was a strange mixture of southern Irish and American.

'Oh, thank you, Sean. You are a good man.' She smiled at him and turned to Jane and Jack. 'When you're finished here, feel free to pop back in for another cup of tea. I have to leave for work at about 12:30 but will be in or about until then. You'll both be very welcome.'

'That's kind of you, Kathleen,' Jane replied.

The woman turned and walked away back towards the gate.

'Now then you two,' Buckley said briskly. 'I didn't want to say in front of Katherine, but today is not a good day for me renting out boats. My men and I are up against a deadline, repairing and cleaning a boat for a new customer. An important one. This is our first job for him, and it could be the first of many, so I don't want to let him down. He's due to pick it up tomorrow. I'm sure you understand.'

His smile was still fixed, but the tone of voice had moved to one of emphasis and was clearly not negotiable.

'If you both come back tomorrow, just after lunch, I'll have a little motorboat ready for you. She handles beautifully and is very stable.' He nodded in the direction of one of the smaller boats in the yard.

'That's fine,' said Jack smiling back. 'We'll go up to the Bandon area for the rest of today. Kathleen has recommended it. By the way, how much will it be to hire the boat?'

'Normally I'd charge twenty-five pounds for a half-day, but as you're friends with Kathleen, I'll let you have it for twenty. Is that OK?'

'Sure,' replied Jane. 'That's really kind of you, Mr Buckley. Thanks very much.' She turned to Jack and took his hand. 'Come on then, Jack, let's leave Mr Buckley to his work.'

Jack nodded at Buckley and let himself be led away by Jane. The feel of her hand in his was very strange. Her hand was gentler and softer than he'd imagined, and the feeling was disconcerting. It immediately took him back to the feelings he had when holding Roisin's hand. He was lost in his head for a few seconds.

As they reached the main gates of the boatyard, Jane turned back to look at Buckley and the boatyard, raising her hand as if she was going to wave goodbye. Jack noticed Buckley had already re-joined his two men, and their conversation had resumed. He seemed oblivious to the tourists now.

Jane gazed around her and spoke quietly. 'What do you think? Sounds like his plans for the rest of today, and possibly this evening, are fixed.'

Jack's mind was entirely focused again.

'I think we can assume that he doesn't want to be disturbed. It looks like we're on for tonight.' Jane nodded. 'Let's tell Kathleen that we're off exploring for the rest of today and we'll be back tomorrow midday for the boat ride. That message might find its way back to Buckley at some point if they talk again when we've gone. We can radio in the intel, and they can get things ready for the op. We'll park up nearby, to keep the road to the village under surveillance.'

Jane nodded her agreement and went off to Kathleen's house. She returned a few minutes later and found Jack sitting at the driver's wheel.

'OK done,' she said. 'She seems happy with the arrangements. She invited us in for more tea, but I politely declined.'

'Right, let's go. Keep your eyes open for vehicles coming the other way.' Jane climbed into the passenger seat, pulling the door closed behind her. He fired the engine, did a three-point turn and the camper van left the tiny village.

When they got to the small fork where they had turned onto the road to Kilmacsimon, Jack slowed to a stop. He pointed to a house close to the junction, set back about seventy-five yards, with a long tree-covered path leading up to it.

'I spotted it as we drove in earlier. I suggest we park along it, as far out of sight as we can, and report in. We can easily say we've been checking the map if anyone appears – from the house or elsewhere. If we're not disturbed, we can monitor the junction and make a note of vehicles that use it. Particularly the ones going to and from the Quay.'

'I'm impressed,' Jane responded. 'We'll make a surveillance expert of you yet. A bit of clever parking will ensure we'll be virtually invisible.'

'Agreed.'

Jack steered the van around the junction, driving slowly up the wooded track. He manoeuvred the camper so that it could not be seen from the road or from the house. Through branches, they could see the junction, but no one could see them.

Jane set up the radio, depressed the transmitter button and gave their call sign.

'Tourist Two to Control. Can you confirm please.' Jane spoke clearly and confidently. She released the button.

The response was immediate and equally clear.

'Control here, Tourist Two. Go ahead please.'

Jane depressed the button again and proceeded to report their findings.

'We've got the junction about half a mile from Kilmacsimon Quay under surveillance and will monitor the traffic from this point on,' she concluded. 'Nothing suspicious at the moment.'

She released the button, and again the void was filled by the clear if metallic response. 'Thanks, Tourist Two. Stay in position and report accordingly. Please await further instructions.'

'Will do. Out,' replied Jane. She put the radio under the dashboard in its hiding place.

'So we have quite a few hours to wait then,' Jack said.

'Seems so.'

He turned to face her.

'Jane, I just want to say that I'm glad you're on my side. And I'm glad you're here now. I've really appreciated all you've done for me since Roisin died, keeping me informed of the investigation and everything. It helped that you seemed to understand everything I was going through.'

'Well, in a way, I do.'

Jack was taken aback. He'd often wondered what motivated her.

'Do you mind if I ask why you chose to join the RUC and Special Branch?'

She looked out of the window for a few seconds before turning back to him.

'It was a simple decision.' Her face was impassive. 'My Da was an RUC Police Inspector. He was leading an investigation into an IRA murder in Belfast and was close to making an arrest. One evening, while I was studying for my A levels upstairs, two masked gunmen broke into the house. They shot my Da three times in the head before he could reach his gun. I ran downstairs and found him lying face down in a pool of blood on the kitchen table. I made the decision very quickly afterwards. No university for me. I'd join the RUC and join the fight against these terrorist bastards. That's the story. No more, no less.'

She looked intently at him.

'Jack, I understand revenge, really I do. It's a powerful motivator.'

He stared at her. She did understand.

Chapter 52

The weather deteriorated as the afternoon progressed. Light showers that happened late morning were replaced by torrential rain in the afternoon and they took it in turns to take comfort breaks behind the van as the need arose. They silently ate the sandwiches and drank the flasks of tea that had been provided by the kitchens at Collins Barracks.

'Can I see the list to-date?' Jack asked Jane as the light began to fade. Jane handed him the notebook.

Kathleen, in a small blue Renault, had turned right towards Bandon at twelve thirty-six on route for her shift at the library. She had returned at five thirty-five pm, presumably having finished work.

He looked at the list and verbalised his thoughts.

'So, only five vehicles have turned here to head to the Quay. All of them in the last hour or so. They might all yet return soon, heading back towards either Bandon or Innishannon. Or we could assume they are private residents returning at the end of the day.'

Jane nodded.

'Logical. They might also be having a drink in the bar,' she said.

Jack smiled. At another time he would have enjoyed a pint. He re-read the details of the four vehicles from the notes in front of him. The make, model and registration number of each had been recorded.

He laid down the notebook, placing the pen into its spiral binding as he did so.

'Interesting.' The tone of Jane's voice made him look up.

A small blue and white oil tanker with Irish Oil Deliveries emblazoned on the side was turning into the minor road. It was much smaller than the large oil tankers seen on main roads. Presumably, so it could access the farm tracks in this area.

They stared at each other and reached the same conclusion.

'Fuck.'

'Fuck indeed,' Jane replied.

She reached for the radio. Her thumb clicked the transmit button.

'Tourist Two to Control. We might have something.'

'Explain please.'

Jane did so.

'It could well be the vehicle we've been expecting,' said Reynolds. 'Just gone by you into the Quay, you say?'

'Yep, and the light is fading fast. What do you want us to do?'

There was a pause of a few seconds, and then Reynold's voice could be heard.

'We've been liaising with your chaps in Belfast, and we all agree there is a strong possibility something is happening tonight. More intelligence has come to light. We're pretty sure its heavy-duty arms and explosives coming in. They'll probably use the cover of darkness to load the weapons. We need to locate that van to eliminate it, and its driver, from our enquiries,' said Reynolds. 'Can you get down to the village unseen? How long to walk there?'

Jack held up one hand, fingers separated.

'Maximum of five minutes,' Jane responded.

'OK, then. Get back to the Quay. Report in and let me know what's happening as soon as you can. You never know, it may be legit and simply delivering oil. We're on full alert here and can have support there within ten minutes if needed.'

'Understood. Talk again when we have something to report.'

Jane switched the radio to mute and put it in her small backpack. She checked her gun, deftly slipping the ammunition clip into the handle, and listened for the reassuring click. She applied the safety catch and tucked the gun into the back of her jeans, pulling her coat down over it to conceal it from view.

Jack followed the same procedure with his own Browning and pocketed a spare loaded clip.

Jane picked up the other spare clip and placed it in her coat pocket. 'OK. Ready,' she said, meeting his eyes and gave him the slightest of winks. They quietly got out of the camper van, and Jack locked the doors.

Their eyes were used to the dark by now. Jane put her arms through her bag's straps, and it nestled in the small of her back. She led the way down the track towards the road and the junction. Jack followed, his eyes constantly scanning the area for signs of movement. There was none.

He caught up with her and whispered quietly.

'If we hear a car, I'll grab your hand, so be ready.'

Jane nodded.

They started walking the short distance towards Kilmacsimon Quay. A steady walk, not hurried, alongside the right-hand side of the road. The silence was eerie. The moon was obscured by the clouds. Only a dim glow remained.

They passed an entrance flanked by two gateposts on their right.

The tree-lined driveway beyond it rose up in a slight incline and curved to the right. Jack deduced that the house at the end was quite a large one but under cover of darkness he couldn't see it. Through the gloom, he could see a plaque on one on the gateposts. He peered forward. It read Kilmacsimon House. He estimated that the house must be situated up the hill above the boatyard and the cottages as the road to the Quay remained flat.

As they walked on, he realised they must be very near to the start of the cottages. He remembered the slight curve in the road. Jane walked close beside him, and he heard her quiet breathing. They glanced at each other, a silent appreciation of what they might be walking into. Jack's heartbeat was fast and strong. All his senses were on full alert.

The row of cottages appeared to their right. About half of them seemed to be occupied with light showing around closed curtains. Jack looked at Kathleen's cottage, part of him prepared to greet her if she emerged. The door to the bar on their left was closed, but again it appeared that people were inside as he heard a slight murmur of voices. He wasn't sure if it was the sound of a TV or people inside talking.

They quietly edged their way past, and the slipway appeared on their left. The gates to the boatyard were now closed and it seemed that a vehicle was parked immediately beyond them. Nothing would have been able to enter, even if the gates had been open. Jack assumed it was to further obscure the view.

He examined the area around them. The accumulated light of the cottages and the bar together with the dim moonlight allowed him a reasonable perspective.

They approached the closed gates of the boatyard. Although not a clear view, he could see the lights were on in the office of the boatyard.

'Things still going on,' whispered Jane. 'Can you hear a motor running?'

Jack strained his ears and squinted in the direction of a faint mechanical sound. He could make out the rhythmical sound of a pump.

Jane pointed to one side of the boatyard office. It was the small oil tanker they had observed earlier, and it appeared to have a long pipe stretching from it to the boatyard's oil tank reservoir. Oil was presumably being transferred from the tanker into the storage tank. Probably motor oil of some description. Boat engines would need oil, of course.

'Almost normal,' said Jack keeping his voice low, 'but why are the gates closed, and why do they have a vehicle blocking the entrance? The tanker would want to drive out again after it had finished.'

Jane shrugged her backpack from her shoulders and swung it quickly in front of her. She reached inside and extracted the radio. Her fingers adjusted the volume control, and she switched it on, crouching down against a nearby wall.

'Tourist Two to Control.' She spoke very quietly but clear into her handset. The response was immediate.

'Control to Tourist Two. Go ahead.'

'We're at the gates to the boatyard. They are shut, and a vehicle is blocking the entrance. The oil tanker is in the boatyard. At the moment it appears to be transferring oil to a tank near the office. We can hear its pump working, and there are people in or near the office.'

Jack moved closer to Jane so he could hear more clearly. Captain Reynold's voice was clear.

'It could be the oil tanker has been modified in some way. It's very possible that Buckley is at this moment loading weapons into the tanker and the oil pump is merely a diversion. Head back to your vehicle, and we'll take it from here. Well done both. Chopper taking off as we speak.'

'Message understood. We're withdrawing now.' Jane was calm and efficient. She switched off the handset and looked at Jack.

'OK, seems we've done as much as we can, over to the big boys now. Let's get out of here. It's going to get noisy here in a few minutes.' She returned the radio to her bag and stood up.

Suddenly the air reverberated with a deafening crack and Jack saw Jane crumple and fall to the floor, her bag falling in front of her. She didn't move. She'd been hit by something.

His hand reached behind him for the revolver tucked into his jeans, but before his hand reached it, he heard a woman's voice from behind him.

'Not so fast you English bastard. Keep your hands where I can see them. Make a wrong move, and you're as dead as she is.' Jack did as he was told and eased his hands into the air. As he did so, he turned in the direction of the voice.

Kathleen stood facing him, pointing a revolver straight at him. She was about ten feet away. The woman shouted loudly, 'Sean, get out here. I've got a problem. The two from this morning.'

The pumping noise had stopped and Jack could hear loud voices from the boatyard office. They'd obviously heard the gunfire too. He realised he only had seconds.

'Kathleen – or whatever the fuck your name is – give it up. It's over. A military helicopter is on its way here from Cork. It'll be here in minutes. Give yourself up and no one needs to get hurt.'

'You're a fucking English liar!' she screamed. 'It's only you two. And she's no good to you now.' The hatred in her voice was clear as crystal.

Jack took a breath. It was clear she hadn't heard Jane make the call on the radio. He just needed a couple of seconds to distract her so he could reach for his Browning. He was debating his options when Kathleen suddenly recoiled backwards with a sudden jerk. The arm holding her own weapon flew sideways, and Jack knew she'd been hit but couldn't make out where from.

'Get her gun!' rasped Jane. He caught a brief image of her lying on her stomach, both hands on her Browning pointed directly at Kathleen. At the same moment, he heard a shout from the boatyard.

'Kathleen, are you OK?'

He came to his senses and sprinted towards the woman as she called out.

'The couple from this morning – they're army! I'm hit!'

Her shouts were cut off as Jack flew at her, knocking her to the ground. The hand carrying the gun swung back towards him. Jack instinctively aimed a savage kick at her. He timed it well, and his boot connected with her forearm. He heard a bone break and knew it must have hurt. She screamed in pain. The gun left her hand and flew off into the dark.

Simultaneously, Jack withdrew his own gun from his waistband and kicked the woman again, this time in the stomach and again in the head. She opened her mouth and tried to scream again but the blow to her stomach had winded her. She fell sideways clutching her face as blood flowed between her fingers. He didn't need to see her face to know that he'd broken her nose and that blood was erupting from the wound. He squatted on top of her and looked to see if she had a weapon in her other hand. She didn't. He leant forward, grabbed a chunk of her hair and twisted it savagely until taut while at the same time pressing his mouth against her ear. She grunted.

'Listen,' he spoke quickly into her ear. 'One more word from you and you're dead. Understand?'

She obviously understood and remained quiet. His fingers kept twisting the hair into her scalp. Her arm, he was certain, was broken. Her gun was gone, and she'd been hit somewhere by a bullet from Jane.

'Jane, you OK?' he asked in the darkness.

'I'm hit, Jack. Leg, I think. Thigh. I can move a little but can't get up.'

Jack made sense of the shapes in the darkness and saw that she was sitting upright, legs splayed to keep herself balanced and her back against the outside of the boatyard wall.

'Stay there. Don't move. I've got Kathleen. She's wounded. Hold on.'

With an almost savage strength, he dragged Kathleen's body over towards where Jane was and threw her body against the wall about five feet from where Jane was positioned. He assumed that Buckley and others were close, just the other side of the car parked behind the boathouse gates.

'Jane, hang on here and keep your eye on this one.' His voice was steady.

Kathleen was lying prone, face to one side, gasping in huge gulps of air, obviously in a lot of pain.

Jane swung her Browning towards Kathleen's body. He saw that she was breathing heavily, also in pain.

'Jack, I think they're just behind the Land Rover. I think I counted three including Buckley. There could be others. The tanker driver. Be careful.' Her words were clear but not loud. As always, she had assessed the situation and given him a few seconds to prepare.

'I've got this one covered,' she added. 'Don't worry about her. If she gives me any trouble, I'll shoot her.' She meant it, and if Kathleen could hear, she would know it was the truth. 'Our boys will be here in minutes.'

Jack orientated himself and threw himself to the other side of the boathouse gates for some protection. He was relieved to find himself leaning up against a concrete column. As he did so, he heard the sound of bullets bring fired from behind the parked car. A hail of gunfire ripped through the wire mesh towards the bar's closed door. It remained shut. Any people inside had had the sense to stay in there when the first shots were fired.

He'd done the right thing by moving to the left of the gates to get some protection. Buckley and his men wouldn't know for sure how many opponents they were facing and were, at least for a few seconds, trapped inside the boatyard. He knew he had to keep them there until the helicopter arrived. Contain the threat.

He stayed crouched and tried to work out where the firing was coming from. He sidestepped to the left using the wall as cover. The firing stopped for a few seconds, and he heard shouts from the side of the Land Rover nearest him. The firing started again, and it was still aimed at the gates. That was his opportunity.

He swivelled and raised his head above the wall for a split second. He was confident they hadn't seen him in the dark. He thought he saw two figures crouching by the Land Rover on the side nearest to him.

He checked his Browning was ready to fire and sprang into action, raising his head above the wall again but this time aiming his Browning too. He pulled the trigger and deliberately sprayed the area. His clip emptied quickly.

His bullets hit their marks. There were two separate grunts, and he was sure he heard two bodies hit the gravel surface. Indeed, the firing from the side of the car nearest him ceased abruptly. His own shot count told him he needed to reload.

He ducked down behind the wall again, pulled out the empty clip and inserted the full one. Rhythm and routine, it took only seconds. He was working automatically, the way he'd been trained.

He heard Buckley's voice shout, 'Gerry, Donal, you OK?' There was no answer.

Jack shouted, 'Give it up Buckley. You're trapped. There's no way out and backup is seconds away.'

There was silence. In the distance Jack thought he could hear the sound of a helicopter. It was clearly approaching the direction of Kilmacsimon Quay.

'Hear that Buckley? You have seconds to give up your weapons. Your whole operation was compromised days ago, and you're a dead man unless you give it up now. In a few seconds, it'll be out of my hands, and the soldiers in the helicopter have instructions to shoot to kill.'

'OK, OK! I'm putting my gun down!' Buckley shouted. 'I'm behind the Land Rover. Look. Don't shoot!' The fear and panic in his voice was clear.

Jack raised his head again and could see something moving in the space where Buckley had suggested he was.

The crack of a bullet hit the wall a few inches from Jack's head. Tiny clumps of concrete spat into his face. As more shots hit the wall behind him, Jack instinctively knew it hadn't come from where Buckley was standing. He ducked down again.

He remembered the fourth man. The tanker driver.

'Buckley. I have someone else just beyond the gate. Move towards it with your hands raised and slowly open the gate. Come through and lie on the floor with your hands behind your head. If you make one wrong move, we will not hesitate to shoot you. Do you understand?'

'Yes. Understood. I'm not carrying. It wasn't me that fired that last shot. It was the driver. Up near the office.'

'Walk! And do it now!' Jack shouted.

He sprang back towards the gates. He couldn't count on Jane being conscious or being able to see Buckley. He had to do it himself. He wasn't too worried about the fourth man. He'd be dealt with by the helicopter's occupants in the next few minutes.

One of the boatyard gates slowly swung open. The shape of Sean Buckley with his hands raised slowly appeared.

'I'm here. Don't shoot!' he said.

Jack kept the Browning pointed at him.

'Get down on the floor. Facedown. Hands behind your head. Now!' Jack shouted. Buckley complied.

'Don't move. Not a fucking muscle. Understand?'

'It's OK, Jack, I've got him covered.' Jane's voice was tense. 'The woman is either dead or unconscious. She's not moving. I can cover him now.'

She threw the radio over to him. 'Call it in.' He bent down and picked it up with his left hand, the Browning in his right. He depressed the on/off switch and held it to his mouth.

'Tourist Two to Control. Over.'

'Control to Tourist Two. Go ahead. Chopper ETA five minutes.'

'RUC Officer down adjacent to main gates of boatyard. She needs medical support. Leg wound. Buckley apprehended along with an

IRA woman. She's either unconscious or dead. Two associates of Buckley shot dead. One more gunman contained in the yard.'

There was silence for a few seconds.

'Understood Tourist Two. Hold on. Out.'

Jack was switching the radio off when another volley of shots ripped through the boatyard gates. The sound was louder than before. The fourth man was closer this time.

'I need to locate the shooter,' he said to Jane.

'Be careful! There's not much he can do by himself. Don't take any risks with the cavalry coming over the hill.'

Jack stood up quickly and looked beyond the gates to see a man running towards the water's edge dodging between the boats in the yard. He could also make out the silhouette of a rifle in the man's hand.

'He's going to get away!'

'Leave it Jack. We've done our job. They'll pick him up or kill him.'

He glanced above the wall again and his eyes went to the last position he'd seen the man. He scanned the area. Suddenly he saw a movement approaching the water's edge. The man was dragging a small boat from the boatyard to the edge of the river. He called back to Jane.

'He's planning to get away on the water. If the helicopter misses him, he can't be followed!' Jack did the calculations in his head. If he was quick he could get there. Ignoring Jane's warnings he ran, keeping as low as possible, to the end of the boatyard wall which stopped abruptly two yards from the water's edge. It gave way to a small pebbly beach, and he found himself ankle deep in water. He estimated the man was about forty feet in front of him in an arc somewhere between twenty feet from the water line to the water's edge. The moon reflected the odd ripple of the water but other than that the darkness remained.

He moved forwards as quietly as he could, feeling the resistance of the water against his ankles. His Browning was held in the firing position and he strained with his eyes, trying to seek out the dark figure. He knew the odds were in his favour. The man would need to grab his rifle, raise it and aim. And he was almost certainly more concerned with getting the boat to the water's edge than firing his weapon.

He realised that the eerie stillness would, in moments, be replaced by the arrival of the helicopter. Would they spot him? Or would he reach the safety of the dark water?

At that moment he heard a muffled grunt about ten yards in front of him. He crouched even lower and tried to make sense of what was in front of him. Then he saw it. The man had his back to him and the boat he was dragging was less than six feet from the water. His back showed a rifle shape slung between his shoulders, presumably strapped in place over his chest and stomach. Jack could hear his gasps of breath. The boat was a wooden one with two oars tilted upwards and held in place by oarlocks. It would be heavy to drag, and the exertion needed to move it on land was clearly considerable.

Jack estimated that at this distance he could hit the man without any trouble. He was about to squeeze the trigger when something stopped him. He would not kill someone if he didn't need to.

'Stop right where you are!' he called. 'Hands off the boat! Put them both in the air. Very slowly.'

The man froze at the sound of Jack's command. He let go of the boat and one of his arms raised.

'I said both arms up,' Jack calmly reiterated. 'Make no mistake, I have a pistol pointing right at your back.'

He took a few more steps forward as the man slowly raised his other hand.

'Now, turn round slowly so that I can see you. Remember, one false move and you're a dead man.'

The man turned slowly to his right and his face became clearer.

Jack felt the blood drain from his body.

He froze.

The man had a new beard and longer hair than in the most recent photograph Jack had seen. But even so, it was unmistakable. Standing in front of him, a few feet away from him with his arms in the air was Declan McGill.

Jack was momentarily speechless.

'So, who the fuck are you then?' McGill seemed calm. The Belfast accent was clear and strong, and Jack realised the man was no longer breathing heavily. He was obviously in good physical shape.

'My name is irrelevant,' replied Jack, moving closer still. 'Just be aware that I've been hunting you down for almost a year now. You may not realise it, but you are a very lucky man. You should be dead by now.'

McGill's face showed confusion.

"You're a fucking Brit. I can hear it in the way you speak. Who the fuck are you?'

'I'm a friend of Rory O'Malley. You know, your Belfast IRA buddy. We picked him up a few days ago and he told me a lot about you.'

'No way, Rory is strong. He would have said nothing to you bastards. He's no tout.'

'Like I said, I've been on your case for a long time. Good to meet you again Declan. Can I call you that? You can call me Jack.'

'Jack fucking who? We haven't met before.' McGill was trying to make sense of the situation. He squinted through the darkness.

'Oh, but we have. Do you remember a night at The Red Devil? You almost had your throat cut by me in the toilets.'

Jack thought he saw a brief flash of recognition cross the man's face. It was quickly replaced by anger.

'What the fuck? What's your problem you English cunt?'

Jack kept the gun aimed straight at McGill.

'Do you remember killing a young nurse near the hospital just over a year ago? A Catholic girl. You and your ASU were responsible.' He watched McGill's face, looking for signs of recognition or remorse. There were none. 'I have it on good authority that it was you that pulled the trigger.'

'You're talking bollocks.'

'A soldier was injured as well. A few weeks before Christmas it was.'

Through the darkness, Jack could tell that he'd struck a chord with his foe. The façade disappeared.

'Yeah, I remember that. It was an accident. I was aiming at the fucking soldier. She got caught in the crossfire. That's how it is sometimes in war. Unintended consequences.' He showed no sign of regret.

Jack felt remarkably calm. He'd heard it all before.

At that moment, the increasingly thunderous sound of the army helicopter's rotor blades could be heard above the trees surrounding the boatyard. Searchlights from the body of the helicopter suddenly erupted from the darkness and unseen eyes surveyed the territory below. The whole boatyard was illuminated like a football stadium.

The helicopter hovered over the centre of the boatyard and ropes were lowered from its undercarriage. Armed soldiers descended onto the ground and sprinted, crouching low, to various points on the perimeter of the boatyard. Jack and McGill watched the events unfold.

'It's like this Declan,' Jack said, taking another step towards McGill, his finger firm against the trigger of the Browning. 'That nurse was my girlfriend. Her name was Roisin. I loved her and you took her away from me. You murdered her.'

As Jack uttered the words, McGill rushed at him through the water. The Browning's muzzle fired two shots in quick succession. Both entered McGill's body in the chest, flinging him backwards like a flailing mannequin. He was dead before his body hit the water.

Jack stared at the body as it lay face up in the shallow water. He felt nothing. He'd done his job. No more innocent people would be murdered by Declan McGill.

He dragged the body from the shallow water and propped it up against the rowing boat. He then removed the rifle from the back of the body and placed it carefully into McGill's lifeless hands. Once done, he turned and walked quickly back to the boatyard gates.

As he reached them, he saw Jane talking with a senior NCO. She was still sitting against the wall and another soldier was examining her wound.

'Have you filled them in?' Jack asked.

'Yes, but what's happened to the fourth man? The driver.'

'He was trying to escape in a rowing boat. He resisted arrest and I had to shoot him. He's dead.'

'Well, that tidies things up. Do you know who he was?

'No idea,' replied Jack. 'Just another IRA terrorist.'

Epilogue
Belfast – three days later

Jane's thigh wound proved serious but not life-threatening. The bullet was removed within an hour at the main hospital in Cork, and the doctors had told her that she'd make a full recovery. Jack had been impressed with her stoicism.

During a de-brief with Turner, warm congratulations were heaped on them both – as well as the team that had so efficiently supported them. The operation was referred to as a surgical military strike and a very successful one based on equally successful covert intelligence. Turner also informed the group that Roy Mason's security advisers had decided, at the eleventh hour, that the Stormont meeting would take place in London rather than in Northern Ireland. The risk of attack was too high.

'We weren't to know that,' Turner explained, 'and the fact that this team categorically prevented a major attack on a member of the British government in Northern Ireland has been recognised.'

It was agreed that Jack's student days were over, at least for the foreseeable future. His cover had almost certainly been blown, and he would be an easy target for extremists from either side if they learned of his true identity.

In a private meeting with Turner, following the de-brief, Jack had been informed of his next assignment. It was an undercover role investigating the funding of IRA weapons and explosives in the United States.

Jack relished the opportunity. He'd always wanted to see the US first hand, and he had to admit that he liked the thought of getting out of Northern Ireland for a while at least. The insane and brutal violence in the province still continued, and all he wanted to do – all he could do – was play his part in advancing the process of peace. Preventing the importation of weapons would go a long way to doing that.

He still missed Roisin, and everything seemed to remind him of her. Her absence still felt like an open wound, and he knew that the naïve young man he had been before meeting her, no longer existed. He'd become something else.

He and Turner had been on the same wavelength about most things. But one thing still troubled Jack. Turner had been emphatic when talking about Rory's supposed death, that his family had to believe, for security reasons, that he'd been shot dead. His new life over the water was to be kept a secret.

Jack privately disagreed. He knew that news of Rory's death would seriously affect the O'Malley family. They were still badly affected by Roisin's death. He was sure that they'd never really recover. Finding out that Rory was an active member of the IRA and a gunrunner would have been bad enough but to hear he was shot dead, executed, would be crushing.

Jack decided on another course. One that would sit better with his conscience.

He still had the Newcastle phone number and knew he had to get back to Newcastle to see them face-to-face before the news of the shootings was released.

He found a quiet place to make the call and dialled the number. The phone rang three times before being picked up.

'Hello, O'Malley's. Siobhan speaking.'

'Hello Siobhan, it's Jack here.' He paused, waiting for a reaction.

'Oh, Jack, it's so good to hear from you. How are you?' She seemed upbeat.

'I'm fine thanks. I was planning to come down to Newcastle later today. To visit Roisin's grave and bring her some flowers. I wondered if I could meet you and Seamus?'

'That would be lovely Jack. We have nothing planned for today. Why don't you stay for lunch too and we can talk properly? It will be so good to see you again, and Roisin would be happy too that you're keeping in touch.'

'That would be great Siobhan, thanks. Would 1 pm be too early? I have to be back in Belfast later that evening – I've borrowed a friend's car for the day.'

'That's fine, Jack. We'll see you then. Looking forward to it. I'll let Seamus know.'

The way she spoke reminded Jack so much of Roisin and tears filled his eyes. He wiped them away and cleared his throat.

'Thanks, Siobhan. See you later then.' He replaced the phone handset.

Siobhan and Seamus welcomed him warmly as he knew they would. They ushered him into the family kitchen and sat him down at the table with a small beer.

He let them talk for a few minutes knowing that the reconnection was necessary for them. As the conversation began to slow, he took a large gulp of beer and replaced the glass on the table in front of him.

'I have something to tell you both. Something that you both need to know and something that must remain between the three of us.' He spoke firmly and gazed intently at both of them in turn.

They stared back at him, aware of the change in his voice.

'Please listen to what I have to say and when I've finished, you can ask me whatever you like. Is that OK?'

They nodded and glanced at each other, nervously.

He composed himself.

'When Roisin was killed, I made a decision. I wanted to do something to get back at those responsible. The IRA. I contacted the military here in Northern Ireland and offered my services as an undercover operative.'

Siobhan and Seamus looked confused, and Siobhan was about to speak when Seamus said, 'Go on, Jack.'

'During my training, I was reliably informed that Rory was an active member of the IRA.' He deliberately paused.

'Oh, sweet Jesus.' Siobhan burst into tears. 'Surely that's wrong. He always swore to us that he had nothing to do with any violence. Didn't he Seamus?' She turned to face her husband.

'Aye indeed he did darling, but I never believed him. Those bastards seduced Rory some time ago. I believe what Jack has told us.' He nodded for Jack to continue.

'I have more to tell you both, and before I do, I have to ask you to keep what I say to the three of us. You can't tell anyone as its dangerous for the whole family. I'll explain.'

He had their attention. They nodded again.

'You will hear in the news tomorrow that Rory was shot dead in a firefight with British Forces in Aughnacloy a few days ago.'

They both gasped. The colour drained from Siobhan's face.

'It isn't true,' said Jack quickly. 'He's alive.' He paused to let the news sink in. It's a cover story to protect him from IRA reprisals and to protect you, his family. I was able to speak to him while he was in custody. He's alive. You have my word.'

Seamus spoke. 'So, you're telling us that he's still being held. In secret. I'm presuming that he has cooperated with you and that a deal was done. Is that correct?'

Jack nodded. He was impressed with the speed at which Seamus had understood the situation.

Seamus turned to his wife.

'He's alive Siobhan. That's something. Jack is taking a huge risk himself by telling us this.' He turned back and looked at Jack. Jack spoke slowly.

'My superiors expressly told me not to tell you. Your grief would be the most compelling cover. But I couldn't do that to you. Losing Roisin was bad enough for you both.'

'When will we be able to see him, Jack?' Siobhan said, in-between her sobs.

Seamus took her hand and turned again to face her.

'Siobhan listen. I can answer that for Jack.' He glanced quickly at Jack and then back to her. 'Maybe never is the answer. Certainly not for many years. They're given new identities and not allowed to contact anyone they know. If the IRA finds out where he is, he'll be assassinated for sure. Jack has told us this so that we can prepare ourselves as best we can before the news comes out tomorrow.'

Siobhan had a look of bewilderment on her face.

Seamus turned again to Jack.

'Thank you, Jack. It's a lot for us to comprehend but knowing he's alive is the most important thing. I tried so hard to persuade him to move away from the path of madness that he was on. I knew deep down that something sinister like this would happen one day. I just hoped he'd somehow avoid it. What do you want us to do?'

Jack was ready with the answer.

'When the news of his death is announced, you have to respond as if you think, and believe, he is dead. Only that way can you protect him and your family. I'll do my best to get a message to him that I've told you the truth, but I can't guarantee that or when it will be.'

Siobhan had stopped sobbing and seemed to have grasped the importance of the words.

'Thank you, Jack. To know he's alive is the important thing. We won't let you down.'

She looked at her husband.

'Seamus and I need some time now on our own to prepare ourselves for what happens next. Will we be required to identify a body?'

'Yes. Similar height and build and coloured hair but not Rory. It's been done before and will be again.'

She nodded.

'OK, then. We'll be ready. One more thing, Jack.'

'What's that?' Jack asked.

'Roisin would have been very proud of you for doing this. She loved you so much.' Seamus was nodding.

'I really hope so. Thank you. Both of you.'

Half an hour later he drove into the cemetery in Newcastle. He parked the car in the designated spaces in front of the small Catholic church. He got out and then carefully locked the door. The sky was cloudy, and the Mourne Mountains looked impressive and a little foreboding.

The graveyard, to the side of the church, was as he remembered it. Large and yet orderly. The grass around the graves was well maintained, the flowers and plants adding colour. The gravel paths throughout, well weeded and tidy.

Jack remembered vividly where her grave was. Near the outer wall of the cemetery representing the newer burial plots.

Her parents had obviously kept it immaculate since her death.

He stood at the foot of her grave, facing the gravestone and closed his eyes for a few seconds. He wanted to see her; to feel her and hear her voice again. Impossible. All he had were his memories, a few photos and a few items of her clothing. That would have to do. His eyes were full of tears as he spoke quietly.

'Roisin. I love you now as much as I did when you were alive. You made me so very happy, and I thank you for that. The man that took you away from me is dead now.' Something inside him felt her frown.

'I've done the best I can for your parents. They're going to miss Rory, but at least they know he's safe, somewhere in the world.' She smiled.

He leant down and lay the flowers at the base of the gravestone. 'I have to go now,' he smiled. 'Just thought I'd tell you in person.'

He opened his eyes, and after a few more seconds turned and walked back to his car.

HISTORICAL NOTES

Absence of Certainty is a work of fiction. Names, characters and most incidents are either a product of the author's imagination or are used fictitiously. Any resemblance to actual people, living or dead, events or locales, is entirely coincidental. The Hillcrest Bar bombing in Dungannon actually happened as did Bloody Sunday. Those incidents are deliberately inserted into the novel to reference the period in which the book is set.

The Troubles was a violent sectarian conflict in Northern Ireland, lasting for thirty years, from late 1968 to 1998. The overwhelmingly Protestant Unionists (loyalists) desired the province to remain part of the United Kingdom; the overwhelmingly Roman Catholic Nationalists (Republicans) wanted Northern Ireland to become part of the Republic of Ireland.

The other significant players in the conflict were the British Army, the Royal Ulster Constabulary (RUC), and the Ulster Defence Regiment (UDR). Their official purpose was to play a peacekeeping role, most prominently between the nationalist Irish Republican Army (IRA), which viewed the conflict as a guerrilla war for national independence, and the Unionist paramilitary forces, who saw the IRA's aggression as terrorism.

Marked by street fighting, bombings, sniper attacks, roadblocks and internment without trial, the confrontation has been called a civil war. Some 3,600 people were killed, and more than 30,000 more were wounded during the conflict.

The period in the book (1975 to 1978) was characterised by the IRA moving from 'insurgency' to 'terrorism,' i.e. smaller scale and clandestine. Bombs detonated in British cities were intended to create terror.

Sectarianism was common. The loyalist paramilitaries became increasingly indiscriminate, killing hundreds of Catholic civilians, and bombing towns and cities south of the border.

At the same time, Republican groups targeted Protestant civilians both in Northern Ireland and in the United Kingdom; bombs detonated in British cities were intended to create terror and draw attention to the Republican cause.

GLOSSARY

APC – Armoured Personnel Carrier

A large armour-plated vehicle used by the British Army.

ATC – Air Training Corps

The UK cadet force affiliated to the Royal Air Force. Cadets aged between thirteen and nineteen years old.

Browning HP

A powerful 9mm handgun used by paramilitaries in the Troubles. They were sourced from a variety of regions, i.e. America, Middle East, Europe. Other types of handgun were also used.

Castlereagh

The RUC holding centre in East Belfast where paramilitary suspects were taken for interrogation. It had a fearsome reaction throughout the Troubles for the very harsh treatment (sometimes torture) of suspected terrorists. It was 'tolerated' by the British government for many years as it was regarded as effective in getting confessions. In 1977 (the period of this book), RUC detectives based there at the time said that they genuinely believed that they were turning the tide, and that their dubious methods were starting to win the war against the IRA.

Counter Insurgency

An approach used to combat the violent activities of terrorist groups against the authorities. During the Troubles, the British army sought to employ tactics using both civilian and military sources to gain information about paramilitary organisations and thereby disrupt their plans.

IRA – Irish Republican Army

The leading Republican paramilitary group. Formed in 1970 following a split within the Republican movement. Those who remained with the original organisation became the Official Irish Republican Army (OIRA) while the new, more militant, group called themselves the Provisional Irish Republican Army (PIRA). Following the OIRA ceasefire of 1972, the Provisionals became known as the IRA. A splinter organisation called itself the INLA – the Irish National Liberation Army.

Loyalist Paramilitary Groups

Illegal groups prepared to use physical violence in an attempt to ensure the continuation of the union between Northern Ireland and Britain. The main loyalist paramilitary groups during the Troubles were: the Ulster Defence Association (UDA) and its associated group the Ulster Freedom Fighters (UFF); the Ulster Volunteer Force (UVF) and its associated group the Red Hand Commando (RHC); and the Loyalist Volunteer Force (LVF).

RUC – Royal Ulster Constabulary

The Northern Ireland police force, founded in 1922. The RUC was responsible for dealing with politically motivated crime as well as ordinary law enforcement. During its existence, the RUC was made up almost entirely of officers drawn from the Protestant community; many Catholics had little trust in its impartiality.

Numerous members of the RUC also had links with loyalist paramilitary groups. On 4th November 2001, as part of the Good Friday Agreement, the force was renamed the Police Service of Northern Ireland (PSNI).

SAS – Special Air Service

An elite regiment of the British army specially trained for covert operations. The SAS was deployed on numerous occasions in Northern Ireland although British authorities denied this at the time.

Tiochaidh ár Lá

An Irish slogan commonly used by supporters and members of the Republican movement. It translates into English as 'Our day will come'.

Tout

Someone in the community who passes on information to the Northern Irish Security Forces.

UDR – Ulster Defence Regiment

A regiment of the British Army recruited from within Northern Ireland, and almost entirely Protestant. The regiment was established in 1970 and disbanded in 1992. Margaret Thatcher, as opposition leader, was warned that paramilitaries such as the UVF had infiltrated the UDR.

UVF – Ulster Volunteer Force

A loyalist paramilitary group (see above) established in 1966 by a former British soldier. It waged an armed campaign for almost thirty years.

14 Intelligence Company

Sometimes referred to as 14 INT, 14 Company, 14th Intelligence Detachment or 'The Det'. The Company was a British Army Special Forces unit established during the Troubles to carry out undercover surveillance operations in Northern Ireland. Members of the armed services were selected to join 14th Company, and for the first time, women could become members of a UK Special Forces unit. Candidates were required to pass a rigorous selection process, designed to weed out anyone without the necessary qualities to deal with the unique challenges of life as an undercover operative. Excellent observational abilities, stamina and the ability to think under stress were vital for undercover surveillance work. Since many operations require agents to work alone, a sense of self-confidence and self-reliance was also a prerequisite.

ACKNOWLEDGEMENTS

My thanks go to my wife Bridget, my children Fi, Jack and Laura, and several good friends, all of whom welcomed the original idea and the early versions of the manuscript with enthusiasm and emotion. They all contributed to getting it 'over the line'. Simply put, I could not have done it without them.

About the author

(Allan McGregor)

Allan is half-Kiwi, half-Brit and was brought up in Nottingham. He's the youngest of four children.

His strong interest in flying came largely from his father who sailed into Portsmouth from New Zealand in the middle of WW2 and became a pilot in the Fleet Air Arm and was posted to a variety of global locations before WW2 ended. After the war ended, he stayed in England and the rest, as they say, is history. Allan learnt to fly gliders and powered aircraft in his teens in the Air Training Corps and took that interest with him to Manchester University where he joined the University Air Squadron and flew from RAF Woodvale near Ormskirk.

After graduating, he embarked on a business career spending time in big companies up to his late 30's and then in the early 1990's set up his own business specialising in leadership development and coaching.

He has always loved reading and writing, and Absence of Certainty is his first novel. As a result of his first marriage, he spent considerable time in Northern Ireland during the troubles and has drawn on that experience in his novel. It was whilst there that he began to develop the idea of an action-adventure novel set in those times. He enjoyed a very different perspective of the Province to most English people and that always stayed with him.

Allan has 3 children aged 30+ (and 4 young grandchildren) and currently lives just west of London with his partner Bridget (a former head teacher). He enjoys badminton, cycling and walking his two black labradors in the hills and woods around his village. He's also a qualified football referee. He played himself to the age of sixty but was obliged to interact with his sport in a different way after he had a spinal diskectomy in 2018. He's also an active volunteer and trustee for a local cycle re-cycling charity.

Printed in Great Britain
by Amazon